"I regret that we

as well as I

"I cannot echo that sentiment, sir." Hugh's amused tone had deepened the color staining Beatrice's porcelain complexion. "*My* only regret is that I ever became acquainted with you at all." Stolen kisses and caresses, snatched during their brief moments alone, were at the forefront of her mind, putting a disquieting throb low in her belly. Bea feared he might also be recalling their passionate moonlit trysts, and his next soft comment proved her intuitive.

"I don't believe you wish we'd never met when we had such a delightful time."

"Then you should curb your conceit because it is the truth," Beatrice retorted, avoiding the sultry glint in his eyes. "Once again I must ask you what you want. I cannot believe you have simply come to see me to reminisce...."

* * *

The Rake's Ruined Lady
Harlequin® Historical #1196—August 2014

Author Note

In Regency England it was the accepted way of things for the firstborn daughter of a gentleman to be married off before the younger became a bride. In the duet of books featuring the Dewey sisters, unfortunately the opposite is the case. Elise is the first to find her soul mate in my novel *A Date with Dishonor,* while her elder sister Beatrice remains a spinster ensconced in the countryside with her father.

Beatrice would readily admit that in the past she has jeopardized her reputation by behaving wildly in affairs of the heart, thus spoiling her chances in the marriage mart. In *The Rake's Ruined Lady,* Bea stars as a heroine who is sure she has learned from her mistakes with scoundrels. At twenty-five she knows she is past her prime but is confident of finally settling into wedded bliss with her fiancé...until the upstanding doctor jilts her for another woman.

Following this setback Beatrice is ready to give up on love altogether, until an old flame, cognizant of her youthful folly, bursts back into her life.

Hugh Kendrick is not the man he once was. The modest fellow with whom Bea fell head over heels in love has transformed into an arrogant diamond magnate, recently returned from India.

Beatrice knows that this time around she should avoid the handsome rogue at all costs, fearing she could easily be tempted to again disgrace herself with him. When Hugh pursues her she must resist his skillful seduction or risk joining his harem of doting mistresses....

I hope you enjoy reading about Bea's inner dilemmas and the challenges she faces on her rocky road to love as much as I have enjoyed writing her story for you.

Mary Brendan

The Rake's Ruined Lady

Recycling programs for this product may not exist in your area.

ISBN-13: 978-0-373-29796-2

THE RAKE'S RUINED LADY

This edition published by arrangement with Harlequin Books S.A.

For questions and comments about the quality of this book, please contact us at CustomerService@Harlequin.com.

HARLEQUIN®
www.Harlequin.com

Printed in U.S.A.

Available from Harlequin® Historical and
MARY BRENDAN

Wedding Night Revenge #203
The Unknown Wife #205
A Scandalous Marriage #210
The Rake and the Rebel #211
Δ*A Practical Mistress* #865
Δ*The Wanton Bride* #894
***A Date with Dishonor* #1157
***The Rake's Ruined Lady* #1196

*The Meredith Sisters
ΔThe Hunter Brothers
**The Dewey Sisters

MARY BRENDAN

was born in north London, but now lives in rural Suffolk. She has always had a fascination with bygone days, and enjoys the research involved in writing historical fiction. When not at her word processor, she can be found trying to bring order to a large overgrown garden, or browsing local fairs and junk shops for that elusive bargain.

Chapter One

'Of course I do not understand!' Beatrice Dewey's blue gaze was fixed on her fiancé's face in shocked disbelief. 'How is any woman supposed to comprehend that the man she believes will shortly be *her* husband must marry another?' She pressed pale, quivering fingers to her brow. 'Repeat to me your news, please, and furthermore tell me why I should accept it.'

Colin Burnett's deep sigh displayed his regret. He stretched a hand towards Beatrice but she evaded his comfort in a swish of pastel muslin.

'Tell me, Colin! An explanation—a dozen explanations if I wish to have them—is the least you owe me.' Beatrice turned back to him, eyes sparking icy fire.

Ten minutes ago Mrs Francis, the Deweys' housekeeper, had interrupted Beatrice's letter-writing to announce that Dr Burnett had called on her. Beatrice had joined her fiancé in the front sitting room with a sunny smile, proving her gladness at this unexpected visit. Her happiness had started to wither before he'd uttered a single word: she'd read from Colin's demeanour that something was dreadfully wrong.

Not for a moment had she believed him jesting when he had quietly informed her that their wedding must be called off. Colin was not one for levity; neither was he a man who liked a drama. Beatrice could tell this predicament was causing him equal embarrassment and sorrow, but was conscious that he seemed nowhere near as wounded as was she at the idea of them parting.

'You know if there were any other way around this I would take it. I want you as my wife, Beatrice. I love you—'

'I don't see how you can love me…not really,' Beatrice interrupted harshly, 'if you are prepared to jilt me because you'd sooner have money.'

'It is not just about the money, my dear.' Colin sounded pained, and a trifle exasperated by her accusation. 'My family's reputation and estates are founded on the baronetcy. The Burnetts were granted the title as long ago as the Norman Conquest and it has passed through our male line ever since.' He cast his eyes heavenwards, seeking inspiration. 'If I reject the title and estates everything will be returned to the crown. How am I to explain that to my relations?'

Beatrice gave an impatient shrug. Her fiancé's logical reference to history and his kin, when her heart was breaking, was simply increasing her indignation.

'My uncle was not an easy man to fathom,' Colin continued doggedly, thrusting his fingers through a shock of auburn hair. 'He was known as an eccentric, but had I for one moment realised what madness he planned I would have privately set lawyers the task of finding a loophole to wriggle out of his stipulations. As it is, I must bow to his whim or lose everything.'

'So instead of forfeiting your birthright and choosing to remain much as you are: a country doctor of modest means—which is the person I fell in love with—you would dance to a dead man's tune to have his fortune and his title?'

Now her shock was receding anger was bringing Beatrice close to tears. She wouldn't beg the man with whom she'd planned to spend her life to honour his proposal, neither would she attempt to shame him into doing so. If he went ahead and married his cousin Stella instead of her then Beatrice knew she would have learned something vitally important and deeply upsetting about Colin's character. And also about her own: she had previously believed she'd become a reasonable judge of people.

'If you have chosen to comply with the terms of your uncle's will, then there is nothing more to be said,' Beatrice whispered. 'All I would ask before you leave is that you find the courtesy to explain to my father why he has wasted his money on my wedding day.' Hot brine squeezed between her lashes and she averted her face.

'I will of course make any financial reparation necessary,' Colin vowed stiltedly.

As he took her elbow to turn her towards him Beatrice flinched from his touch as though scalded. 'I think you should go now, sir.'

'Please don't hate me, Beatrice…I couldn't stand it…'

'I have a lot more to stand than you, I think.' Beatrice gazed stormily into eyes that were pleading for compassion. 'Please do not beg me for anything. Especially that I should not hate you for squandering three years of my life and destroying my future happiness.' She distanced herself from him, an odd lethargy enveloping her. 'In truth I do not hate you, Colin…I am coming to realise that I pity you for allowing a person you barely knew to dupe you and dictate to you.' She smiled sourly. 'I've let you kiss and caress me, yet despite our intimacy I never really knew you. I'd not imagined you capable of acting in such a callous and selfish way.'

Beatrice noticed the faint colour rising in his cheeks at her wounding criticism.

'It is because I refuse to act selfishly that I must give you up.' Colin cleared his throat. 'I have a family duty to uphold…'

'What about your duty to me?' Beatrice cried. But she knew it was too late. If he were to change his mind and refuse his birthright to marry her instead things would never be right between them. She could never recapture the person she'd been just twenty minutes ago, when excitedly smoothing her hair and gown before speeding down the stairs to joyfully welcome her fiancé and ask him to stay to dine with them.

He too would be different: outwardly Colin might claim to have forgiven her for making him forfeit his inheritance. Inwardly his bitter disappointment might fester and grow until it destroyed the love he professed to still have for her.

'I made a mistake in giving you my heart, but in time

I will appreciate you handing it back to me. The pain will pass now I have come to understand your character better.' Beatrice paused, a part of her relishing the hurt she had brought to his eyes with that brutal comment. But she was not by nature spiteful and the feeling soon faded. 'My father is in his study. Please call on him before leaving and do the honourable thing. He is not a wealthy man, as you know, and has scrimped to buy my trousseau.'

'My uncle was fifty-five and if he knew he was not long for this world he kept it to himself. Had he been old and infirm I would have had more cause to check on the terms of my inheritance.' Colin strode to block Beatrice's path as she made to exit the room.

'I've had explanations enough,' Beatrice rebuffed coolly. 'There is no need for you to tarry longer. I hope you find your new wealth and status make up for what you and I have lost.' She withdrew a small garnet ring from her finger and held it out. 'Yours, I believe. Now, please let me pass.'

Colin's lips tightened at Beatrice's frosty tone but he took the gem and pocketed it, standing aside. 'I've suffered too…I'll never forget you…'

Beatrice heard his plaintive farewell as she closed the parlour door. With her eyes filled with burning water she approached the stairs. She would wait in her bedchamber till Colin left, then go and see her father.

Beatrice knew her papa would need comforting over this calamity as much as she did. Walter Dewey had liked Dr Burnett as his physician and as his future son-in-law. Colin had promised financial reparation and she hoped her father would not be too proud or too angry to accept the cash.

Her sister, Elise, would be shocked to discover she was not shortly to be a matron of honour. Elise lived in Mayfair and had done her best to persuade her kin to join her as permanent house guests following her marriage to Viscount Blackthorne. Alex had a fabulous mansion on Upper Brook Street. But Walter Dewey had insisted a quiet pastoral life suited him. Beatrice had also been happy to remain in bucolic bliss in Hertfordshire as her physician fiancé was living and working in the vicinity of St Albans.

Now Beatrice wondered if Colin had always wished to improve his prospects from that of country doctor, and if so whether he might immediately move to town with his intended wife to enjoy what remained of the season.

At twenty-five, Beatrice accepted that in the eyes of the world she was past her marriageable prime. Most of the friends she'd made during her debut were now married with children. Colin's future bride was not known to Beatrice—unsurprisingly, as she'd just learned her rival was some seven years her junior and had just made her come-out. Bea had digested that much about Stella Rawlings before shock had snatched away her senses, leaving her momentarily deaf to the horrible details of Colin's visit.

The light tap on the door brought Bea's head up off the pillow. She had been dozing on her bed's coverlet while waiting for the sound of the doctor's departure from her house, and her life. Beatrice knuckled her tired eyes as she went to the door, realising she'd cried herself into a deeper sleep than she'd wished to have.

'Papa!' Beatrice frowned in consternation. 'You should not have come upstairs!' She sent a searching glance over her father's stooped shoulder. 'Did Mr Francis help you with the climb?'

Walter Dewey waved away his daughter's concern as he made slow progress into her bedchamber assisted by a wooden walking stick. 'Norman is out hunting rabbits for our dinner.' He explained the manservant's absence. 'My small struggle is nothing to the pain I know you must be suffering my dear.'

Walter eased himself down into the armchair by the window. Raising his tired eyes to his daughter's wan face he shook his head to indicate he felt lost for words.

'Dr Burnett has gone?' Beatrice croaked.

'He has, and with my opinion of him ringing in his ears.'

Beatrice dropped to her knees by her father's chair and took a dry, withered hand between her soft palms. 'Please don't be upset over it, Papa,' she whispered, fearful for his health. She could hear his laboured breathing and see a greyish circle outlining his lips. 'My heart will mend…'

'You have a resilient ticker, then, my love,' Walter remarked wryly. How many times now has it been broken in two by some fellow?'

Beatrice knew her father was referring to her past romances that had foundered—usually because the gentleman involved had no money and could not afford to get married. How ironic that this time she must remain a spinster because the reverse were true. Her fiancé had recently received his inheritance and with it a demand to jilt her.

'Had this confounded Sir Donald not died when he did, leaving his odious terms and conditions, you would shortly have been Mrs Burnett.'

Walter gazed levelly at his daughter's upturned face. Beatrice had always been a beauty; some said she was fairer than her younger sister, who had bagged herself a nobleman three years ago. Walter thought them equally wonderful, in their own ways, although he wished Beatrice resembled her younger sister in one aspect: Elise had chosen to give her heart just the once, and very wisely.

Two previous rogues—besotted by Beatrice's golden-haired loveliness, Walter was sure—had encouraged his elder girl to think they would propose, then bitten their tongues at the last minute. In both cases it had transpired that they must fortune-hunt for a bride, being penniless.

Out in the sticks and cut off from the cream of polite society he might be, but Walter was cognizant with marriage mart standards: Beatrice's chances of finding a spouse diminished with every failed romance and every year that passed.

In Walter's opinion Beatrice was as lovely at twenty-five as she'd been when half a decade younger. Her creamy complexion was smooth and unblemished and her blonde hair appeared as shiny and abundant as it had been when she was a teenager. Her figure was enviably slender, yet curvaceous enough to catch a man's eye, and her vivacity made people take to her instantly. Yet still his elder girl remained at home with him because he'd never had the means to provide either of his daughters with a dowry.

Elise had married a millionaire who'd stated bluntly that the privilege of marrying Walter's daughter was payment enough. Unfortunately a similar good and generous fellow had never crossed Beatrice's path, catching her eye.

Colin Burnett had come closest to walking her down the aisle, and thus Walter despised him the most.

'Do you think Burnett truthfully had no idea of the clause in his uncle's will?'

Beatrice gave a little nod. 'I believe him sincere on that; as for greatly adoring me and never forgetting me, that I now find harder to swallow.' Her father's thin fingers closed comfortingly on hers. 'Did Colin offer to pay back the cash you spent on wedding preparations?' Bea asked huskily.

'He did,' Walter confirmed, bringing his daughter's hand to his cool lips.

'It is only fair you are not left out of pocket because of him. You will take what is due to you, won't you, Papa?' Beatrice used the heel of her hand on her cheek to remove a trickle of tears.

'Indeed I shall!' Walter forcefully concurred. 'I admit there was a moment when I felt like telling him to take himself and his money off to rot in hell...but I didn't.' He rumbled a chuckle. 'He might be getting off scot-free from a breach of promise suit but he won't wriggle out of my expenses so easily. Mark my words, my dear, Burnett will get his comeuppance for treating you so shabbily.'

'Letters for me?' Elise Blackthorne jumped up from her dressing table stool as her maid approached, proffering a silver salver.

Excitedly the viscountess rifled through the post, ignoring elegant cards inviting her to society parties, to find what she was looking for. She frowned; it was from Hertfordshire but bore her father's spidery script rather than her sister's neat slanting hand.

'I shall not need you for an hour or so, Maria.' Before the maid left her bedchamber Elise asked, 'Is the viscount eating breakfast?'

'He has gone to the stables, my lady. Shall I send one of the boys to give him a message?'

Elise shook her head, satisfied she would see Alex before he went about his business for the day. She still felt sated from his lovemaking that morning and knew she should get dressed. If he came back to find her in a lacy negligee they might once more tumble onto the silk sheets, limbs entwined. Elise wanted to get to Pall Mall early today because the dressmaker there had recently given her a fitting and she was impatient to see the beautiful blue satin gown she would wear when matron of honour at Bea's wedding.

Elise corresponded regularly with her sister and relished reading about all the wedding preparations. A local seamstress was making Bea's gown, although the bride to be was keeping the style of it a secret. Mrs Garner had a workshop based in St Albans and had served the Dewey family for over a decade. Walter had never had the means to provide his daughters with many new clothes when growing up and their debuts had thus been modest affairs.

'What have you got there?'

Else twisted about at the sound of her husband's husky baritone.

Alex came closer and dropped a kiss on her bare shoulder. His fingers continued to caress his wife's satiny skin as he glanced at the parchment in her hand, recognising the writing.

'Your father has sent you a letter.'

Elise twisted about in the circle of her husband's arms. 'I'm just about to read it, Alex, so don't…' Her breathy plea was cut off as his mouth slanted over hers and he drew her closer.

'Oh…Alex…' Elise giggled, but her protest was half-hearted as she melted against him.

'It's your own fault,' he growled. 'What's a man to do when his gorgeous wife parades about half naked?'

'Whatever he likes, I suppose,' Elise breathed against his preying mouth.

'Right answer, sweetheart…' Alex purred and, swinging her up in his arms, headed for the bed.

Chapter Two

'There was a time when it was hard to shake you off my shoulder; now I need to make an appointment to see you?' Alex Blackthorne's ironic comment drew an apologetic grin from his best friend. However, the fellow's narrowed gaze remained fixed on the razor sweeping a path through stubble towards a lean cheekbone.

Hugh Kendrick swirled the implement in a china bowl filled with soap-floating water before turning to face the viscount. 'You know I'd sooner come to watch the fight with you, but I've promised Gwen a trip to Epsom races this afternoon.'

Alex sank into a hide chair in his friend's bedchamber. Obligingly he shifted to one side, allowing Hugh's startled valet to rescue an elegant jacket that his master had discarded over the back of the upholstery.

'Besides, if your wife wasn't out of town you wouldn't want my company, would you?' Over the top of the towel mopping his face Hugh hiked a dark eyebrow at Alex.

'True…' Alex sighed, flicking a speck from a thigh breeched in fawn cloth.

He was feeling at a loose end since Elise had gone to Hertfordshire to visit her family. It was puzzling that Walter Dewey had written a letter containing a coded message that he would like Elise to visit as soon as she was able.

Alex felt rather guilty now for distracting his wife from immediately reading her note on the morning it had arrived. It had been some hours after the post was delivered that Elise had finally retrieved the paper from amongst their warm, crumpled bed sheets. Mere moments after breaking the seal she'd thrust the letter beneath Alex's nose, announcing that she'd deciphered her father's few odd sentences and was certain that a crisis had occurred. Elise could never bear to be parted from her infant son, so Adam had gone to Hertfordshire too, and at Alex's insistence Maria had accompanied mother and child in one of the luxurious Blackthorne travelling coaches.

'You look browned off,' Hugh remarked, shrugging into his shirt. For several minutes he had been contemplating Alex's frowning expression as he stared into space with his chin resting atop fingers forming a steeple. Hugh guessed his friend was already missing his beloved wife and son.

The two men had been friends for decades, despite the fact that for most of that time their statuses had been poles apart. Hugh had been the underdog, with nothing much to claim to his credit other than his popularity and his family connections. His late father had been an upstanding fellow, a minor peer of the realm who had seen the best in everybody. Unfortunately that blind faith had been particularly strong where his heir was concerned. Others, however, could see what a corrupt, calculating character was Toby Kendrick. On taking his birthright following his father's demise, Hugh's brother had become even more of an unbearable wretch.

But Hugh no longer had reason to feel resentful over the bad hand life had dealt him as the second son of a gentleman who believed in primogeniture. Neither had he reason to feel lucky that Viscount Blackthorne had chosen him as a life-long comrade. Hugh might not have a title to polish, but he now had every other advantage that his illustrious friend enjoyed, including a fortune that his acquaintances coveted and that dukes would like their debutante daughters to share in through marriage.

'It's odd for my father-in-law to call Elise home.' Alex finally stirred himself to answer while standing up. The last time his wife had been summoned in such a way Beatrice had sent word because their father had fractured his collarbone in a fall. Naturally Walter had wanted to have both his beloved daughters by his side… just in case the injury had proved fatal.

'Do you think some harm might have again befallen him?'

'Walter wrote the letter himself, so I doubt he's bedridden.' Alex shrugged. 'It's probably all about Beatrice's wedding day. Elise is matron of honour…' He grimaced bewilderment at the workings of the female mind.

Hugh glanced up to find his friend's eyes on him. 'Yes…perhaps it's just about the wedding,' he muttered, resuming buttoning his cuffs.

'You don't ask about Beatrice any more.' Alex began adjusting his cravat in the mantel glass now Hugh had left the space free.

'Does she ask about me?' Hugh countered, picking up his jacket and pegging it on a finger over a muscular shoulder. He preceded his friend towards the door.

They were heading towards the top of the stairs before Alex answered. 'You can't blame Beatrice for wanting to forget all about you after the way you behaved.'

Hugh's mouth tilted sardonically. 'Indeed...so it seems a bit pointless asking about her, doesn't it?' He plunged his hands into his pockets. 'A lot of water has passed under the bridge since then...'

'And for you...most of it flowed in India...' Alex remarked dryly.

'So it did...' Hugh said in a similar vein. 'I hope everything goes well on the big day.'

He moved ahead of Alex, descending the stairs at quite a speed.

On reaching the cool marble vestibule of Hugh's grand town house the friends waited for the butler to announce that the curricle had been brought round. A moment later they clattered down the stone steps, then stopped to exchange a few words before going their separate ways.

'Come along to Epsom with us if you're kicking your heels. You might back a few winners and cheer yourself up by raising your bank balance.' Hugh was speaking ironically; he knew very well that his friend's accounts were in no need of a boost. It was his spirits that were flagging.

The startling change in his own fortunes still gave Hugh cause to smile inwardly. Just two years ago he'd had reason to watch carefully every penny he spent. Now he could purchase a stable of prized Arabs and watch them race at Epsom—or anywhere else—if that was his whim. Yet Hugh realised that his enthusiasm for a day out with his favourite mistress was waning and he felt oddly deflated.

'You expect me to play gooseberry to you and the lovely Gwen?' Alex scowled. 'I don't think I will, but thanks for asking.' He clapped a hand on Hugh's shoulder. 'See you in White's later in the week, I expect.'

'It's a bit late to let Gwen down with an excuse.' Hugh sounded irritated by his conscience.

'Quite right…keep the lady happy,' Alex mocked.

Gwen Sharpe was a celebrated Cyprian known to select as lovers affluent gentlemen who could provide her with the finer things in life. Hugh certainly fitted the bill, following a bizarre stroke of luck that had made him one of the wealthiest men in the country.

'I'll be back before ten tonight. Do you fancy a visit to the Palm House to cure your boredom?' Hugh called over a shoulder as he approached the kerb to take the curricle's reins from his tiger.

Alex snorted a laugh. 'I'm a married man…are you trying to get me hung?'

Hugh shook his head in mock disgust. 'You're under the thumb…that's what you are.'

'And I'll willingly remain there…' Alex returned, grinning.

The Palm House was a notorious den of iniquity

where gambling and whoring went hand in hand. Men of all classes—from criminals to aristocracy—could be found mingling in its smoky environment from midnight till gone daybreak. At early light the club would spew forth its clientele, the majority of whom would stagger off with sore heads and empty purses.

Hugh set the greys to a trot, wishing he could shake off the feeling that he'd sooner return home than go to Epsom with Gwen. His mistress was beautiful and beguiling, if gratingly possessive at times. Any man would want to spend time with her… And yet Hugh, for a reason that escaped him, wanted solitude to reflect on a romance that had long been dead and buried. The woman he'd loved three years ago was now about to become another man's bride, so what purpose would be served by brooding on what might have been?

With a curse exploding through his gritted teeth Hugh set the horses to a faster pace, exasperated by his maudlin thoughts and the fact that his friend had chosen this morning to remind him that his sister-in-law's marriage was imminent. Beatrice Dewey was firmly in his past, and Gwen and Sophia, the courtesans he kept in high style, would serve very well for the present. If in need of deeper emotion he could head out to India and spend some time with somebody he'd grown to love…

'What do *you* want?'

'That's a nice greeting, I must say.'

'Are we to pretend I'm pleased to see you?' Hugh folded the newspaper he'd been reading whilst breakfasting and skimmed it over the crisp damask tablecloth.

He lounged into a mahogany chair-back, crossing his arms over the ruffles on his shirt. Sardonically, he surveyed his older brother.

Uninvited, Sir Toby Kendrick pulled out the chair opposite Hugh, seating himself with a flourish of coat-tails. He then stared obstinately at a footman until the fellow darted forward.

'Coffee—and fill a plate with whatever is over there.' Toby flicked a finger at the domed silver platters lining the sideboard whilst giving his order. He turned sly eyes on his brother, daring Hugh to object.

The servant withdrew with a jerky bow, a fleeting glance flying at his master from beneath his powdered wig. Hugh gave an imperceptible nod, sanctioning his brother's boorish demand to be fed.

All of the servants knew—in common with the *ton*—that Hugh Kendrick and his older brother did not get on.

Sir Toby's dislike of his younger brother had increased since Hugh's wealth and standing had eclipsed his own. Toby had relished what he deemed to be his rightful place as loftiest Kendrick. Now he'd been toppled, and in such a teeth-grindingly, shocking stroke of luck for his brother that Toby had been apoplectic when first hearing about it. Knowing that he wasn't alone in being bitter was no consolation to Toby. His brother was popular, and more people had been pleased than jealous of Hugh's success.

Their mother and their sister had been overjoyed—no doubt because they'd both benefited from Hugh's generosity. Toby had received nothing from Hugh other than a bottle of champagne with which to toast his luck.

In the event Toby had refrained from smashing the magnum to smithereens on the step and downed the prime vintage at record speed, drowning his sorrows.

'No broiled kidneys?' Toby used a silver fork to push the food about on the plate that had just been set before him.

'I don't like kidneys,' Hugh replied. He sat forward in his chair. 'Neither do I like being disturbed by visitors at his ungodly hour of the day.' He got to his feet. 'Are you going to tell me what you want? Or have you just turned up for a free breakfast and the opportunity to try my patience?'

Toby shoved away the plate of untasted splendid food, a curl to his lip. 'All that cash and you can't find yourself a decent cook?' he chortled.

'As you've no appetite, and nothing of moment to say, it's time you went on your way.' He addressed the footman. 'My brother is leaving. Show him out.' Turning his back on Toby he strolled to the huge windows that overlooked Grosvenor Square, idly surveying the busy street scene.

The servant attempted to conceal his satisfied smirk on springing forward to do his master's bidding.

'You're getting a bit too high and mighty, aren't you?' Toby barked, his cheeks florid.

'Perhaps I spent too long studying you when growing up,' Hugh drawled over a shoulder.

Toby whacked away the footman's ushering arm, stomping closer to Hugh. 'Very well...I have something to discuss,' he snarled in an undertone.

'Go ahead; but be brief. I have an appointment with my tailor.'

'Might we repair to your library and be private?' Toby suggested sarcastically.

Hugh glanced back at the servants clearing the breakfast things. He sighed. 'If we must…' He strode for the door without another word and once in the corridor approached the library at the same exasperated speed.

Toby trudged behind, his footsteps muffled by the luxurious carpet. Inwardly he squirmed at having to come here, cap in hand, and beg his brother for a loan. Not so long ago he had been the one the others in the family came to when in need of cash. It had given Toby immense pleasure to make them dance to his tune for their coins; even his mother had had to humble herself to extract her allowance from him. But now she had no need to because Hugh had provided her with a generous pension—something her dear late husband had omitted to do.

Sir Kenneth Kendrick had relied on his son and heir to provide fairly for his successors, proving that he might have doted on Toby but he had never come to know his eldest son's true nature.

'I need two hundred pounds urgently,' Toby blurted as soon as the door was closed behind him.

'Is that a request for a loan?'

'You know damn well it is,' Toby spat. He swiped a hand about his mouth, aware he'd need to control his temper if he was to get the cash and keep the duns at bay. Hugh might be open-handed where his mother and sister were concerned, but his generosity to Toby was a different matter.

Hugh leaned on the library table that almost spanned from one end of the oak-panelled room to the other. He drummed his long fingers in slow rhythm on the leather-topped furniture. 'I've already handed over a thousand pounds in less than six months.' Hugh watched his brother's lips whiten in anger at that reminder.

'I didn't realise you were keeping a tally of the paltry sums.' Toby flung himself down in a chair, affecting ennui.

'As I recall, one thousand pounds wasn't a paltry amount when I came to you many years ago and begged for your help in securing Sarah's future.'

Then Toby's meanness had run so deep that he'd denied his only sister the cash she desperately needed after she'd been compromised during her debut. With their father gone it had fallen to Hugh, impecunious at that time, to rescue Sarah's reputation. He'd managed to scrape together a dowry—the majority of the cash borrowed from Alex Blackthorne—thus tempting a decent chap, lacking prospects, to put a ring on his disgraced sister's finger.

Inwardly Toby railed at himself; he'd laid himself wide open to that barb. 'The little madam deserved to be taught a lesson for acting like a strumpet.'

'Our sister did nothing wrong other than to trust one of your friends to act as a gentleman. She was seventeen and not worldly-wise,' Hugh coldly reminded him.

Toby snorted derision. 'Well, she was worldly-wise after her folly…so a lesson well learned about promenading after dark with randy men. You—and she—should thank me rather than criticising.'

Hugh moved his head in disgust. 'I wonder sometimes if we are related. You really are the most obnoxious character.'

'Are you questioning our dear mama's virtue?' Toby guffawed. 'She'll not thank you for hearing that repeated. Perhaps I might tell her.'

He eyed his sibling calculatingly, feeling confident that Hugh would relent rather than risk upsetting their widowed mother. The dowager was approaching sixty-five and would be distraught to know her elder son risked a spell in the Fleet because his debts were out of control.

'I've had enough of you…take yourself off…' Hugh snapped in exasperation, turning for the door.

'What's wrong? No money left? Sent too much out to India, have you? Toby's voice was low and sly and he concealed a smirk at the look of intense hatred he'd brought to his brother's face.

'I'll arrange for a bank draft later in the day,' Hugh said, just before quitting the room. 'Now, if you don't mind, I need to be elsewhere…'

Toby strutted after him, looking exceedingly pleased with himself.

'If you come again demanding me to bail you out of gambling debts you'll be wasting your time. I won't care what you say…'

'Won't you, now…?' Toby drawled provocatively. 'Gambling debts?' He smoothly changed the subject. 'It's nothing so vulgar, my dear fellow. Serena has expensive tastes in jewellery, if you *must* have the details…'

Toby wasn't referring to his prospective fiancée's taste but to that of his mistress. Hugh knew his brother had set up Serena Worthing in a smart apartment, and even with a marriage contract under discussion it seemed Toby had no intention of putting her off to concentrate on his future wife.

'Well, whatever it is…whoring, drinking, gambling… you'll pay for it yourself in future.'

'If ever our positions return to what they were…what they *should* be…I'll remember this conversation and all those others where you've had the damnable cheek to moralise.' Toby pointed a stout finger at his brother. 'Before you got rich and Blackthorne got married the two of you were constant petticoat-chasers. Blackthorne might have eased off now, but you're worse than ever since you got back from India.' Toby thrust his face close to Hugh's jaw. 'Tell me…what it is about an exotic beauty that fires a man's blood so…?'

'You sound jealous of my popularity with the ladies.' Hugh shoved his brother away and strode on along the corridor. 'Show yourself out.'

Chapter Three

'I'm sorry Papa worried you enough to bring you racing to Hertfordshire yesterday. I had no idea he'd summoned you home just because the wedding is off.' Beatrice bounced her baby nephew on her knee. 'Of course it is wonderful to have you visit, Elise, and this little chap has grown so big since I last saw him.'

Elise had been pouring tea into bone china, but on hearing the quaver in her sister's voice she put down the pot and crouched down by the side of Bea's armchair. 'You don't need to be brave with me, my dear. I know how dreadfully hurt you are.' She pressed Bea's fingers in comfort.

Beatrice avoided Elise's astute gaze, blinking rapidly at the window to one side of her. 'It is all right…really it is…it has been nearly a week now since…' She tried to name the person who'd caused her heartbreak but found his name stuck to her tongue.

As her nephew gurgled, giving her a gummy smile, Bea fondled his soft pink cheek with a forefinger.

'Another few days and I will be right as rain—won't I, Master Adam?'

'Well, I know I would not be, if it were me who'd been so cruelly jilted,' Elise announced pithily. She shook her head in disbelief. 'I'd never have imagined Dr Burnett to be a callous or a fickle fellow.'

'I'm glad I wasn't the only one who mistook his character.' Beatrice sighed. 'I can't forgive him for abandoning me in favour of family duty, yet since I've had time to calm down I understand why he did so.'

'Then I think you exceedingly over-obliging!' Elise exclaimed. 'Love should override all else in my book.'

'In a perfect world…perhaps…' Beatrice returned philosophically. 'I think matrimony and Beatrice Dewey are destined to remain strangers.'

'Never say so! There is a husband for you…he just has not shown himself yet.' Elise attempted to draw her sister from her glums with a provocative comment. 'As I recall, there was nobody more determined to be a wife and mother than you.'

Beatrice chuckled wryly at that reminder. Indeed, there had been a time when she'd driven her poor sister to distraction, so keen had she been to settle down with a nice fellow and raise a little family of her own. After several false starts she'd met Colin and finally thought her ambition was within her grasp. Now, for some reason, she felt tired of struggling towards that particular dream…

'You girls are up early.' Walter Dewey entered the sunny front parlour, supported by his stick. He gave his daughters an affectionate smile, thinking it nice to have them both together again at home, and with the added bonus of his handsome little grandson.

In Walter's opinion the child was a perfect blend of his parents: he had the viscount's brown eyes and sturdy build and his mother's sharp chin and fair hair.

'Did you sleep well?' he asked Elise. 'I heard young Adam having a grizzle just before dawn broke.'

'He was wet so I changed his nappy,' Viscountess Blackthorne said, as though it were the most natural thing in the world to tend to her baby herself rather than give Adam to his nurse.

Following their parents' acrimonious divorce, Elise and Bea had been reared by their papa in straitened circumstances, so were accustomed to being useful and practical in mundane matters. Both young women were quite happy to dress themselves and knew how to cook and clean. When younger, the sisters had taken to painting their bedrooms and made a capable job of it, much to their papa's surprise and delight.

'Don't look at me like that, miss,' Walter mildly reproved, having caught Beatrice frowning at him. 'I know you believe I'm at fault because your sister has better things to do than commiserate with us that you've been put back on the shelf—'

'I certainly do not!' Elise cut across her father. 'There's nothing more important to me than being here with you, although the reason for it is upsetting.' She gave her sister's cheek an affectionate stroke. 'Bea is certainly not on the shelf, Papa! How can she be when she is so pretty and looks not a day over eighteen…?'

'Oh…Elise!' Beatrice choked. 'A very nice compliment but it really is too much.'

'Perhaps I exaggerated just a little. You could pass easily for twenty-one and that is certainly not over-egging it.' Elise cocked her head to assess her sister's countenance. Beatrice was still one of the loveliest young women of her acquaintance, and in the *haut monde* Viscountess Blackthorne certainly came into contact with some vaunted beauties.

For the first time in days Beatrice chuckled with genuine amusement. 'Papa's right: I might be on the shelf…' she pulled a little face '…but I'm not sure it worries me; at present I'm fed up with gentlemen and romance.'

'That will pass.' Walter flapped a hand. 'Every young lady craves her own home and family.'

'Are you trying to get rid of me, Papa?' Beatrice teased her father.

'You know I am not! You may stay with your old papa for as long as you wish…but to tell the truth I was looking forward to walking you down the aisle before these old legs finally give out on me.'

'And so you shall, Papa,' Elise reassured him, getting up from her place by her sister's chair. Having tested the tea that she'd abandoned in the pot, Elise found it now unpalatably lukewarm.

'Your Aunt Dolly will be very sad to have this news,' Walter muttered, sinking into a seat.

'She loves a wedding,' Elise reflected, settling by her papa on the sofa.

'She travelled here to attend your nuptials uninvited,

as I recall.' Walter dredged up a chuckle at the memory of his widowed sister turning up out of the blue on the eve of the wedding, expecting to be housed and fed.

'And Mrs Vickers accompanied her,' Elise chipped in, fondly dwelling on her countryside wedding at the local church. It had been a quiet, yet wonderful occasion, with just her family about her. She glanced at her sister, wondering if Bea was musing sadly on the fact that Colin Burnett had acted as Alex's groomsman that fine afternoon.

'I rather liked Edith Vickers,' Beatrice remarked brightly. She had indeed been thinking of Colin's role in her sister's happy day and pounced on the first thing that came into her head to chase memories of him from her mind. 'How is Mrs Vickers? Do you ever see her?'

'Oh...of course...you would not know for I've not had a reason to mention it.' Elise frowned. 'Sadly, Mrs Vickers passed away.' She leaned forward to impart an exciting titbit. 'There was quite a brouhaha when it came to light that she had not been as hard up as she'd believed herself to be. When Edith's husband died his creditors pounced and left her in very reduced circumstances. But they left alone the deeds to a strip of land in India because it was deemed to be barren. Mrs Vickers bequeathed it to her nephew, Hugh.'

'Hugh Kendrick?' Walter snarled.

He recalled that name. When Beatrice had gone with her sister to London several years ago Mrs Vickers's nephew had shown undue interest in Beatrice, raising her hopes that he might propose. Walter had been enraged to know the fellow hadn't the wherewithal to take on a wife so must fortune-hunt for a bride. He'd been angry at himself, too, knowing that if only he had put by a dowry for his daughters his elder child might have been settled before the younger, as was the proper way of things.

'Oh, I'm sorry to hear of her passing.' Beatrice wiped dribble from her nephew's mouth with her hanky. 'I expect Aunt Dolly misses Edith. They were good friends, weren't they?'

'So…the land was not worthless?' Walter guessed, returning to the crux of the matter.

'It was not,' Elise confirmed, clapping her hands in glee. 'Alex was delighted for his friend when he found out about his good fortune. Of course there were many green-eyed people not so pleased at the turn of events, and Sir Toby Kendrick led the pack—'

'What happened?' Walter butted in impatiently, his gnarled hand clutching tightly at his stick, turning the knuckles white. Walter loved a good tale of Lady Luck turning up unexpectedly. Many a time over the years he had wished that elusive minx would smile on him when his marriage and his business had crumbled, leaving him desolate with two teenage girls to bring up alone.

'The strip of land contained some mines, long ago abandoned as dry. Hugh went to India and had them reinvestigated from curiosity and they turned up a seam of fine diamonds. So now Hugh Kendrick is very rich, and I for one am overjoyed for him.'

Beatrice blinked in astonishment at her past love's extraordinary stroke of luck. 'Yes…good for him…' she said quietly.

'Good for him?' Walter barked. 'Another fellow who broke your heart, as I recall.'

'I do seem to attract rogues.' Beatrice's tone was rueful rather than bitter. 'I'm sure it's my own fault,' she added with a twinkling smile. 'You have warned me not to be so impetuous, haven't you, Papa?' Bea knew that in the past, especially in her pursuit of Hugh Kendrick, she'd been not only impetuous but foolhardy.

Walter glanced at his jilted daughter. He'd been right to call Elise home, he realised; just a few days ago Beatrice's low spirits had worried him. Now, with her sister close by, she was recovering far better than Walter had dared hope. It had always been a great comfort to him that his girls were good friends as well as close kin. He knew of families where siblings resented one another—especially when one child did better than the other. But Beatrice had only been happy for her younger sister when she had caught herself a handsome aristocrat to wed, and Elise with her open, sweet nature never attempted to lord it over her less fortunate sibling.

'It's a shame Edith didn't pop off a few years ago,' Walter said. 'Her rogue of a nephew would have received his bequest earlier and been in a position to call on me for your hand.'

'Papa!' Beatrice cried, half-amused, half-outraged. 'Poor Edith! I am sad to hear of her demise no matter what benefits it turned up.' She gestured airily. 'Besides, it all turned out for the best; after that little sojourn in London ended, and with it my friendship with Mr Kendrick, I had only been home a few days before I was feeling relieved that he'd thrown me over.' She tickled

Adam, making him giggle, while adding self-mockingly, 'I quickly met Colin and fell in love all over again.'

'On the rebound,' Walter muttered darkly. 'And look where that got you.'

'Hugh *is* still a bachelor,' Elise piped up, subtly siding with her father.

She had also thought at the time that her sister had transferred her affection to Dr Burnett far too quickly after Hugh's rejection. Not that Hugh had carelessly withdrawn his suit; at the time he had confided in Alex to feeling mortified at not being in a position to propose to Bea. Elise had thought him brutal in making a clean break with her sister, yet had come to realise it had been the decent thing to do. The couple's mutual affection had started stirring gossip, and the town tabbies loved nothing better than to amuse themselves shredding an innocent's reputation.

A girl who too obviously set her cap at a gentleman, then failed to get him to put a ring on her finger, invited opprobrium. Worse still, if it had been discovered that Beatrice had advertised for a husband in a gazette, like a vulgar hussy, the Dewey sisters would have been hounded out of town during the season they'd been house guests of the Chapmans. In the event a scandal *had* broken, but Elise and Alex had been the butt of it and it had quickly died away when Elise received Alex's marriage proposal.

'I understood Hugh Kendrick had set his sights on Fiona Chapman's inheritance.' Walter had been reflecting, as had his daughters, on the drama of three years ago.

'Fiona deterred him from proposing, I believe, knowing as she did that his heart wasn't in it.' Elise glanced at Beatrice, who seemed oblivious to the hint and continued playing pat-a-cake with Adam.

'That young woman must have been kicking herself ever since.' Walter growled a laugh. 'I expect she has had the scolding of her life from Maude.' He mentioned Fiona's mother with obvious fondness. The Chapmans were good people and had remained loyal to the Deweys through good and bad times over the decades.

'Verity is increasing with her first child.' Verity Clemence, née Chapman, was a very dear friend of Elise's. 'I have only just found out!' She answered Bea's unspoken question, flashed by a pair of expressive blue eyes. 'I believe the babe is not due till late autumn.'

'She must be thrilled, and so must be Mr and Mrs Chapman.' Beatrice sounded wistful. 'It will be their first grandchild…'

A bang on the door caused the room's occupants to abruptly cease their lively conversation and look at one another in surprise. Elise jumped up to peer discreetly out of the square-paned window. 'We are on the point of having a visit from Mrs Callan and Victoria,' she groaned.

'The grapevine has done its work, then,' Beatrice acknowledged wryly.

'Would you sooner I sent them away?' Elise feared that her sister was right: the vicar's wife and daughter had come to pry about the broken engagement rather than politely socialise.

'Everybody will know sooner or later, so I must get used to the idea of facing down the stares and whispers.'

Bea stood up, handing Adam to his mother. 'Let's get it over with now, while I'm feeling ready to deflect any amount of sly comments.'

Elise's smile combined admiration and encouragement for Bea. 'I'll tell Betty to show them in.'

A few minutes later Elise was back with her family in the front parlour, exchanging a resigned smile with Bea as they heard voices in the hallway heralding their visitors' imminent appearance.

'We came as soon as we heard,' Mrs Callan announced with theatrical sympathy, surging into the room. She halted abruptly, causing her plump daughter trailing in her wake to collide with her. Nudging Victoria, to alert her to the presence of aristocracy, Mrs Callan bobbed low to the viscountess, who was rocking her son in her arms.

'We are indeed honoured to see you today, Lady Blackthorne. Ah…you have brought your little son to see his grandpapa.' Ethel Callan fluttered a hand to her throat to indicate her regret in what she was about to say. 'Of course it is a shame that such calamitous news brings you back to Hertfordshire.'

'I come to Hertfordshire gladly, for good or bad news.'

'Oh…of course…' Mrs Callan approached Beatrice, taking her hands in a thin, dry grip. 'Shocked! It is not too strong a word!' She gave Bea's fingers a vigorous shake. 'Deeply disappointed also, to discover that nice Dr Burnett would heartlessly abandon you like that.'

'We have discovered he is not so nice, have we not, Mama?' Victoria piped up.

'Dr Burnett had his reasons for doing what he did

and I have accepted them, so that is that.' Beatrice's voice was cool and held an air of finality as she firmly withdrew her hands from the older woman's clutch. She was not about to be drawn into complaining about her loss. Whatever she said would be repeated ad infinitum in the village.

'Do take a seat, madam, and you also, Miss Callan.' Walter's fist was quivering on his stick as his annoyance increased. Just as he'd been daring to hope Beatrice seemed more cheerful these two were likely to overset her again with their false pity. He knew for a fact that Victoria had done her utmost to snare the doctor herself. It had gone round the locality that the minx had concocted ailments simply to get the fellow to make a house call. Her father had moaned to Walter that he owed Burnett a tidy sum on account of his spinster daughter's antics, and no gain made from it.

Ethel Callan settled down, with much smoothing of skirts, in a vacant chair by the fireside, and her daughter perched on the sofa next to Walter.

'We were just about to have some fresh tea,' Beatrice announced. 'I'll ask Mrs Francis to bring two more cups and a fresh pot…' Her voice tailed off as another rat-a-tat on the door was heard. Inwardly she groaned, fearing yet more ladies had come to gleefully commiserate with her. 'I'll go this time.' She sent Elise a subtle wink that conveyed she'd sooner her sister fielded questions for a short while.

Chapter Four

In the hallway Beatrice spied the comforting figure of Mrs Francis ambling towards her from the direction of the kitchen.

'I'll attend to the door.' Bea gave the housekeeper a smile. 'Would you make some tea for us, please, and bring it along directly? The sooner we have been hospitable the sooner our guests might decide to be on their way.'

Betty Francis twitched a smile, understanding the quip. 'Don't you worry. I'll be quick as I can with the refreshments, but maybe I'll just dawdle a moment and see how many cups we might need.' The woman's grey head pointed grimly at the door. Betty knew very well why people were calling on them, and wouldn't be surprised to see Squire Thaddon's wife outside with some of her friends, keen to join the inquisition that was taking place in the front parlour.

'I suppose that might be wise,' Bea said wryly.

'The rumour mill's been grinding overtime, no doubt

about that,' Betty muttered darkly. 'Might be you'll open up and I'll need to break out another tea service.'

Betty Francis and her husband Norman had been with the Deweys for approaching twenty-five years and felt very protective of the family. Betty had been like a mother to the girls when the hussy Mr Dewey had married ran off to her lover. If she bumped into the doctor Betty would cheerfully wring his neck for breaking Miss Beatrice's heart. But she'd heard from the butcher's boy, who'd pedalled over earlier in the week, that Colin Burnett had wasted no time in upping sticks and moving away.

With one hand Beatrice smoothed her sprigged muslin dress, while the other tucked blonde tendrils behind her small ears. Forcing an insouciant expression, she opened the door. Extreme astonishment caused her smile to freeze on her full pink lips.

'Hello, Beatrice; you look well…'

'Why…Mr Kendrick…I…that is…we were expecting somebody else,' Beatrice finished faintly, having finally snapped herself to attention.

'You remember me…I'm flattered.'

Beatrice attempted to rouse herself from her stupor. Her heart had begun to thud erratically and the pearl buttons on her bodice were quivering with every breath she took. But if her visitor noticed her bosom's alluring movement he gave no sign; Hugh Kendrick's eyes were politely fixed on her blanching face.

'I'm sorry to startle you, and hope I've not arrived at a bad time…'

'No…not at all…' Bea fibbed. 'Please…do come in,

sir.' She belatedly remembered her manners and drew to one side, aware that Betty was hovering behind, watching and listening to their strained conversation.

'Just one more cup, then, please, Mrs Francis.' Beatrice was thankful to have a reason to turn to the housekeeper and compose herself, simply to avoid a pair or relentless hawk-like eyes.

She *had* recognised Hugh straight away, yet marvelled at having done so. The person before her little resembled the gentleman she had fallen in love with three years ago. His thick hair was still conker-brown, worn rather long, and his eyes were deepest hazel, fringed with ebony lashes; but there all similarity ended. Once he'd had an appealing fresh-faced demeanour and had worn modestly styled attire. Now his lean, angular face was sun-beaten and bore lines of dissipation. His elegantly tailored suit of clothing, dusty and creased from the journey, proclaimed him a man who could afford to be carelessly indulgent.

So far they'd exchanged few words, all of them polite, yet Bea felt unsettled by his lazy confidence. Once Hugh Kendrick would blush endearingly the moment she entered a room; at present she found his hooded amber gaze intimidating rather than flattering. As Beatrice pivoted about to again invite him into her home she sensed a pang of regret that he was no longer a charming young fellow but an aloof stranger who possessed an alarming virility.

'I expect you're busy with wedding preparations.'

His quiet comment caused Beatrice to snap her darkening eyes to him, wondering if he was being deliberately sarcastic. His tone had been as unemotional as were his features, but she quickly realised it was unlikely he'd yet heard her bad news. Her sister had only found out a few days ago on reaching Hertfordshire, and Elise's husband remained in ignorance of what had gone on.

'It's none of my business, I know. My apologies for mentioning it.' Hugh had sensed her frostiness increase at the mention of her marriage. She had good cause to dislike him, and he'd often cursed the reason for it.

But not any more. He'd been too broke to have her—the only woman he'd really wanted—and following several humiliating and vain attempts at fortune-hunting a bride he'd done with love and marriage. Now he could buy himself all the female company he needed, and renew it when he grew bored with the women in his life.

Hugh's mouth slanted in self-mockery as he recalled that a joyful wedding reception had been taking place the last time they'd been in one another's company.

Alex Blackthorne had been married in Hertfordshire at a country church with few people in attendance, but he had bestowed on his bride an extravagant party when they arrived back in Mayfair. No expense had been spared and the lavish affair had seen ambitious society brides emulating it ever since.

During the celebration Hugh remembered Beatrice and her father keeping their distance from him. He had taken against the fellow escorting Beatrice even before Alex told him that Beatrice Dewey had become engaged to Colin Burnett.

'What do you want, sir?' Bea asked coolly, although

her complexion had grown warm beneath his relentless scrutiny. She felt wound as tightly as a spring, but the thrill of being so close to him, enveloped in his musky sandalwood scent, was not easily conquered. If he'd just stop staring at her, she thought crossly, she might manage to calm down and stop turning over in her mind what had happened between them years ago.

At Vauxhall Pleasure Gardens, Hugh had singled her out, paying her such attention that a crowd of envious women had closed in on them to eavesdrop. The giddy elation of that warm midsummer evening and the following days, anticipating her next meeting with Hugh, were not easy to forget. Neither was the memory of her happiness disintegrating when he bluntly told her he couldn't see her again.

'We have some neighbours visiting. I do not want to seem inhospitable, sir, but it might be better if you do not join us.' Mrs Callan's hoarse laugh had jolted Beatrice to the present. 'My father has not forgotten or forgiven that once we knew each other…that is, he recalls that our brief friendship turned sour,' Beatrice hastily amended, blushing. They had most definitely not *known* each other—in the biblical sense or any other. She had mistaken this man's nature and sincerity just as she had with Colin.

'I regret that we parted before I knew you as well as I would have liked.'

'I cannot echo that sentiment, sir.' Hugh's amused tone had deepened the colour staining Beatrice's porcelain complexion. '*My* only regret is that I ever became acquainted with you at all.' Stolen kisses and caresses, snatched during their brief moments alone, were at the forefront of her mind, putting a disquieting throb low in her belly. Bea feared he might also be recalling their passionate moonlit trysts, and his next soft comment proved her intuitive.

'I don't believe you wish we'd never met when we had such a delightful time.'

'Then you should curb your conceit, because it is the truth,' Beatrice snapped, avoiding the sultry glint in his eyes. 'Once again I must ask you what you want. I cannot believe you have simply come to see me and reminisce—'

'I won't keep you long from your friends,' Hugh interrupted smoothly. 'Nice as it is to see you, my dear, it's a far more vital matter that brings me here uninvited.'

Bea was aware of the arrogance in his tone and felt her hackles rise. No doubt now he had increased his prospects he felt she should feel flattered by his attention. Before she could step away from him he'd strolled back towards the door as though he might leave.

'I have some urgent news for Alex. Would you fetch him, please, so I might speak to him?' Hugh's exasperating thoughts made him sound harsh and domineering. Beneath his breath he was cursing himself for finding her country freshness sweetly appealing after Gwen's cloying presence. Once he'd touched and caressed Beatrice often, and with her full consent. Any sudden move from him now was sure to result in a swift slap, so he'd distanced himself to avoid temptation.

'Alex?' A small frown crinkled Bea's brow. 'Why, I cannot get him, sir...he is not here. Elise arrived a few days ago with baby Adam but we have not seen Alex. Is he on his way, then?'

'I imagined he would have arrived by now. He left before me. His butler said he'd travelled into Hertfordshire so I came directly here, assuming he'd be with Elise.'

On the long hard ride towards St Albans he'd been wondering how he'd feel again when he saw Beatrice. In his youth he'd been infatuated plenty of times, impoverished just as frequently, by pert beauties with expensive tastes. But he'd put all of them from his mind. Beatrice Dewey he'd not been able to forget. He'd explained it away by blaming mutual friends for keeping the winsome blonde haunting his thoughts. But Hugh suspected that what presently occupied Beatrice's mind was her brother-in-law's safety. She was no doubt imagining that Alex had come a cropper on the road, and Hugh naturally wanted to soothe her fears on that score.

'If he'd broken an axle, or one of his horses had gone lame, I would have passed him en route,' Hugh softly reassured her. 'Alex might have taken a break at a tavern.'

A furrow appeared in Beatrice's smooth brow, testament to the fact she was not entirely convinced by that argument. 'I shall let Elise know you are here; she'll want to speak to you if you've come on her husband's account.'

Swiftly Hugh moved to apprehend her, catching her wrist in a firm grip. 'It might be best not to tell her anything till I locate Alex. I don't want to unduly upset Elise if there is an easy explanation for the viscount's absence.'

'Yes...I understand...' Beatrice croaked, her skin heating beneath his clasp. She'd proof now that Hugh Kendrick had kindly sought to allay her fears over her brother-in-law's tardiness, despite suspecting all might not be well. But it was the sensation of Hugh's touch—far more assertive than she remembered it to be—rather than anxiety for Alex that was making her captured flesh quiver.

Slowly Hugh withdrew his hand, and this time Bea heard a syllable of the oath he emitted as he jammed his hands in his pockets and walked off.

'Oh, there you are, Bea...I wondered where you had got to...'

It was too late to prevent Elise knowing the truth: Bea's prolonged absence had prompted her sister to nip out of the front parlour in search of her. With Adam cradled against a shoulder, obscuring her view, Elise hadn't at first noticed the gentleman by the door.

'Hugh!' Elise hurried towards him. 'What a lovely surprise to see you! Why have you not joined us in the parlour?' she burst out. Elise's sparkling gaze veered between the couple, lingered on Bea, wordlessly enquiring what had brought about this unexpected and exciting turn of events.

'Mr Kendrick has come here with important news for Alex.' Beatrice didn't want to worry Elise, but knew her sister would eventually discover the reason behind Hugh's visit. 'We expect he'll turn up soon, having stopped for a drink.'

'Alex didn't say he would come after me but I won't be surprised if he does.' Elise smiled contentedly. 'He's probably at the Red Lion. He doesn't like Papa to fiddle and fuss and spend his money on unnecessary comforts just so he might bed down here for a night or two.'

'Of course…that's where he is.' Beatrice sighed in relief. When Viscount Blackthorne had been courting her sister he would often lodge at the inn at St Albans.

Elise was swaying her drowsing son while frowning at Hugh. 'If you've come all this way it must be bad news. Please tell me what it is for I shall only fret if you do not. Has something awful happened in the few days I've been away?'

'I'm afraid that your mother-in-law has scarlatina.' Hugh comforted Elise with a sympathetic smile as one of her hands flew to cover her shocked gasp. 'The physician thinks she will recover well but at her age there is an obvious risk…' His voice tailed off. 'She has been asking to see Alex.'

'Of course…he must go immediately to her side. I should return too.' Elise was very fond of her mother-in-law and knew the woman doted on Alex, her only child.

'It has been wonderful to see you, but Papa will understand why you must cut short your visit.' Beatrice strove to remove Elise's worry over leaving so soon after arriving in Hertfordshire.

The doorknocker was again loudly employed at the same moment that Betty reappeared, shuffling towards them, bearing a tray laden with a silver tea set surrounded by some delicate bone china.

'If it's more nosey Parkers here to tattle they can come back another time,' the housekeeper stated with salty directness. 'We're right out of tea anyhow, till Norman gets back from town with the provisions.'

Being closest to the door, Hugh did the honours, opening it to find Alex on the step.

The viscount gave his chum a quizzical look while proceeding inside, but was prevented from asking the most obvious question. His wife hastily handed her precious burden to her sister, then launched herself at him to hug him about the waist in a show of welcome and comfort at the news she must soon break. Gently Elise urged her husband towards a small alcove by the stairs so they might quietly converse.

'What's it all about?' Walter demanded waspishly, emerging from the parlour and pulling the door shut behind him. 'You're not going to abandon me with those two, are you?'

Leaning heavily on his stick, he fished out his spectacles and put them on so he might get a closer look at what was occurring. He peered from one to the other of the people crowding his narrow hallway. 'Ah…capital! I see my son-in-law has dropped by to join us…why are they whispering?'

Walter didn't wait for a reply to his question about Elise and Alex huddling together a yard or so away. His attention had already moved on to a person he felt sure he recognised. When the fellow's identity popped into his mind his gaze narrowed angrily on Hugh Kendrick's tall, distinguished figure.

'Ha! I *do* know you! So you've heard, have you, and come to speak to my daughter and me? Well, Bea won't have you now, no matter how much money you've got from your diamonds. And neither will I. You had your chance years ago, so be off with you.'

In the ensuing silence Betty shuffled forward with the heavy tea tray, and never before had Bea felt quite so grateful for their housekeeper's peevishness.

'Is some kind person going to open the door?' The woman huffed out. 'My arms are giving out with the weight of this lot.' Betty rested a hip against the wall for support.

Courteously, Hugh unburdened the elderly servant, allowing her to enter the parlour. She gave him a wide smile when he carried the tray inside and put it down on the table, causing the two seated ladies to gawp admiringly at him. Hugh nodded politely before retracing his steps, leaving Betty behind the closed door setting the cups and Mrs Callan and Victoria frantically burbling in low voices.

'You may quit my house, sirrah.' Walter pointed his stick at Hugh. 'Beatrice, come into the parlour, do. I've exhausted every topic of conversation I can think of that avoids mentioning a fickle scoundrel upsetting my daughter.' Again his rheumy eyes settled accusingly on Hugh.

Walter beckoned to Elise and Alex, then disappeared inside the parlour, oblivious to his elder daughter's mortification or Hugh Kendrick's cynically amused expression.

'I'm sorry my father was so rude just then.' Beatrice's voice was hoarse with chagrin and she found she could not meet his eyes. She feared he'd understood her father's oblique reference to her having been jilted. Eventually it would all come out and Hugh Kendrick, along with other acquaintances who resided further afield, would discover Beatrice Dewey's wedding had been cancelled, but she didn't want his pity, or his questions, today.

'I've poured the tea if you want to go in and drink it before it goes cold,' Betty announced, still sounding tetchy as she closed the parlour door and stomped off down the corridor.

'Just take tea with us, Alex, before setting off to see your mother; Papa will like it if you do.' Elise tenderly removed her drowsing baby from Bea's embrace. She'd seen the wisdom in her husband's argument that he could travel faster alone to London. 'I can explain all about the dowager's illness to Papa when the ladies leave.'

Elise gave Hugh a look of heartfelt gratitude, then the preoccupied couple joined Walter in the parlour, leaving Beatrice behind and in two minds as to whether to follow them. But running off and letting Hugh Kendrick see himself out would be rude and cowardly. Beatrice hoped she was neither of those things. Today Hugh had acted as a true friend to her brother-in-law; the least he deserved in recompense was a little hospitality before setting again on the road.

'I'll go to the kitchen and get you some refreshment. You should have some tea at least…'

Hugh caught at her shoulder as she turned to go. 'Your father's churlishness doesn't bother me, but I'd like you to explain to me what caused it.'

Beatrice tipped up her chin, met his eyes squarely. 'I

have already told you that he has not forgotten or forgiven you for pursuing me when I was younger.' The sensation of his long fingers again restraining her was making her skin tingle and burn. She glanced significantly at the tanned digits curved on rose-sprigged cotton. 'If you don't mind waiting in there I will fetch your tea.' Beatrice indicated a door further along the hallway.

'Am I to be held in solitary confinement?'

Hugh sounded less amused now—haughty, even, Bea realised as his fingers fractionally tightened on her before dropping away. But though her defences were rising she knew he had a point. 'I admit it is unfair treatment, sir, when you have performed a mission of mercy for your friend. I beg you will tolerate my elderly father's foibles. It is not just you he is set against; he is protective of his daughters and hostile to any person who might have harmed us.'

'Is Dr Burnett such a person?' Hugh asked bluntly.

'I will explain to Papa how generously you have behaved when our visitors have gone.' Fearing he might repeat his question about Colin's role in all this, Beatrice quickly took two backward steps before carrying on towards the kitchen.

Chapter Five

'Who's the handsome stranger?' Betty asked in her forthright way, having assessed Beatrice's tortured expression. 'I've not seen him here before but I reckon he knows you...and rather well in my opinion.' She wiped her damp hands on her pinafore then plonked them on her ample hips.

Beatrice had closed the kitchen door and then her eyes while leaning against the panels, her head tilted up in an attempt to control her whirling thoughts. She pushed away from her support and with a sigh took a seat at the floury-topped table. 'He's a good friend of the viscount's,' she finally answered, picking up a warm biscuit from the dozen or so cooling on a rack. Beatrice loved a freshly baked treacle biscuit and usually would have taken a greedy bite and got a ticking off from Betty for not letting it set properly. But she put it back, unable to quell the queasiness in her stomach spoiling her appetite.

'So...this fellow is also a friend of yours, is he, Miss

Beatrice?' Betty crossed her arms over her chest, awaiting a reply.

'Once he was...or I thought as much. But I was wrong about him as well.' Beatrice frowned at her fingers, clasped in front of her on the table. She'd banished Colin from her mind and refused to mention his name. 'Would you put the kettle on, Betty? Mr Kendrick has done the viscount a good turn by conveying news from London. He deserves some tea before setting off home.'

The housekeeper gave Beatrice an old-fashioned look. 'I'll do that for him, and I'll even bring him along a few of those.' She tipped her head at the biscuits. 'No matter what your father thinks of the fellow, I took to him— 'cos he's a gentleman not too high and mighty to give a hand to the likes of me.'

'He hasn't always been a wealthy man, so I expect he is used to fetching and carrying for himself,' Beatrice murmured, almost to herself.

'Sometimes them that comes late to luxury are the worst sort, with their penny-pinching and lording it. They don't want to go back to scrimping and scraping, and doffing caps, you see. He's not like that. I'd stake my life on it.' Betty imparted her wisdom on the subject of upstarts.

Bea planted an elbow on the tabletop and sank her sharp little chin into a palm. She couldn't agree with Betty's estimation of Mr Kendrick's modesty. She'd seen a very imperious glint in his eyes earlier that had impressed upon her, almost as much as had his cool tone of voice, that he was no longer the ordinary man she'd once known...and loved.

'Off you go, then, and keep him company and I'll be along directly.' The housekeeper nodded at the door.

'I think I'd sooner stay here with you and wait till the tea's brewed.'

'I know you would,' Betty said. 'That's why I reckon you should go and sit with him and show him what you're made of.' She wagged a finger. 'You, Miss Beatrice, are not a coward. If I can tell he frightens you I reckon he already knows.'

'He does *not* frighten me!' Beatrice asserted, sitting straight in the chair and blinking at Betty.

'In that case you'll remember your manners and have a nice chat about the weather with him while the kettle boils,' Betty returned bossily. 'I'll be by in about ten minutes with a hot pot of tea and a plate of biscuits.' She turned away. 'But those two in the front parlour aren't getting any; Vicar's wife maybe, but not a charitable bone in her body by my reckoning. And the daughter's not much better.'

Betty glanced over her shoulder as she heard the chair scrape back. Her puckered features softened in a smile as she watched Beatrice marching towards the door, a determined set to her full mouth.

'Tea won't be long...do sit down, sir.'

Beatrice had entered the morning room to find Hugh standing by the unlit fire, contemplating the view through the window. His long fingers were drumming on the oak mantelpiece, making him seem impatient, and Bea wondered if he'd decide to leave without waiting for refreshment. The idea that he might depart before she'd proved to him her indifference to his arrival prompted her to burst out with some conversation.

'I hope that the dowager will soon recover. I have only met her once or twice but found her to be very nice,' Beatrice rattled off. She had decided to steer their chat in the direction of mutual concerns. In that way she might avoid his hard stares and lazy mockery. 'My father will be sad to hear that she's ailing. He also likes Alex's mother...'

'I'll attempt to find out how she managed to charm him,' Hugh remarked dryly. He strolled to an armchair and sat down.

Beatrice perched on a seat opposite, inwardly sighing that she'd suffered an early defeat. 'How are your family keeping, sir?' she asked brightly, recollecting that he had a younger married sister. 'Have you nephews or nieces?'

'One of each,' Hugh replied, sitting back and planting a dusty boot atop one knee. His fingers curled close to his mouth and he regarded her through dropped lashes. He knew she was anxious to avoid answering personal questions but, vulgar as his curiosity might be, he wanted to hear from her own lips that her wedding was off.

Elise's urgent summons to the countryside, taken together with Walter Dewey's recent bitter comments about scoundrels upsetting his daughters, pointed to the fact that Beatrice was not after all getting married. Hugh wanted her to tell him herself, because in that way he could judge her reaction and whether she had instigated the break-up with Dr Burnett.

'How old are your sister's children?' Beatrice doggedly continued, keeping an eye on the clock. Betty had said she would bring the tea in ten minutes; Bea was sure that five must already have passed. Yet the hands seemed to have crawled only fractionally about the face of the timepiece ticking on the wall.

'Luke is seven and Lucinda five.'

'Such nice names,' Beatrice remarked, on realising he wasn't about to add anything to the drawled information. Abruptly she got to her feet. 'I should open the door wider for Mrs Francis or she will struggle entering with the tray. Indeed…I should carry it for her…'

Bea had a plausible excuse to escape the strained atmosphere, but Betty's warning about acting cowardly rang in her ears, holding her on the spot. Today there'd been nothing in Hugh Kendrick's behaviour to which she might take serious offence. So far he'd been unfailingly civil… And yet she knew Betty had spoken the truth: she *was* fearful of him, and not simply because he might at any moment launch an unwanted question at her.

The fever on her flesh where his hands had been, the butterflies circling in her stomach, all were indications that she was not immune to this man, and she dearly wanted to be. It might be three years since they'd kissed and caressed one another but the memory of it was strengthening with every minute that passed. There was an unbearable tension between them and she knew he too was dwelling on that shared intimacy.

Never had Colin Burnett kissed her so hard and long that a vivid colour had stained her lips for hours. Never had he, during their long engagement, pulled open her bodice and drawn whimpers of delight from her when his mouth teased her breasts.

In a brief courtship Hugh Kendrick had done those things and more before it had all turned to ashes.

But he was different now, and she must be too. Behind the screen of his long lashes amusement was competing with lust in his hazel eyes. He might still desire her but he no doubt found his younger self—and hers—risible in hindsight. He now possessed riches… and power and influence. She could tell that from his every mannerism and utterance. He was no longer a man used to being denied what he wanted, whereas once everything…even she as his wife…had been out of his reach. Now, of course, he could pick and choose from society debutantes for a bride.

Well, she wouldn't want him as a husband now! Beatrice inwardly exhorted herself. Her papa was right: even had he raced here on hearing she was free, to beg her to accept his proposal, she'd not have him! He'd had his chance and could go away, back to his fine life, and leave her in peace. She had earlier said to her father and sister that she'd done with men and marriage and she'd meant it. The idea of living out her days as a spinster, doting on her nephew rather than her own offspring, was not a *vastly* depressing future.

She moistened her lips, feeling calmer and ready to force out a little more conversation. 'I shall no doubt hear Betty approaching.' Beatrice returned to her chair and sat down. 'There is no need to leave you alone again.'

'Thank you…'

Beatrice shot him a look, noting his ironic tone, but if he wanted to interrogate her, let him. She now felt prepared for any challenge he might throw down.

'The weather is cool for the time of the year.' Bea again broke the silence, irked that she was the one making all the effort to be sociable. 'Have you a little conversation about your journey?' she suggested with faux sweetness. 'For instance…did you drive here or come on horseback?' She again glanced at the snugly fitting dusty jacket encasing his broad shoulders. She imagined his valet would be horrified to see the state of it.

'Horseback; it seemed the quickest way to travel with urgent news.'

'And did it rain during the journey?' Beatrice asked, causing him to smile.

'Just a few spots…'

'Oh…well, I'm glad you kept dry at least.'

'I appreciate your concern.'

Again Beatrice flicked an acid look at him from beneath her lashes, then glanced at the clock. Fifteen minutes had passed. She hoped Betty was not deliberately hanging things out because she had taken to Hugh Kendrick and wanted him to stay a while…

'Do I make you nervous, Beatrice?'

Bea snapped her sapphire eyes to his watching gaze. 'Of course not! What makes you think that, sir?'

'I fear you are about to wrench apart that handkerchief.' He jerked a nod at the scrap of linen, taut between her rigid fingers.

She'd unconsciously been twisting it for minutes. Quickly she tossed aside the thing that had betrayed her.

'I should leave and let you get back to your guests.' Hugh stood up.

'No!' Beatrice jumped to her feet, instinctively stepping towards him. 'Please—' She broke off, unsure of what she had been about to say but realising that she honestly did not want him to go yet. 'I could not in all conscience allow you to journey home without something to drink. Would you prefer a glass of port? You have come a very long way with unpleasant tidings.'

'I believe you were already dealing with an unpleasant matter and I've made things worse.' He drove his hands into his pockets, tilting his head to watch her averted expression. 'Were you, Beatrice, dealing with a family crisis when I turned up?'

'No…' She swung a beautifully poised mien towards him. 'I am no longer marrying Dr Burnett, so there has been something for us, as a family, to discuss, but it's done now.' She fluttered a gesture. 'No crisis at all… far too strong a word for the situation…'

Hugh stared out of the large casement at the garden. 'The man's a damnable fool.'

Beatrice moistened her lips, mortified that from her casual explanation he'd easily deduced that she'd been jilted rather than the other way around.

He pivoted on a heel, gave a self-deprecating laugh. 'You seem unlucky enough to attract such types and I'm sure you don't deserve to, my dear.'

'You know nothing about me now. Please do not feel obliged to embroider your condolences.'

Beatrice realised it was high time to show him out before the annoying lump in her throat choked her. Why was she feeling close to tears because he'd said something nice about her and offered his sympathy?

Without asking if he would oblige, the housekeeper came in, holding out the tray for Hugh to carry to the table. She also gave him a smile and, Beatrice was sure, a wink. A moment later Betty had withdrawn, leaving a silence that was shattered within seconds by the clock chiming.

Beatrice busied herself pouring tea. 'Please be seated again, if you wish.' Suddenly voices in the hallway drew her attention. 'The vicar's wife and daughter are leaving…'

'I'm sorry I kept you from them,' Hugh murmured, choosing to prop himself against the mantelpiece rather than take a chair.

For the first time since he'd arrived they exchanged a proper smile.

'Please don't apologise, sir, for their company was no loss on my part, I assure you.' Bea put a cup of tea near the five bronzed fingers splayed on the mantelshelf.

'I'm certain your father and sister did sterling work on your behalf.'

'They are both protective of me and will see off the tattlers.' Beatrice sipped tea, placing down her cup with an unsteady hand that rattled together china. 'Mrs Callan and her daughter wished to let me know how shocked and sorry they are to hear I'm to remain a spinster, so are bound to be disappointed to have lost my company after just a few minutes. But I would not have our neighbours...or anybody for that matter...think that I am hiding away, embarrassed and heartbroken, so must go over to the vicarage later in the week to allow their sympathy full rein.'

Hugh smiled. 'And are you? Heartbroken, I mean? You're too fine to allow that dolt Burnett to embarrass you...'

'Why bother asking how I feel now? You didn't care before!' Bea cried, before sinking her small teeth in her lower lip to stem the list of accusations ready to be launched at him. Abruptly she turned and snatched up the plate of treacle biscuits, bitterly regretting that she'd let her suppressed anger at *his* defection, rather than Colin's, simmer and boil over. 'Please, have a biscuit. Betty would like you to...' She slid the plate next to his untasted tea on the oak mantel.

'Of course I damn well cared!' Hugh gritted out, curving his fingers over her forearm to keep her close when she would have swished away. 'Did you believe me that callous?'

Bea prised away his fingers from her body, flinging him off when he would have kept her hand imprisoned in his. But there was a smile pinned to her lips when she said, 'I'm sorry, sir...please think nothing more of it. I'm just a little on edge after recent events or would not have spoken so.'

She made a concerted effort to still her madly drumming heart. She would not allow him, or any man, to make her act like a hysterical harpy. She had, just an hour or two ago, felt relatively at peace with the prospect of returning to her life as a spinster and living at home with her father. Now, since Hugh Kendrick's arrival, old yearnings and emotions that she'd thought she'd successfully conquered were again pricking at her mind, making her feel restless.

'I must not keep you any longer,' she blurted. 'I expect you will want to speak to Alex before he heads off to see his mother...'

A skewed smile was Hugh's reaction to being summarily dismissed. 'Perhaps I should not have made my presence known to your guests earlier,' he said quietly. 'Will our absence from the parlour have given rise to more speculation and added to your troubles?'

Bea had been occupying her nervous fingers by shifting crockery to and fro on the tray. Now she turned about with a frown. 'I admit I had not thought of that...' *And I should have.* The phrase rotated slowly in her mind. She'd concentrated on the Callans being absorbed by her jilting, but of course they'd also be intrigued to have the details of what had kept Miss Dewey and Mr Kendrick elsewhere in the house during their visit. Mrs Callan was renowned for an ability to craft a salacious rumour from little other than her own imagination...

'Your family are sure to have explained the situation,' Hugh reassured her. 'It would indeed be a travesty if you were to be the subject of conjecture because of me when nothing at all exists between us...does it?'

'Nothing at all,' Bea fervently endorsed. 'And, as you say, my sister and father would have made that quite clear when explaining that I was attending to your needs...your hospitality,' she quickly amended, managing a fleeting smile despite his amused expression acknowledging her infelicity. 'Besides, in a short while people will no longer be interested in me but chasing new and more interesting tales.'

Unfortunately Beatrice knew that was not strictly true in this neck of the woods: London might boast fresh scandals every week, but in the sticks it might be six months or more before the old biddies found something as entertaining as Beatrice Dewey's being jilted to chew over at their afternoon get-togethers. They'd also be intrigued to know that soon after the cancellation of her wedding to Dr Burnett she'd been having a private talk with a handsome stranger.

Bea raised a hand to her throbbing brow, realising she was not quite as indifferent to cruel gossip as she'd believed herself to be. If a rumour started, and travelled to London, that shortly after being jilted she'd tried to charm Hugh Kendrick, she'd be mortified...especially if he got to hear of it...

'I'm setting off in a moment. Do you fancy a lift back to town? You can tether your mount to the curricle.' Alex had given a cough to herald his arrival before fully entering the morning room and addressing his friend. Behind him came his wife, using a knuckle between Adam's soft lips to pacify him.

'He is hungry, and wet too. I shall take him upstairs.' Elise gazed into her husband's face. 'Promise you will come and say goodbye before leaving.'

Alex cupped his wife's cheek with a loving hand. It was answer enough for Elise and she went off, content.

'So...you are still here, Mr Kendrick.' Walter limped into the room. 'I believe I mistook the reason for your arrival, sir. I've learned you have done my son-in-law a good deed and for that I'm grateful.'

Hugh bowed, accepting the oblique apology for his host's earlier brusqueness.

'Drink your tea, then, and stay to dine if you wish. I can see that Beatrice has been keeping you company and holds no argument with you. So I cannot either, I suppose,' Walter grumpily concluded.

'Thank you, but I am setting on the road again.' Hugh graciously declined Walter's off-hand invitation.

Walter shrugged and ambled off towards his study.

'I shall also take my leave,' Beatrice said. 'I wish you both a safe journey, and please give the dowager my best wishes for a speedy recovery.'

Her brother-in-law received a spontaneous hug, Hugh a formal bob. A moment later she was slipping from the room, only fleetingly hesitating at the door to discover if Hugh was watching her.

He was. And it hadn't gone unnoticed by Alex either.

'Don't even *think* of a dalliance there, or you'll have me to answer to this time, not her father.'

Hugh dispassionately met his friend's steady gaze. 'I get the distinct impression that Miss Dewey finds it difficult to tolerate my company. There'll be no repeat of what went on, trust me.' He hesitated, then strolled to the window. 'Does she know about my life in India?'

'I've not had reason to tell my wife all of it, so I doubt Bea knows much at all other than that you're now rich from your Indian mines. Neither, I hope, is she interested in any of it.'

Hugh nodded slowly, lips thinning in a grim smile.

'Are you thinking of cutting off your ties abroad?'

Hugh's sharp glance answered Alex before he heard his friend's reply. 'My ties in India are permanent and non-negotiable.'

'That's what I thought...' Alex said deceptively mildly. 'So I repeat...stay away from my sister-in-law or suffer the consequences...'

A moment later it was as though no tense exchange had taken place between them.

Alex said, 'I want to get going. Norman Francis will bring your horse round from the stable and we can be on the road in ten minutes...'

Chapter Six

'Why don't you come with me to London?'

While speaking Elise continued folding a lawn petticoat, then packed it away in readiness for departure later that morning. Her maid was attending to the baby's things, neatly piling them alongside her mistress's garments in the travelling trunk.

When Beatrice continued cooing at Adam, Elise renewed her effort to persuade her sister to have a sojourn in town. 'You'll enjoy the shops in Oxford Street and I'll introduce you to some nice people.' She waved aside Bea's dubious frown. 'There are some nice ladies, I swear. In fact I'd say some of the matrons in this neighbourhood are worse tattlers…'

'I can't think who you might mean,' Beatrice replied drolly.

'In any case it is high time you said hello to the Chapmans. Verity would love to see you. She'll tell you all about the babe she is expecting…' Elise bit her lip, realising it was insensitive to enthuse over another woman's marital bliss to a dear sister who had recently been jilted. 'Fiona is naturally still at home with Mr and Mrs Chapman, and I'm sure she'd adore having your company.'

'There's no need to fuss over me, Elise.' Beatrice raised her eyes from the baby's rosy face to give her sister a serene smile. 'I'm better now, honestly, and will bear up here with Papa.' She held the baby aloft, rolling him to and fro and making him giggle. 'The shock of it all has been short lived, I assure you. Isn't that so, Master Adam?'

'The shock of what, exactly?' Elise quipped. 'Seeing Hugh Kendrick or losing your fiancé?'

'I no longer think of Colin as a loss but as a hazard I avoided.' Bea got up from the clothes-strewn bed where she'd played with her nephew and handed him to his nurse. Helpfully, she started to assist her sister with packing. She felt her profile growing warm beneath Elise's determined stare. 'Oh, all right, I admit Mr Kendrick's appearance did shake me up a bit. But I'm over that too.'

'I wasn't hinting that you should come with me so you might see Hugh again,' Elise fibbed. She had seen the way the couple had reacted to one another yesterday and it had stirred in her an idea that they might still harbour feelings for one another. Hugh had not taken his eyes off her sister and Bea had certainly not seemed indifferent to him in the way a woman should if an old flame—now completely forgotten—turned up out of the blue.

Following his upturn in fortune Hugh was highly sought after by top hostesses and fond mamas with debutantes to settle, but Elise knew he wasn't courting any well-bred young lady. Of course she heard the gossip, like everybody else, and knew he associated with female company of a very different class. Although Elise liked Hugh, he was an unashamed philanderer, and that fact dampened her enthusiasm for Beatrice again falling for him. The last thing Elise wanted was for her beloved sister to again have her dreams shattered by a man.

'I suppose I ought to tell you that Hugh is known as an incorrigible rake who keeps company with demireps. I have to admit, though, that Alex's reputation was vastly embellished upon by excitable ladies before we were wed.' Elise smiled wryly; she'd not forgotten how jealous she'd felt, hearing about Alex's paramours.

'Thank you for the warning,' Bea said mildly. 'I'm not surprised to know it; he seems very different now from the man I once knew. Anyhow, his sordid habits and so on are of no interest to me. I don't care how he spends his time.'

Elise gave her sister an old-fashioned look. 'You might have sounded a little more convincing, my dear.'

Beatrice raised her eyes heavenward, miming exasperation, making her sister chuckle.

'Papa won't mind at all if you stay in town with me for a week or two. Mr and Mrs Francis attend to all his needs—'

'No…' Beatrice interrupted, giving her sister a winning smile. 'But thank you for the invitation.' She knew what Elise was up to: finding her a replacement for Colin. Although Bea was swayed by an offer to visit dear friends in the metropolis, the idea that Hugh Kendrick might believe she'd followed him home to put herself in his way was terrifying enough to quash the temptation to accept.

Elise huffed in defeat. 'I don't know what you are afraid of. I have told you that Papa and I fielded every question that Mrs Callan batted over about your association with Hugh. I made a point of letting them know he had courted our friend Fiona Chapman to put them off the scent.'

'And I do thank you for it. But I am not afraid, Elise, of gossip or of Hugh Kendrick.' Bea knew that was not quite truthful and hastened on. 'So, I will remain here, quite content, though I pray your mother-in-law will recover.' Bea looked reflective. 'She was very kind to us at your wedding reception and made sure Papa and I had servants dancing attendance on us. She introduced us to so many people, and Papa was glad to renew his acquaintance with her that day. He told me he had liked her late husband too.'

'Susannah is a dear soul…' Elise frowned, folding linen with renewed vigour. 'I must quickly get back and visit her. I'm sure the doctor is right, though, and she's already on the mend.'

Beatrice comforted her sister with a hug. 'She will be fine, Elise. The dowager will be up and about again in no time…'

'I should like to attend.'

'Are you feeling up to the journey, Papa?' Beatrice asked in concern.

The post had arrived just ten minutes ago. Alex's bold black script had been on one of many letters Bea, with heavy heart, had brought to her father's study. Walter had opened it at once. There had been a note for her too, from Elise, but Beatrice had slipped that into the pocket of her skirt and would read it later.

The other letters, she surmised, were replies from the guests who'd been informed by her father last week that the wedding would not be taking place. She recognised Mr Chapman's hand, and also that of her Aunt Dolly on two of the five sealed parchments. Bea felt sure all would contain messages of sympathy and encouragement for her, but she didn't yet want to know about any of it.

Neither did Walter, it seemed. Bea's father left untouched the pile of post and continued sighing and polishing his glasses with his handkerchief.

'Are you sure the journey will not excessively tire you?' Beatrice rephrased her question in an attempt to draw her father's attention.

'I will bear a few discomforts to pay my respects to Susannah Blackthorne.' Walter dabbed a handkerchief at his watering eyes. He put his glasses on, then held up Alex's letter so he might again scan the sad news that his son-in-law's mother had passed away. The funeral was to be held in a few days' time and Alex had offered to send his coach for Walter and Beatrice so they might join the mourners at Blackthorne Hall. He had added that he hoped very much they would attend as his mother had enquired after the two of them only recently.

'You will come as well, my dear, won't you? I should not like to travel alone.' Walter raised hopeful eyes to his daughter.

'Of course I shall come with you, Papa!' Beatrice replied. 'I would not want to miss it.'

Walter nodded, content. 'I shall write a reply and get Norman to quickly despatch it to Berkshire. I don't like imposing on the viscount's generosity but we must accept the use of his transport.'

'Alex will be cross if you do not! I expect he and Elise are feeling very low and will be glad to see us as soon as maybe.'

'As a family we lately seem to be in the doldrums more often than not.' Walter dropped the letter to the desk, drawing forward his quill and a plain parchment. 'Susannah was a very vivacious woman…and more than ten years my junior.' He dipped the pen into ink. 'I'm getting quite ancient now…'

'Don't be so maudlin, Papa!' Beatrice dropped a light kiss on the top of her father's sparsely covered crown. 'You are a mere spring chicken.'

She could tell he was feeling quite depressed at the news of the dowager's death. Bea had noticed that as he aged her father acted increasingly sentimental when hearing about sad or happy events.

As Walter's quill began scratching on paper she turned for the door, informing him, 'I'll start to pack a few things.'

Beatrice took down her carpetbag from the top of the clothes press. She blew dust off it and set it on her bed's coverlet. It seemed she would be taking a trip to stay with her sister after all, but glumly wished something nicer had prompted it.

As the viscount's well-sprung travelling coach bounced over a rut the letter in Bea's hand fluttered from her fingers to the hide seat. She retrieved it and recommenced reading. It had arrived that morning, before she and her papa had set on the road for Berkshire, and had been sent by Fiona Chapman. Bea had known the identity of the sender as soon as she spied her name written in elegant sloping script. But it had only been moments ago when her papa, seated opposite, ceased chattering and started dozing that she'd drawn her friend's note from her reticule and unsealed it.

As expected, the message bore very kind and sincere wishes to boost her morale following her jilting. Bea had already received fulsome sympathy from Aunt Dolly and Fiona's father. Walter had shown to her the letter from Mr Chapman and Bea had had to smile at Anthony's robust defence of her reputation. In his honest opinion Walter's daughter was too good for the physician in any case, and the whole matter was a blessing in disguise for Beatrice. Anthony had emphasised that observation with a very large and forceful exclamation mark that had punctured the paper.

'My sentiments exactly,' Walter had barked, perking up on reading it. Then he'd promptly helped himself to port from the decanter on the edge of his desk.

But now, as Beatrice's blue gaze landed on the final paragraph of Fiona's letter, she gasped at the startling news it contained. Mr Kendrick, Fiona wrote, had put a flea in Colin Burnett's ear over vulgarly flaunting his new fiancée before anybody in town had been given the news that he'd jilted his former bride-to-be. Bea's eyes sped on over the paper. The clash had taken place at her sister Verity's home, Fiona informed her, and Mr Kendrick had threatened, *very discreetly*—Fiona had underlined those two words—to throw the doctor out if he didn't go before people started asking awkward questions. Colin had bowed to Mr Kendrick's dictate and slunk off with his tail between his legs, Fiona penned in conclusion, before signing off with affection and good wishes.

Beatrice felt her heart thudding in consternation and her cheeks glowing despite the breeze from the window. The last thing she'd wanted was any fuss about the affair, because it would be sure to give an impression that she was bitter and jealous over it all. And whereas for a short while those emotions *had* overtaken her, they had now faded away. Or so she'd thought…

Beatrice slowly reread that ultimate paragraph. She *was* irked that Colin could treat her so shabbily when less than a month ago he'd said it was her he loved and would marry if only he could. She pondered then on Stella, and whether the girl was pretty, and if Colin had quickly fallen in love with her.

In which case, Beatrice impatiently scolded herself, *he is the most dishonest and fickle man alive and you should pray you never again are foolish enough to be taken in by his like.*

Having mentally shaken herself, she turned her thoughts to Hugh Kendrick. So he had championed her, had he? She wondered why that was. Their recent meeting had been frosty, if civil. She stared through the coach window and twisted a smile at the passing scenery. Perhaps the aim of his gallant intervention had been to impress Fiona. Beatrice recalled that he had courted her friend a few years ago; perhaps Mr Kendrick was of a mind to do so once more as they were both still single and Fiona was a minor heiress. At her sister's wedding reception Hugh had partnered Fiona in the ballroom and Bea recalled thinking they had looked happy together…

Bea folded the note without again looking at it, putting it back into her reticule, then rested her head against the squabs. Behind her drooping lids two couples were dancing and laughing. The gentlemen had both once professed to want her as a wife. Beatrice huffed a sigh, wishing for a nap to overcome her so she might have a respite from her irritating fantasies.

Wearily she again watched the verdant landscape flashing past, but the same thoughts were haunting her mind. Colin and Stella would be the first to get married: no long engagement for him this time, as he now had enough money to set up home immediately. If Hugh Kendrick were intending to propose to Fiona, and her friend were to accept him, Bea would make sure she was one of the first to send congratulations…

'You are sighing louder than the wind outside.' Walter had one eye open and was watching his daughter's restless movements from beneath a thick wiry brow.

'It is rather gusty…' Bea pulled the blind across the window to protect the coach interior from draughts.

'Have you read your letter?'

'Mmm...' Bea guessed her father was keen to hear what was in it.

'I have lately shared my missives from London with you,' Walter wheedled, giving her a twinkling smile.

Beatrice smiled, swayed by his mischievous manner. 'Oh, very well... Fiona Chapman has written to me more or less echoing her father's thoughts on Dr Burnett.'

'Oh...is that it? No other news?' Walter queried. He'd watched his daughter from between his sparse lashes while she'd been reading and had been sure he'd heard a muted cry of dismay. Not wanting to immediately pry, he'd waited till she seemed more herself before letting her know he was awake.

Walter had felt very protective of Beatrice since the doctor had broken her heart. The more she put a brave face on it, the more he desperately wanted to make it all come right for her. He'd guessed the cause of her distress was reading about some antic of Burnett's reported in her letter.

'I've just had news that Colin turned up at Verity's house, but it was made clear he was unwelcome, so he left.'

Walter struggled to sit upright. 'Did he, by Jove?' Gleefully he banged his cane on the floor of the coach, grunting a laugh.

Bea nodded, suppressing a smile at her father's delight on hearing about her erstwhile fiancé's humiliation. 'Miss Rawlings was there too.'

Walter thumped the cane again, in anger this time. 'How dare he treat you like that? Damned impertinence he's got, squiring another woman so soon. I've a mind to bring it to his notice.'

'I believe Mr Kendrick has beaten you to it, Papa…'

'So it was that fellow, was it?' Walter nodded. 'That's twice he's done us a favour in a short space of time. Hugh Kendrick has just gone up considerably in my estimation. I suppose I must find an opportunity to tell him so.' He grimaced, remembering how rude he'd recently been to Hugh.

Beatrice settled back into the seat, niggling anxieties again assailing her. Just how much of a good deed had Mr Kendrick done her? She feared that embarrassing rumours about the jilting might even now be circulating, and would only be worsened by talk of two gentlemen—both past loves of hers—arguing in public over her.

Chapter Seven

'Alex seems to be bearing up well.'

'Oh, he is a stoic soul and keeps busy all the time to take his mind off things.' Elise met her sister's eyes in the mirror. 'But I believe at a time like this he misses having brothers or sisters to talk to.'

Beatrice was seated on her sister's high four-poster bed, watching the maid put the finishing touches to Elise's coiffure. At breakfast that morning Alex had seemed very composed, despite it being the day of his beloved mother's funeral. It was the late dowager's daughter-in-law who was having difficulty turning off the waterworks.

As Elise stood up from the dressing stool, pulling on her black gloves, Beatrice relinquished her soft perch and embraced her sniffling sister. 'Alex has you to comfort him, my dear...and I'll wager he's told you already that's enough family for him.'

Elise nodded, wiping her eyes. 'Susannah wouldn't want any wailing; she said so before falling into a deep sleep. Of course she knew the end was near, but she slipped away peacefully.' Elise suddenly crushed Bea in a hug. 'Thank you for coming.'

'Did you honestly think I would not?' Beatrice asked gently.

Elise shook her head. 'I knew you would not let me down.'

'You have never let *me* down, have you?' Bea stated truthfully, remembering a time when Elise had been unstintingly loyal. Elise, though exasperated with her, had continued risking censure despite Bea's shockingly selfish and daft actions. To her shame, Bea knew her behaviour had been at its worst during her infatuation with Hugh Kendrick. She'd made quite a fool of herself over him, much to Elise's dismay. But today Bea was determined to banish thoughts of her own upset from her head. And that was not an easy task as Elise had let on that Hugh Kendrick was due to attend the funeral if he could escape his commitments in London.

'Come...dry your eyes again,' Bea prompted gently. 'If we are to visit the nursery before we go downstairs Adam will not want to see his mama blubbing.'

Having left the darling baby in the care of his nurse, the ladies joined the other mourners. A hum of conversation, interspersed by muted laughter, met the sisters on entering the Blackthornes' vast drawing room. It was crowded with people and Beatrice was glad that the atmosphere seemed relaxed despite the sombre occasion. They headed towards their papa, who was standing by the wide, open fire. Walter was alternately warming his palms on his hot toddy and on the leaping flames in the grate. It was mid-May, but the weather was cool for the time of the year.

'I hope the showers hold off,' Alex said, turning from his father-in-law to greet his wife and sister-in-law.

Elise slipped a hand to her husband's arm, giving it an encouraging squeeze.

'Are you warm enough, Papa?' Bea asked. 'Would you like a chair brought closer to the fire so you may be seated?'

'I'm doing very well just where I am, thank you, my dear. My old pins and my stick will keep me upright for a while longer.'

'You must sit by me in the coach when we follow the hearse to the chapel—' Elise broke off to exclaim, 'Ah, good! Hugh has arrived; he's left it to the last minute, though.'

Beatrice felt her stomach lurch despite the fact she had discreetly been scouring the room for a sight of him from the moment she'd entered it. Casually she glanced at the doorway and felt the tension within increase. He looked very distinguished in his impeccably tailored black clothes, and she noticed that several people had turned to acknowledge his arrival.

'Has it started to rain?'

Alex had noticed the glistening mist on his friend's sleeve as Hugh approached.

'It's only light drizzle, and the sun's trying to break through the clouds.'

Hugh's bow encompassed them all, but Bea felt his eyes lingering on her so gave him a short sharp smile.

'Come, my dear...' Alex turned to Elise, having noticed a servant discreetly signalling to him. 'The carriages are ready and it's time we were off.'

The couple moved ahead and Beatrice took her father's arm to assist him. Hugh fell into a slow step beside them, remaining quiet as they filed out into the hallway.

'You must get in the coach with Elise, Papa.'

'And you will come too?' Walter fretted.

'If there is sufficient room I will; but you must ride with Elise in any case.'

Beatrice was used to walking. Living in the country, she often rambled many miles in one day, especially in the summer. She walked to the vicarage to take tea with Mrs Callan and her daughter when no immediate excuse to refuse their invitation sprang to mind. She'd also hiked the four miles into St Albans when the little trap they owned for such outings had had a broken axle and no soul passed by in a cart and offered her a lift. A march to the chapel at Blackthorne Hall was an easy distance to cover for someone of her age and stamina. But her father would struggle to keep his footing on the uneven, uphill ground.

Bea glanced at the people in the hallway; many looked to be decades her senior. From glistening eyes and use of hankies she guessed that Susannah had been truly liked by her friends, neighbours and servants.

'I've no need of a ride, Alex,' Bea whispered, nodding at some elderly ladies close by, dabbing at their eyes. 'There are others more deserving.' She stepped outside onto the mellow flags of a flight of steps that cascaded between stone pillars down to an expanse of gravel. At least half a dozen assorted crested vehicles were lined up in a semi-circle, ready for use. The glossy-flanked grey and ebony horses appeared impeccably behaved as they tossed regal black-plumed heads.

Beatrice noticed that a column of mourners was snaking towards the chapel. Pulling her silk cloak about her, she started off too, at the tail-end of it.

'The sun seems reluctant to escape the clouds.'

Beatrice's spine tingled at the sound of that familiar baritone. Hugh Kendrick was several yards behind but had obviously addressed her as no other person was within earshot. He seemed to be casually strolling in her wake, yet with no obvious effort he had quickly caught her up and fallen into step at her side.

'It is an unwritten law that funerals and weddings must have more than a fair share of bad weather.' Bea's light comment was given while gazing at a mountain of threatening grey nimbus on the horizon. To avoid his steady gaze she then turned her attention to the rolling parkland of Blackthorne Hall that stretched as far as the eye could see. The green of the grass had adopted a dull metallic hue beneath the lowering atmosphere.

'Were you preparing for showers on your own wedding day?'

Beatrice was surprised that he'd mentioned that. A quick glance at his eyes reassured her that he hadn't spoken from malice. She guessed he wanted to air the matter because, if ignored, it might wedge itself awkwardly between them. She was hopeful he shared her view that any hostilities between them should be under truce today.

'I was banking on a fine day in June, but one never knows...and now it is all academic in any case.'

A breeze whipped golden tendrils of hair across her forehead and she drew her cloak closely about herself. She scoured her mind for a different topic of conversation but didn't feel determined to rid herself of his company.

'It seems the dowager was liked and respected by a great many people. My father has sung her sincere praises and those of her late husband.'

'They were nice people. The late Lady Blackthorne was always kind and friendly to me. I was made to feel at home when I spent school holidays with Alex here at the Hall.'

Bea smiled. 'You have known each other a long time?'

'More than twenty years.'

'I expect you were a couple of young scamps.'

'Indeed we were...' Hugh chuckled in private reminiscence, then sensed Bea's questioning eyes on him. 'Please don't ask me to elaborate.'

'Well, sir, now you've hinted at your wickedness I feel I must press for more details.' A teasing blue glance peeked at his lean, tanned profile.

'Just the usual boyish antics...climbing trees, catching frogs and tadpoles, building camp fires that rage out of control,' Hugh admitted with a hint of drollery.

'A fire...out of control?' Beatrice echoed with scandalised interest.

'It was a dry summer...' Hugh's inflection implied that the drought mitigated the disaster. 'Luckily for us the old viscount remained reasonably restrained when learning that his son and heir together with his best friend had burned down a newly planted copse of oak saplings while frying eggs for their supper.'

Beatrice choked a horrified laugh. 'Thank goodness neither of you were injured.'

'I burned myself trying to put the fire out…' Hugh flexed long-fingered hands.

Bea had never before noticed, or felt when he'd caressed her, that area of puckered skin on one of his palms. She recalled his touch had always been blissfully tender. Quickly she shoved the disturbing memory far back in her mind before he became puzzled as to what he might have said or done to make her blush.

'It was quite an inferno,' Hugh admitted. 'It frightened the life out of the viscountess; she made Alex and me amuse ourselves indoors for the rest of the holiday. We rolled marbles with bandaged hands till we were sick of the sight of them. Even when the physician told us we were fit to be let out we were kept confined to barracks. But I wasn't sent home in well-deserved disgrace.' His boyish expression became grave. 'I could give you many other instances of Susannah's kindness and tolerance.'

Beatrice realised that Hugh was as moved by Susannah's passing as had been the weeping ladies in the Blackthornes' hallway. But of course he would not show the extent of his feelings: once, when a personable chap rather than a diamond magnate, he might have been less inclined to conceal his sadness behind a suave mask. Quietly she mulled over the theory of whether gentlemen felt it was incumbent on them to foster an air of detachment as they became richer.

'And what mischief did you get up to in your youth, Miss Dewey?'

Bea glanced up with an impish smile. 'Young ladies are never naughty,' she lectured, before tearing her eyes free of his wolfish mockery.

'I seem to recall a time, Beatrice, when you were very naughty indeed...'

'Then I advise you to forget it, sir, as it is now of no consequence,' she snapped. She tilted her chin and strode on, but no matter how energetic her attempt to outpace him he loped casually right at her side.

'But you don't deny it happened?' he provoked her.

'I have nothing to say on the subject other than you are very ill-mannered to bring it up.'

'My apologies for upsetting you...'

He'd spoken in a drawling voice that made Bea's back teeth grind together. 'You have not done so,' she replied, in so brittle a tone that it immediately proved her answer a lie.

'Of course we were talking about childhood. I alluded to a time when you were most certainly a woman, and I admit it was not fair to do so.'

Bea said nothing, despite his throaty answer having twisted a knot in her stomach. She again contemplated the countryside, presenting him with her haughtily tilted profile.

'So, did you enjoy your schooldays? How did you spend them, Beatrice?' His tone had become less challenging, as though he regretted having embarrassed her by hinting at her wanton behaviour with him.

'When we lived in London Elise and I were schooled at home by Miss Dawkins,' Bea responded coolly. A moment later she realised it was childish to remain huffy. He'd spoken the truth, after all, even if it was unpalatable. 'I was almost fifteen when we moved to Hertfordshire, so there was little time left to polish me up. Papa did engage a governess for Elise, and the poor woman did her best to prepare me for my looming debut.' An amusing recollection made her lips quirk. 'She despaired of my singing and piano-playing and told Papa he had wasted his money buying an instrument that neither of his daughters would ever master.'

'What did Walter say to that?' Hugh asked, laughter in his voice.

'I cannot recall, but I expect he was disappointed to have squandered the cash; we were quite hard up by then—' Beatrice broke off, regretting mentioning her father's financial struggle. Hugh, in common with many others, would know that her parents had divorced amidst a scandal that had impoverished Walter Dewey. It had been a terrible time for them all and she didn't intend to now pick at the painful memory.

'I expect you missed your mother's guidance during your come-out.'

Hugh abhorred hypocrisy so avoided judging others' morality. He was no paragon and had had illicit liaisons with other men's wives, although neither of his current mistresses was married. He therefore found it hard to understand why Arabella Dewey had left her husband

and children. In polite society the customary way of things was to seek discreet diversion when bored with one's spouse. But it seemed Arabella hadn't been able to abide Walter's company. Hugh found that rather sad, as he sensed the fellow was basically a good sort and the couple had produced two beautiful girls.

Arabella had passed on years ago, when still in her prime, but not before she'd scandalised the *ton* by abandoning her husband and teenage daughters to run off and live with her lover.

'Aunt Dolly did her level best to take me under her wing and turn me into a sweet debutante,' Bea finally answered, having reminisced on that dear lady's efforts to obtain invitations to top social functions so she might attract a suitor.

'Thank goodness she failed,' Hugh muttered. He put up his hands in mock defence as Bea glowered at him. 'It's a compliment, I swear. In my experience debutantes tend to be vapid creatures.'

'I'm surprised you know any well enough to be able to judge.' Unfortunately Bea's sarcasm had not been spoken quietly enough.

'What do you mean by that, Beatrice?'

What *did* she mean by that? Beatrice thought frantically. She'd rather not let him know that Elise had told her he was a notorious rake.

Ignoring his question, and his scorching stare, she chattered on. 'My father paid handsomely to get us vouchers for Almack's that year, but it wasn't a successful season for me.' She stopped short of elaborating on her failure: some hostesses had spitefully shunned them because the gossip over her parents' divorce was still doing the rounds.

'What did you mean by your comment?' Hugh demanded, undeterred. His firm fingers circled her wrist, turning her towards him. 'Why would I not know such young ladies?'

Beatrice shook him off, then set on her way again. 'I know you liked Fiona Chapman, but she is rather too old to be called a deb.' She was thankful that excuse had popped into her head. Moments later she regretted having drawn her friend into it; in mentioning Fiona's age she'd sounded bitchy and jealous. Besides, Fiona was only a year her senior…

'I still like Miss Chapman very much,' Hugh said levelly.

'And so do I like her very much. Actually, I had a letter from her just days ago,' Beatrice blurted in emphasis.

She sensed the same quickening of her heart as she had on first absorbing the disturbing fact that Hugh and Colin had argued about her in public.

'Did the letter have good news for you?' Hugh asked. He'd immediately guessed what information Fiona might have passed on.

'I think you probably know the answer to that.' Beatrice twisted towards him, eyes blazing accusingly. She was tempted to give him a piece of her mind about risking her reputation in such a way, but the lych gate was now in view and beyond it, standing by some ancient leaning headstones, was her father, supported by his stick. He raised a bony hand, signalling to her to come to him, just as Elise also gave her a wave. With a curt dip for Hugh she sped ahead to join her family, filing into the chapel.

Chapter Eight

'I suppose I must speak to the fellow,' Walter grumpily announced.

Beatrice removed her father's port from his fingers, setting it on the table before he spilled it down his front.

They were sitting side by side on a small fireside sofa and had been observing the company attending the wake. Alex and Elise were the perfect hosts, moving through the room talking to the mourners. From elderly estate servants, now retired, to the Duke of Rodley, who'd arrived on horseback from the next town with two bottles of best cognac strapped to his saddle, all were being graciously thanked for their kind messages and tributes.

'Would you like me to fetch you some pastries from the buffet, Papa?' Beatrice had noticed her father again reaching for his depleted glass of port. He was drinking too much, as was his wont. Over the years Walter's daughters had had to ask their manservant to take their father to bed when he'd been unable to rouse himself due to over-imbibing.

'Another fruit tart might be sufficient, my dear. I have room for just one.' As his daughter rose from the sofa, he added, 'And will you bring the fellow over to me so I might talk to him before he leaves?'

'Do you know that he's soon leaving?' Bea asked, glancing at Hugh's dark figure surrounded by some jolly people.

'The viscount told me his friend Kendrick intends returning to town today. I imagine he will not set on the road after dark…not in this weather.'

Walter turned to the dismal grey afternoon beyond the enormous casements. The fire to one side of them had been hissing and spluttering as the driving rain dampened the apple-scented logs. After the funeral service they had been lucky to return to the Hall before the worst of the rain set in.

'Will you fetch him over?' Walter nagged. 'I'd sooner not struggle up out of this chair to go to him and eat humble pie with strangers present.' Walter sighed. 'Yet it must be done. My conscience will not allow it to be otherwise.'

Hugh's group were loudly toasting Susannah's life. Alex's mother had left strict instructions that she wanted no maudlin speeches at her wake but a thanksgiving for the blessing of a wonderful life shared with an adored husband and beloved son.

Moving gracefully through the throng towards the dining room, Bea angled her head in an attempt to drag Hugh's attention from his lively companions. He now seemed oblivious to her presence, and yet before, when walking to the chapel with him, it had been impossible to escape his taunting amber gaze. She'd no intention of approaching him to loiter meekly at his shoulder, waiting for an opportunity to interrupt.

On passing over the threshold into the dining room she glanced over her shoulder, and her heartbeat quickened as his eyes clashed on hers. She felt a burst of elation that had nothing to do with being a step closer to carrying out her father's task. She'd experienced similar excitement years ago, when she'd easily lured his attention every time she quit or entered a room.

Turning her head, Bea carried on towards the buffet table—but not before she'd noticed him concealing his private smile with a sliding forefinger.

He'd made no move to leave the group and Bea fumed. If her wordless plea for an audience wasn't plain enough for him to act on he could forgo having her father's apology and her farewell before he left for London!

'Are you still hungry, Beatrice?' Hugh's eyes skimmed over her slender figure swathed in black silk. 'You certainly look as though a little more sustenance might benefit you.'

'You…you think I am too thin?' Beatrice stammered. His comment had irked, and his swift approach had startled her. Her gaze dropped to the intricate folds of his cravat, pinned with a sizeable diamond. Sourly she wondered whether he'd dug it up himself.

'You seem less…buxom than I remember.'

Bea's soft lips parted in a mixture of astonishment and indignation. She'd never realised he'd thought her fat.

'Well, I'm happy with my appetite!' she breathed. 'I

never eat too much, and I think it impertinent of you to make such a comment.'

'Am I to pretend I know nothing of your body when I can recall it quite clearly within my embrace and pressed to mine?'

'Please say no more!' Bea hissed. 'I find that remark even more unmannerly,' she spluttered, blushing scarlet.

'I apologise, then; I merely intended a passing observation that your figure appeared more curvaceous when you were younger.'

He was quelling his humour with a frown, and she guessed he was deliberately riling her because of their prickly parting at the chapel earlier. 'Please do not explain and add insult to injury. Your opinion of my looks is of no consequence to me in any case.'

Beatrice turned to the pastries and began loading a plate with them while her cheeks continued to burn.

'If you are about to accuse me of being a glutton, this food is for my papa.' In her agitation, it had slipped her mind that Walter desired just one fruit tart. Swishing about with a laden plate she moved on.

'Did you want to speak to me on a matter?'

Beatrice halted, moistening her lips. She'd also forgotten she'd drawn him to her side with a come-hither glance.

'I...I did want to have a word with you. My father would like you to join him for a chat before you go.'

'Of course I'll speak to him.' Hugh glanced back towards the drawing room, locating the sofa on which Walter was ensconced. 'It would be my pleasure.'

'Thank you,' Bea replied stiltedly.

'Shall I accompany you now?' Hugh suggested mildly.

'If you wish to, sir.'

Hugh's heavy sigh brought Bea's eyes darting to his bronzed face.

'I beg you will not put yourself out for us, though,' she said acidly. 'My father would not want that.

'It is *you* putting me out, my dear. Have you forgotten my name that you continue calling me sir?'

'Indeed I have not, *Mr Kendrick*,' Bea returned sweetly on passing him.

'Will you let me know what Mr Dewey wants to talk about so I might prepare my defence?' Hugh asked wryly, falling into step with Bea as they wound a path around knots of people.

'You are not about to be ticked off, I assure you.' Bea was unable to repress a smile at his ironic tone. 'I believe Papa wishes to apologise to you.'

'And how have I redeemed myself in his eyes?' Hugh politely led the way past a long sofa encircled by chattering ladies. A few yards on, at a quieter spot, he turned back to Bea. His hand was idly planted against the wall, completing her casual entrapment by his powerful body.

'Papa was most grateful to you for coming to Hertfordshire to convey the news about the dowager's ill health. I expect he wants to impress that on you.'

'I recall he said something similar to me at the time,' Hugh murmured, his eyes lingering on Bea's mouth as her pearly teeth attacked her lower lip. 'I doubt he'd make an issue of repeating it. So what else is on his mind?'

'If we carry on to him I'm sure he will tell you,' Bea returned.

Barely were the words out when a sudden clap of thunder made her gasp and stumble. She would have dropped her pastries but for Hugh's steadying hand on her shoulder. Beatrice felt her heart thudding unevenly and the silk of her sleeve seemed to grow unbearably hot beneath his palm. She gave an embarrassed laugh.

'Heavens! That frightened the life out of me.' She glanced about to see that she hadn't been the only lady startled by the storm. Fans were whizzing and a few smelling salts bottles were being wafted amidst nervous giggling. A small crowd had gathered at the windows to watch lightning zigzagging across the heavens.

Bea's gaze was captured by eyes that had lost their golden tint and now burned like coal embers. His fingers began moving in a slow caress, increasing pressure, as though he would feel her skin beneath the barrier of fabric. Her eyelids became weighty, slowly falling beneath the narcotic effect of his secret seduction.

'Please don't… I…' She finally listened to the inner voice protesting wildly at her behaviour. She sensed he might dip his head and kiss her while she acted like a mindless idiot enthralled by his touch. And at such a time and place as a wake! Despite her chagrin she felt unable to physically move away from him and raised her eyes to beseech him for leniency.

As Hugh withdrew his fingers in a slow stroking movement Bea expelled a breath, darting glances hither and thither, relieved that people were still too preoccupied with the storm to have noticed their indecent intimacy.

Hugh took the plate from Bea's shaking hand. 'I'm glad I wasn't responsible this time for giving you the jitters...or was I?' he challenged.

In a moment he was resuming their conversation as though nothing had happened, although Bea felt strangely light-headed.

'As you seem reluctant to help me prepare for a chastisement, let me stab a guess at the bee in your father's bonnet.' He paused before asking abruptly, 'Did you tell him what was in Fiona's letter?'

'Of course...' Bea replied after a second spent wondering how he could change so quickly from charmer to interrogator.

'Ah...so I imagine I'm about to be told to mind my own business where Colin Burnett is concerned.' Hugh's moulded mouth slanted sardonically.

'Actually, you are wrong,' Bea answered, flustered, because just as she'd been recovering her equilibrium he had again upset it. He had a knack of being too forthright for comfort. It was something else he'd acquired along with his money, she was sure, but she wouldn't be intimidated by it any more than she'd allow his practised philandering to steal her composure. 'It is I who would ask...insist...you do that. My father, on the other hand, seemed pleased to hear about your uninvited interference in my affairs.'

Bea stared pointedly at his imprisoning arm until lazily he removed it from where it had been propped against the wall. She took immediate advantage of her liberation and carried on towards her father, forcing herself to a leisurely pace so it would not seem she was cravenly taking flight.

'Papa seems in good spirits.' Elise sipped tea following this observation.

'I think he has sunk rather too far into good spirits.' Bea put down her bone china cup.

The sisters were side by side on a window seat and had been watching fat clouds travelling over the insipid sky through the square-paned glass. They had turned their attention to their father, still huddled on the sofa by the fire, now with a group of male companions. By his side on the velvet upholstery was the Duke of Rodley. His grace had been topping up Walter's glass with his fine cognac for at least fifteen minutes while gregariously holding court. Opposite, in a wing chair, sat Hugh Kendrick, also with a replenished brandy balloon and an air of indolent interest in the duke's conversation. Just moments ago Alex had also joined the gentlemen. He was leaning on the back of the sofa while, at the duke's insistence, partaking of his late mother's favourite tipple.

A cosy atmosphere had descended on the drawing room. Most of the guests who lived locally had departed, keen to get home since the storm had blown south. Others, with long journeys in front of them, had taken up the Blackthornes' offer of accommodation at the Hall while the roads remained bad.

Hugh Kendrick had not bowed to Alex's insistence

that he stay because it would be madness to risk life and limb in such abominable weather. He planned to get going before dusk, much to his host's disgust.

'I think I shall go and see Adam before dinnertime.' Elise found it difficult to spend long periods apart from her little boy.

'Dinner?' Bea choked a laugh. 'I have eaten very well already, Elise.'

'Oh, the gentlemen will expect their dinner; and their port and cigars,' Elise declared ruefully, thinking of her husband's predilection for a smoke and a drink when they had male company. 'Will you come with me and say goodnight to Adam?'

'I shall peek at him in the nursery later,' Bea promised. 'For now I shall keep the ladies company.' With a nod she indicated the elderly women she'd seen drying their eyes in the hall earlier. Bea had been introduced to them and recalled that the silver-haired individual with a remarkably hooked nose was called Lady Groves. On her black satin bosom was pinned a huge mourning brooch. The name of the other lady had momentarily escaped Beatrice's mind.

'Lady Groves came in her brother's stead as he is poorly,' Elise informed her helpfully. 'My mother-in-law was Lord Mornington's *chère amie* for a very long time. He is heartbroken to lose Susannah and it has made him quite ill.'

'Poor man…' Bea murmured.

'Lady Groves and Susannah were friends; they were about the same age, I believe, and were widowed at about the same time. Mary Woodley, Lady Groves's companion, lost her husband in the Peninsular wars.'

After Elise had gone off to the nursery Bea settled in a wingchair adjacent to the ladies with a cheerful, 'The clouds are fast moving away, thank goodness.'

'I shall be glad to set off home tomorrow if the water on the roads has drained away.'

Mary Woodley was a lesser mortal than her noble benefactress in the eyes of polite society. But Lady Groves saw her companion as her equal and treated her as such, despite her friend's impoverishment. She also treated Mary to those things she could not afford to purchase for herself, due to her subsisting on her late husband's meagre army pension.

'I'd rather stay here a while longer, Mary, so flooding doesn't bother me.' Lady Groves's greedy black gaze roved her sumptuous surroundings. 'It is the first time I have visited Blackthorne Hall but my brother told me it was a wonderful sight.'

'But what about the Whitleys' *musicale,* Gloria?' Mary mildly complained. 'I do not want to miss that in case that flibbertigibbet turns up with her aunt, causing us all to gawp at her. Very strange behaviour...very strange indeed.'

'I heard that Miss Rawlings wasn't even officially invited to the Clemences' that evening.' Lady Groves tutted at such vulgar conduct as gatecrashing. 'Country bumpkins!'

'Miss Rawlings?' Beatrice echoed faintly, too shocked at hearing her rival's name to take umbrage at Lady

Groves's all-encompassing insult to people like herself who hailed from the shires.

'I doubt you would know her my dear.' Lady Groves patted at Bea's fingers, tightly curled on her lap. 'She is a gel about eighteen and new to town—from the Yorkshire area, we believe, don't we, Mary? She is out this year and is being chaperoned by her aunt. Nobody knows much about them, you see…but the bold chit seems determined to change that.'

But I think I might know about her… The words rotated in Bea's head but she managed to keep them from tripping off her tongue. It seemed these two ladies were ignorant of her being jilted, and therefore didn't know that the *'bold chit'* they spoke about had stolen her fiancé.

'Dolly Pearson told me that the aunt says her charge is secretly engaged.' Mary was pop-eyed while giving this news.

Lady Groves snorted her wordless opinion on that. 'If Miss Rawlings *does* have a fiancé I'll wager the fellow is unaware of her flirting.' She inclined forward to whisper, 'I saw her fluttering her eyelashes at…' She left the sentence unfinished but her eyes darted sideways to where the gentlemen were grouped. 'If she thinks she has a chance of snaring *him* she'll be sorely disappointed.'

'No respectable young lady has a hope of catching Hugh Kendrick's eye,' Mary scoffed behind the fingers fluttering in front of her lips. 'He has no interest in debutantes, no matter how irresistible they find him.'

'No wonder he's oblivious to decent gels with those

two doxies fighting over him. Then there's the shocking *other business* to keep him occupied…' Lady Groves rumbled.

'*Other business...?*' Bea echoed the phrase back at the woman.

Lady Groves looked extremely discomfited by her slip, but nevertheless patted again at Bea's fingers before attempting to change the subject.

'Is Mr Kendrick a villain?' Bea insisted on knowing, and received a shocked look from Mary Woodley at such impertinence as cross-examining Lady Groves.

'You are a sweet innocent and need not know the details of a gentleman's behaviour when he is freed from the restraints of a civilised society…' Lady Groves said, fingering her throat in embarrassment.

'I assure you I am not about to swoon on hearing that Mr Kendrick has female friends.' Bea realised she sounded vulgarly inquisitive, and very unladylike, but she couldn't help herself. She craved to know more.

'Miss Rawlings and her aunt *did* leave the Clemences' early with a gentleman but I've no idea who he was,' Mary burst out, returning to gossip she deemed more seemly. 'I was coming out of the retiring room and saw the trio suddenly disappearing down the stairs.'

'I didn't see the fellow, but possibly he was her father, come to take her home before she disgraced herself,' Lady Groves sniffed.

'He seemed far too young for that, Gloria!' Mrs Woodley disagreed. 'Perhaps Dolly might know who he was. She seems to find out everything first, though I doubt she spotted the fellow either, for his arrival and departure seemed as one.'

'Dolly Pearson is my aunt.'

Beatrice could think of nothing more to say at that point. She knew she should feel grateful that the argument between Hugh and Colin had been very discreet, and few people yet knew the details of it. But preying on her mind was the scandal concerning Hugh to which Lady Groves had referred but had refused to explain.

'I do recall, now you mention it, that you are related to Dolly.' Lady Groves beamed, having fully recovered from her shock at Miss Dewey's audacity a moment ago. 'My brother, Lord Mornington, told me that your sister was Dolly's niece. I've always found Mrs Pearson a charming woman,' she added graciously. Glancing at Mary for a comment, Gloria found the woman peering beneath her pale lashes at the group of gentlemen. 'What's the matter with you, Mary?' she asked.

'Do you think Mr Kendrick overheard us talking about him?' Mary whispered, aghast. 'He seems to be staring at us rather too frequently, Gloria.'

Lady Groves frowned thoughtfully, then looked at Beatrice. 'You were talking to him earlier, weren't you, my dear?'

'Yes...I was...' Bea avoided looking his way, although she felt the side of her face burning and wondered if he'd guessed that she'd just heard an intriguing hint about his sordid way of life.

'He is your brother-in-law's good friend, is he not?' Mary Woodley picked up on her ladyship's unspoken thought that Miss Dewey might have caught Hugh Kendrick's interest.

'I believe they've known each other since their schooldays,' Bea answered with a neutral smile.

'Do *you* have a beau, my dear?' Lady Groves had already taken a surreptitious look at the young woman's pretty white fingers and noted they lacked any rings. 'A sweet gel like you must have admirers buzzing around like bees about a honeypot.'

Mary discreetly nudged her companion in the ribs, having just brought to mind a stunning titbit. Dolly Pearson had told her recently that a swine of a country doctor had jilted her niece. No names had been mentioned, and Mary had taken little interest in the tale as she'd doubted she'd know such provincial folk. But it seemed she did! Obviously the niece in question could not be the viscount's wife, and that only left…

'I am not being courted,' Bea answered as cheerfully as she could. 'Well, I did promise Elise I would visit the nursery and see baby Adam before he goes to bed.' She rose gracefully. 'Apparently we are all to be given dinner soon.'

'Such charming hosts,' Lady Groves murmured. 'I hope Mr Kendrick changes his mind and stays. I should like to have a chat with him.'

'I'm afraid *I'm* hoping he will disappoint you,' Beatrice murmured beneath her breath, walking away. She had seen the sudden intelligence on Mary Woodley's face and knew that Dolly hadn't after all kept the news of her jilting to herself. Philosophically, Bea realised people would soon know—and besides, what occupied her now was imagining how debauched Hugh might have become in the years since she'd last known him.

The two ladies exchanged a look as soon as they judged Miss Dewey was at a safe distance.

Lady Groves shook her head. 'I doubt it, Mary. She might be his friend's sister-in-law, and a beauty too, I must add, but rather mature to seriously catch the eye of such an eligible gentleman. She is the senior of the two gels and it must be galling for her to have nothing when her sister has done so well. Miss Dewey could pass for twenty with that perfect complexion...but she must learn to control that forward nature.'

Mary nodded vigorously. 'She is twenty-five; Dolly told me her niece's age and said she'd be lucky to come so close again to her wedding day. I expect the doctor has found someone younger and more demure and that's why he jilted her!'

'Jilted?' Lady Groves sounded horrified. 'Poor child! That *is* a setback. Gentlemen like to think they've won a prize with a wife, not a cast-off—'

'Hugh Kendrick has just watched Miss Dewey leaving the room, Gloria,' Mrs Woodley interrupted excitedly. 'I think he likes her...'

Chapter Nine

A ghostly shroud appeared to be hovering over the sodden ground as Bea stepped out of a side door onto shingle. Following yesterday's downpour a thick early-morning mist had formed and cool droplets tickled her complexion as she crunched over gravel towards the stable block. While surveying the pearly landscape she drew in a deep breath, savouring its earthy effervescence. It was barely seven o'clock and, apart from the servants, nobody else was yet up at Blackthorne Hall.

Bea was kitted out in sturdy boots and one of her sister's riding habits, with a hat sitting jauntily on her fair tresses. As she jumped a puddle, one hand on the brim to prevent her hat flying off, she felt inexplicably joyful, considering the ordeals of the last few weeks. Others might pity her, and think there was little in her life to celebrate, yet Beatrice was determined that failed love affairs would never crush her while she had Elise and her papa close by. And her little family was expanding all the time: yesterday, after dinner, when the gentlemen had taken port and cigars, and Lady Groves and Mary Woodley had settled down in the drawing room to play cards, Elise had quietly confided to Bea that she suspected Adam might soon have a little brother or sister.

While pondering on the lovely idea of a little niece to cherish alongside Adam, Bea realised being a spinster aunt held a certain warm appeal. Vigorously she brushed a splash of mud from the fine cloth of her sister's bottle-green skirt. The viscountess had a collection of the most exquisite silks and satins stitched by feted *modistes* and would press on Bea any garment she might praise—not simply to borrow, but to keep. Bea understood the sweetness behind Elise's generosity but rarely accepted such lavish gifts, quipping that there was little need for pearl-encrusted ball gowns in her neck of the woods.

Having traversed a courtyard, Bea glimpsed the stables situated beyond a walled physic garden. As she approached the neat shrubs and plants some of her child-like delight at being up early on this fresh new morning dwindled. The sight of the herbs had reminded her of Colin. His work as a doctor had necessitated him knowing about natural remedies for ailments and Bea had taken an interest in the healing powers of plants too.

Her fingers brushed against rosemary spikes, filling her nostrils with a pungent perfume. Suddenly she crouched down, unable to pass by without touching the velvety leaves of lady's mantle, cradling their watery jewels. The image of tiny diamonds jolted her upright, thinking of another gentleman who had the power to disturb her peace of mind.

She marched briskly on, trying to shake off the unwanted memory of Hugh's degeneracy. Mulling the secret scandal over in private, she'd guessed, from Lady Groves's hint, that it had occurred abroad, and that Hugh's investment in India held the clue to the outrage he'd committed. When she'd joined Elise in the nursery yesterday she'd asked her sister—quite casually—if she could shed any light on the matter alluded to by Lady Groves. The viscountess had given a little shrug, reminding Bea that Hugh was a notorious rake and saying that she doubted he'd remain celibate just because he was on foreign soil.

Bea had already arrived at the same conclusion: the idea of Mr Kendrick having foreign affairs, as well as a few closer to home, had probably sent the elderly ladies into a tizz…but it certainly didn't surprise *her*.

Of course Bea knew the only way to find out for sure what it was all about was to ask him…and she'd no intention of doing that! Why would she bother when she didn't care a jot what he got up to…?

'You're up early, Beatrice.'

'So…so are you, sir.' Bea had swivelled about and automatically stuttered a reply, despite her amazement at seeing the very person who'd been intruding on her thoughts.

Hugh was emerging from the first stall she'd passed, leading a large chestnut horse. 'Are you riding alone?'

'I am… Elise told me last night she would not stir herself before ten o'clock. She and Alex often like to lie in…' Bea cleared her throat, wishing she'd kept her answer brief.

'I'm sure they do...' Hugh muttered, glancing at the house.

'I thought you would by now be in London,' Bea blurted, unable to curb her curiosity at his reappearance.

'I'm sorry to disappoint you,' Hugh drawled. 'But it was foolish of me to suppose I'd get even as far as Enfield last night. Half the road had been washed away by the flooding so I turned back after a couple of miles.'

Bea found the idea of him, unbeknown to her, sleeping beneath the same roof rather disquieting. And if he had returned to the house he hadn't joined them at dinner yesterday. 'You stayed at the Hall last night after all?'

'I was tempted to,' he said huskily. 'Too tempted...' he muttered at the leather he was tightening on the chestnut's flanks. 'I put up at the Red Lion instead.'

His tawny eyes ran over her smart figure and returned quizzically to her lovely face. He was too polite to voice the obvious: that she was dressed in her sister's expensive finery. Bea's gloved fingers adjusted the tailored jacket; she wasn't too proud to hide the fact that she wore borrowed clothes. Besides, he already knew her father's income wouldn't stretch to such luxuries.

'Elise kindly loaned me one of her habits,' she said carelessly.

'And very becoming it is too.' Hugh fondled the chestnut's ears soothingly as the stallion continued nudging him to gain attention. 'Will you accompany Elise to London when she returns there?'

'No, we are going back to Hertfordshire this afternoon.'

'The roads will still be hazardous to travel on.'

'My brother-in-law has given us a good sturdy coach and the driver is skilled. The journey to Berkshire was very comfy despite the potholes.'

Bea was aware that they were politely skirting about the obvious. Much as she wanted to forget him holding her close yesterday, the incident constantly played over in her mind. And she believed he was also brooding on it. A solid heat seemed to be building between them, despite the yard or two of cool atmosphere separating their bodies.

'Molly, is it, for you, ma'am?'

A young stable lad had poked his head above the door, startling Bea with his question about her choice of ride.

'Yes…thank you…' Bea managed a smile for the youth. 'She suits me very well,' Bea explained as the ensuing quiet stretched. 'I always take her out when I visit. I hope she remembers me…'

'You're not easy to forget,' Hugh muttered. 'You were right in thinking your father wished to thank me yesterday for reminding Burnett of his manners.'

'Are you hinting I should follow his suit?' Bea crisply enquired. 'Because if you are I must disappoint.' She avoided a pair of preying eyes, glad of the distraction of clopping hooves ringing on cobbles as the ostler led a small dappled horse towards her.

Once the lad had assisted her in mounting the mare Bea felt energised and calmer. She smoothed Molly's nose, murmuring affectionately as she heard her snicker softly. The opportunity to ride was a great treat for Beatrice; Walter Dewey hadn't owned any quality horseflesh for many years. In her early teens Bea had shared the use of a pony with Elise and they had both delighted in galloping about under their father's strict supervision. Then the sisters' world had crumbled when their mother had abandoned them and their father had bankrupted himself trying to win her back.

Bea had retained a modest skill, despite the intermittence of being in the saddle, and she wanted to savour her morning constitutional. She dipped her head at Hugh in farewell, trotting on towards the beckoning open space off to the south.

'Do you mind if I join you?' Hugh had swung easily onto the stallion's back, bringing his prancing under control within a matter of seconds.

'Not at all…' Beatrice called over a shoulder. 'Don't feel obliged to try to keep up, though…'

With that bold challenge she prodded her mount into action and Molly sprang forward immediately, covering ground.

As soon as Bea had leapt the small brook that edged the meadow she gave Molly her head. The mare might be small and pretty but she was a wiry little animal, and Bea's exhilaration soared as stinging air battered her soft cheeks. She laughed softly, racing on, but it was just seconds later that she registered the thud of hooves closing on her. She knew when he reined in to allow her to retain the lead as the drumming rhythm subtly changed tempo. Bea allowed Molly to slow down too, reluctant to appear determined to outpace him in some silly contest. She'd known from the start that docile little Molly was no match for the sleek thoroughbred on her tail.

Having reached the valley where the brook fed a fast-flowing stream, Beatrice slackened the reins so the mare could take a drink and crop grass.

Hugh came to a halt some yards away, then dismounted. He strolled over, wordlessly extending his arms, inviting her to get down.

Bea hesitated, then went to him because she could see he imagined her wary of his touch. And she wasn't afraid of him. Neither had she any need to be. In an instant he'd lifted her easily, swung her about with giddying speed, then put her down on the turf and walked off.

Feeling flustered by his efficient handling, she wandered towards the water's edge, glad to stretch her legs, while he tethered the stallion to a branch.

'He's a fine beast.' Beatrice was keen to make conversation. The tense silences between them seemed more awkward than an exchange of barbed remarks. 'He must be new; I don't recall seeing Alex ride him.'

'He's mine.'

'You brought your own horse with you?' Bea turned about.

'I rode him here; I left London quite late and I didn't want to miss Susannah's funeral.' He came slowly closer. 'Travelling across country is quicker than using a carriage on the roads.'

He assessed Bea's thoughtful expression.

'You're wondering why I didn't make it home yesterday, in that case.'

Bea nodded, aware of his eyes roving her flushed

complexion, making her wonder if mud had flown up from Molly's hooves to dirty her face as well as her hands.

'I found I didn't want to go home, Beatrice. I wanted to stay here for a while longer…'

Beatrice turned away, then bent down to dip her fingers into the cold water, sluicing off the soil stains. If he thought she'd ask him if he'd returned to see her, he was mistaken. She'd no intention of giving him an opportunity to scoff on that score.

'Elise is worried Alex will pine for his mama as he has no brothers or sisters.' She sent that over a shoulder before standing and drying her hands on her skirt.

'Siblings can be more of a burden than a support.' Hugh joined her on the bank of the stream.

Bea glanced at his harsh, chiselled features. She was sorry that he felt that way, considering how close she was to her beloved Elise. Hugh had a sister and a brother, and she wondered to which he'd referred when making that damning comment about his kin.

Curiosity loosened her tongue. 'Are you not a close family?'

'I visit my mother regularly, but my sister only rarely now she's settled in the shires with her husband. We have no quarrel with one another.' A chuckle grazed his throat. 'Which is remarkable, considering how Sarah has tested my patience and my pocket in the past.'

'And Sir Toby?' Bea asked after a short silence.

'The less I see of him the better I like it,' Hugh replied. He jammed his fists into his pockets, turning his head to gaze out over the fields. 'He is an unpleasant character and I would advise anybody to steer clear of him. My aunt Edith couldn't abide him, so she said.'

Beatrice sensed the soft clod beneath her feet giving way and scrambled backwards. Hugh grabbed at her whirling hand, jerking her away from the water and to safety higher up the bank.

He didn't immediately relinquish her and Bea made no effort to wriggle her fingers free of his warm grip. She blushed beneath the golden gaze she sensed scorching the top of her head, finally liberating herself with murmured thanks for his assistance. She was determined not to give the impression of being susceptible to his polished charm. And he was very attractive… more so than when she'd fallen in love with him…she grudgingly acknowledged while darting him a glance.

He had the height and dark good-looks that appealed to women and made lesser-blessed fellows resentful. He also now had the wherewithal to purchase expensive tailoring to enhance his broad shoulders… Beatrice abruptly curtailed her wild appreciation. It was now nothing to her how handsome his face, or how snug his clothes! But she could understand why women everywhere—even in exotic locations—might succumb to him…

'I have been remiss in not offering you my condolences,' Beatrice uttered briskly, in order to curb her annoying preoccupation with his attractiveness. 'I had no idea that your aunt Edith had passed away till recently.' She started to walk along the bank. 'Elise told me the sad news when she came to Hertfordshire. I liked Mrs Vickers, although I spoke to her only a few times when in London.'

It had been during that particular sojourn in town three years ago that she had met Hugh Kendrick and almost disgraced herself with him.

With hindsight Beatrice was aghast at what she'd done. Why she had ever thought it a good idea to adopt the soubriquet *Lady Lonesome* when advertising for a husband in a gazette, or to arrange clandestine trysts with strangers to select her mate, she would never fathom. She'd matured in character since, with Colin's staid influence, she was sure. But the memory of what she'd risked—and forced her younger sister to risk as her reluctant accomplice—horrified her.

Bea was very fortunate that her antics had not completely sullied her future and her family's name, already tarnished by her parents' divorce. Few people had ever been aware of her stupid scheme; the man at her side had known because he'd responded to her advert. As a lure she'd pretended to possess a dowry and Hugh Kendrick had been eager to lay claim to it, if not to her...

'Ah...I do recall you first met my aunt and me at Vauxhall Gardens. You were attending a concert with your sister and the Chapman family.'

Hugh sounded as though he'd dredged up the details from the pit of his memory while strolling at her side. In fact he'd not forgotten a solitary thing about that first encounter. Neither had he forgotten that he'd replied to *Lady Lonesome's* advertisement because of Toby's refusal to loan him money to pay his rent and keep a roof over his head.

But there had also been the matter of Sophia Sweetman's expensive tastes depleting his bank balance. Sophia had been under his protection then—until he'd found he couldn't afford to keep her any longer. Now she was again his paramour, and he was able to give her all she wanted this time round, but Hugh wasn't sure he wanted Sophia—or Gwen Sharpe for that matter—no matter what delightful tricks they dreamt up to keep his interest and defeat one another. Annoyingly, he knew that the coltish blonde at his side would have no such difficulty arousing him…

Hugh cursed beneath his breath at the direction his thoughts…and his loins…were taking. 'My aunt liked you,' he said in a voice roughened by frustration. 'When you and your sister left town that year and returned to Hertfordshire she lacked your company.'

'I expect Edith missed having the details of our hasty escape explained to her.'

Beatrice had sensed his irritation. If he were already bored with her company she'd not impose on him longer. She retraced her steps towards Molly, hoping he might offer to assist her in remounting rather than watch her scramble in an ungainly fashion onto the mare's back.

'I missed you too.'

'Did you?' Beatrice jerked around. 'You had an odd way of showing it, Mr Kendrick, as I recall.'

'What does that mean?'

'I believe you were paying attention to Fiona Chapman before I had unpacked my case in Hertfordshire.'

'Were you jealous?'

Beatrice whipped a biting glance to his rugged profile but found a denial refused to trip off her tongue.

Slowly he turned his head, his hawk-like eyes trapping her, bringing her to an involuntarily halt.

'It is a shame you have become arrogant and conceited,' she whispered. 'I think I liked you better as a penniless fortune-hunter.' She marched on, but had covered very little ground when a hand clasped her wrist, jerking her back.

'And I liked you better when you were a country miss keen to please me.'

'That silly girl no longer exists.' Bea twisted her wrist in an attempt to free herself.

'I think she could be resurrected, given time…' he growled.

'And I think you might now be rich, thanks to your aunt's bequest, but the Indian sun has addled your wits.' Beatrice forced a fist between them to prise herself away from him.

Hugh grunted a laugh, dipping his head as though he would kiss her. But he skimmed his mouth past her mutinous face, letting her go. 'Quite possibly something's addled my wits,' he muttered, and walked on.

Inwardly he mocked himself for feeling like a randy youth. He'd been burning with desire for her yesterday and only the thought of an audience with her father had checked his lust. If a roomful of mourners at a wake hadn't put him off pursuing her he knew he should quickly distance himself, in case he lost control while they were alone. He should have gone home yesterday, he realised, and straight to Gwen and a long night of release.

There was nothing to be achieved by wanting her; he was tormenting himself for no reason. Alex would kill him if he seduced his sister-in-law, and Hugh was sure he wasn't ready for a wife. Inwardly, he mocked himself that if he did propose Beatrice Dewey would throw the offer back at him. But she'd accepted Burnett, and Hugh knew there'd been a suitor before the doctor…

'Did Mr Vaughan propose to you?'

Beatrice quit gazing at the mud underfoot. 'Mr Vaughan? How do you know of him?' she gasped in surprise.

'Because you told me,' Hugh replied dryly. 'Don't you remember that conversation, Beatrice?'

Bea bit her lip. No doubt when in Hugh's arms, in a blissful haze, she had confided her secrets to him. Mr Vaughan had been the first gentleman for whom she'd formed a *tendresse*. The lawyer had pursued her when she was eighteen, then repaid her shy devotion by dropping her like a stone to wed the fiancée he'd omitted to mention.

'No…he did not propose. Rather like you, he enjoyed flirting while chasing a dowry to make taking on a wife worthwhile.'

Hugh strode back towards her, caught her face in a fierce grip when she avoided looking at him. 'I told you at the time I was wrong to mislead you when I had nothing to give. If things had been different we would by now have been man and wife. Things for me are different now.'

Beatrice would have pulled back but Hugh caught the tops of her arms, keeping her against him. Oddly, he was calmly certain that whatever he thought he knew about himself, whatever secrets he'd be obliged to expose, he was on the brink of asking her to marry him.

'Things for me are different now, too,' Bea retorted, glaring into hard hazel eyes. 'Once home that year I fell in love properly, with a decent man, and soon realised that I'd felt mere infatuation for you.'

'Is that so?' Hugh asked softly. 'I wonder if I'm able to infatuate you again now your decent man has disappeared…'

This time his mouth closed with hers relentlessly, tracking every evasion until she ceded with a little gasp and allowed their lips to merge. She felt his long fingers forking into her hair, dislodging her hat and a few pins. But though she struggled Bea knew she was defeated. Since the moment he had turned up at her father's house with news of Alex's mother she had unconsciously craved this. Within a second of his caress skimming her silhouette she had melted closer.

Hugh sensed her need and immediately deepened the kiss, manoeuvring her jaw to part her mouth. His tongue teased the silk of her inner lip, sliding and circling with slow eroticism, while a determined hand stroked from her back to her buttocks, jolting her into awareness of the effect she was having on him. His hands cupped her face, forcing her back from him so he could gaze at her features. A flush had spread across a soft cheek where his stubble had grazed her and her mouth, moist and temptingly slack, was scarlet and plump from his passionate assault.

But she was not the sweet ingénue she'd been before. He could read behind the desire in her large eyes that her response was reluctant…measured…and he wondered just how much the doctor had taken before he'd gone away.

'You're easily infatuated, sweetheart,' Hugh murmured. 'I'm beginning to wish I'd bedded down at the Hall last night, after all, and got to know you again.'

His brutal comment was like a dousing with cold water for Beatrice. He couldn't have made it plainer that he thought her a wanton, desperate for his attention, just as she had been years ago when she'd promised him anything he wanted, then cried when he'd coolly told her he must stop seeing her.

A small hand, liberated from entrapment between their bodies, flew up to crack against his unshaven cheek, jerking his head sideways. 'I'm not infatuated and never will be again…not with you, at least. I'm disgusted by your lust and insolence.' She backed away, pressing quivering fingers to her pulsing lips. 'Colin might not be able to marry me under the terms of his inheritance but I'd sooner be his mistress than your wife.'

Hugh stalked her on their way back, until she realised she'd got the stream directly behind her and could go no further.

'I don't recall proposing to you…ever…not then, not now,' he gritted through his teeth, infuriated with himself as well as her.

He would have risked even worse humiliation at her

hands if he'd let those four damnable words circling his mind trip off his tongue.

'But if it's a lover you want…' Hugh continued in a deliberately lewd tone as he trailed just one tormenting digit down a hot silky cheek. 'I'll provide a better service than the doctor…in every way. Just name it and it's yours, whatever you desire.' He grunted a callous laugh as she flinched at his crude proposition. 'So… the decent man's gone off to Miss Rawlings to keep his estates safe, has he?'

'Don't you dare mock him!' Beatrice cried. 'He didn't want to leave me! He had to for his future heirs' sake!'

'Quite the martyr, then, isn't he?' Hugh mocked. 'Yet Sir Colin, as he demands to be known, gives the impression of a man content with his lot in life…whereas I have just realised I am not, because I want what he doesn't.'

Beatrice gulped down an indignant protestation. She had not seen Colin since he'd jilted her, but for her pride's sake she'd clung to a belief that he was missing her as she missed him. She might tell her family… she might tell herself…that she was glad they'd parted, but in private moments she knew it wasn't wholly so. There had been tender interludes during their relationship, if no great passion. For this man to brutally throw her fiancé's faithlessness in her face—even if it were the truth—was galling.

'If Colin seems content it is because he is stoic and sensible enough to know he must accept what he cannot change!' Beatrice hissed. 'Whereas *you* are a disgusting degenerate.'

'Am I? Who told you so?' Hugh enquired with specious softness.

Beatrice pressed together her lips, as though to prevent herself repeating what she'd learned about him from Lady Groves: he was a man who preferred spending time with harlots rather than decent women, despite his popularity with debutantes. If the ladies' comments about the flirtatious Miss Rawlings were to be believed Colin's future wife seemed, with awful irony, particularly taken with Hugh Kendrick. And if that were not enough then there was the *other business* which, if she'd guessed correctly, had taken place overseas.

'Come…if you want to slander me, Beatrice, let me have some details and your source.'

'But I've not slandered you, have I?' she breathed, removing tendrils of fair hair that a stirring breeze had lashed across her vivid blue vision. 'That damning description is accurate and could be added to.'

He shrugged, cruelly amused. 'With a little more information, sweet, I'll be able to judge.'

The temptation to provoke him into admitting he had dallied with exotic women was too great, and he had invited it. 'It wouldn't matter where in the world you were, you'd sooner scandalise decent people than curb your lust.'

'Ah…I see… It worries you that I might have let my eye rove when in India. You told me you weren't jealous, Beatrice…' he goaded, glad that she didn't seem in possession of any firm facts.

'I'm not jealous…' Bea raged.

But he was ready for her fist this time and caught

the small curled digits inches from his face. 'What do you want me to tell you, sweet? All of it?'

'Get out of my way,' she choked in frustration and fury.

Her eyes continued sparking blue fire despite the burn of tears making her blink. She'd never win this verbal battle and knew she was close to breaking down so must withdraw from it. She was not jealous or upset in any way because of Hugh Kendrick, of that she was certain! Her distress came from the unpalatable news that Colin might already have eased his conscience where she was concerned. It was hard to bear, especially as he must replace her with a woman who seemed likely to stray—perhaps before they'd even wed.

As a sob raised her bosom, then grazed her throat, Hugh released her and strode away. Gathering the reins of the two horses, he brought them closer to where Beatrice still stood, holding herself rigidly, on the bank of the stream. When she refused to approach he jerked her closer and, without a word, hoisted her atop Molly with such strength that she had to cling to the mare's neck to prevent herself toppling straight off the other side.

'My offer of *carte blanche* stands,' he said with quiet gravity, gazing up at her steadily, a hand on Molly's bridle preventing her escape. 'Perhaps, in the circumstances, you should consider it.'

'And perhaps you should go to hell!' Beatrice hissed, slapping wildly at his fingers until he removed them. She set off across the meadow at a gallop, the wind drying her wet face as fast as the brine was falling.

When the Hall was in sight she realised that he had

not followed her all the way back. She clattered onto the cobbles of the stable yard and, turning her head, saw him stationed on the brow of the hill, watching her. Involuntarily Bea shivered at his dark, brooding presence outlined against a pale sky. A moment later he'd turned the stallion's head and was heading fast in the direction of London.

Chapter Ten

'You will do as your uncle wished!'

'I don't see why I must.' Stella Rawlings had been pouting at her reflection while fixing a garnet to a small earlobe. Now she swivelled on the dressing stool to give her aunt a sulky look. 'I'm becoming popular and I'd sooner have my pick of the bachelors than have a husband chosen for me.' She stood up and approached the mantelpiece to sort through invitations, selecting one. 'See...the Rutherfords want us to join them in their box at the opera.'

Idly, she waved the parchment. The Rutherfords were close to the heart of the *ton* and every chaperon wanted her ward to have their patronage.

Apart from Maggie Monk.

The woman stomped closer, snatching the card from Stella's fingers and tossing it back whence it came. 'The only reason you're in demand, my girl, is because you've drawn attention from every randy fellow in Mayfair. Bertram Rutherford is rumoured to have at least five bastards.'

Stella flounced to sit on the stool, head tilted to one side while she playfully flicked the eardrop. She'd sooner have had rubies, but at least Colin had bought her a gift to mark the announcement of their betrothal. She twisted the garnet ring on her finger. She'd sooner have had a ruby engagement ring too…but mostly she craved a magnificent diamond…from Hugh Kendrick…

Her grey eyes lifted to her reflection, assessing her features. She knew she wasn't a conventional beauty: her small snub nose was littered with freckles and her full mouth had a natural droop that made her look dissatisfied even when she wasn't. She twirled a ringlet about a finger, wishing her hair were golden-blonde rather than flame-red, but gentlemen liked her generous bosom and curvy hips; they also appreciated her brazenness, even if their wives didn't.

So, in all, Stella Rawlings was satisfied with her looks and the way things were going since she'd arrived in town. She just wished her aunt would accept that Sir Colin should be kept dangling in reserve…just in case she failed to hook a gentleman with a good deal more to offer than a minor title and a modest country estate.

'Did you hear what I said, miss?' Maggie exploded when Stella continued simpering at her reflection. 'You are making a fool of yourself, flirting with every gentleman who ogles you. Lord Whitley is over sixty and yet I thought at one point you were about to sit on his knee, so close did you get to his chair.'

'The old goat would have liked that,' Stella snorted, planting her hands on the dresser and pushing herself to her feet once more.

'Maybe...but his wife would not. You do not irk somebody as important as Lady Whitley at her own *soirée*.'

'Why ever not?' Stella piped up. 'Her husband will ensure she asks me again.'

'How do you know that?' Maggie snapped.

'Because he assured me of it.'

'I imagine Lord Whitley's assured plenty of girls of plenty of things, and none of it came to pass.'

'Oh...hush, Auntie.' Stella changed tack, embracing Maggie to sweeten her temper. 'I'm just enjoying myself and I wish you'd be happy for me.'

Maggie gave a mollified sniff. 'I'll be happy when your fiancé adds a gold band to that garnet ring. Your uncle Donald wanted you to be quickly wed to Sir Colin so your future would be secure and you'd be a titled lady. We must set the date without delay.'

'I don't want to just yet,' Stella insisted sulkily. 'There are better titles going begging than his.' She noticed her aunt's expression darkening so added, 'But if I *do* want Sir Colin I'll keep him...don't worry your head about that.'

Stella felt confident she had her fiancé wound about her little finger, and all it had taken was a sly glimpse of her shapely calves. She'd schemed to give him a taste of what she could offer but hadn't wanted Sir Colin to think her a little trollop, so had pretended to be unaware of him entering the parlour at the very moment she'd been adjusting a garter.

His fulsome apology for intruding had not been able to disguise the burst of lust in his eyes. The following day Sir Colin had presented her with the gift of garnet eardrops. Stella's lips knotted in ruefulness. She should have raised her skirts higher that afternoon...she might then have got the rubies she wanted.

Maggie shook her head in a mix of despair and appreciation, watching Stella sorting through her jewellery box. The eardrops were removed and a different set, bought by a previous admirer, tried on. She'd received that gift of oval amethysts from a besotted old coal merchant in York.

Maggie knew Stella was still a virgin, so Sir Colin had no quibble there. But the girl was adept at getting cash spent on her while preserving the goods. She could understand why Stella wanted more than Colin Burnett could give. But only he could give what Maggie Monk was determined Stella would get...so the girl was marrying him and no other.

'You must come and stay with us in London and let Hugh see that you don't care a fig for him and he'll never force you to be his mistress.'

Before joining her husband in town Elise had decided to have a final attempt at persuading Bea to fight her corner. She had packed up and left Blackthorne Hall and was en route to Mayfair via her childhood home, where she had stayed the night with her family.

'I'm sure Mr Kendrick knows he can't intimidate me.' Bea smiled, despite feeling a fraud. The dratted man's name, even an annoying phantom feeling of his body still pressing against hers, was enough to dry her mouth. But she continued with the task of folding clean linen brought in from the washing line as though undisturbed by the nature of their conversation.

'Well, even if you don't mind Hugh Kendrick bothering you, you must be worried that the gossips in town are having a field-day at your expense.'

Elise hated being so brutal but hoped that resorting to bald facts might galvanise Beatrice into preserving her pride and dignity. Elise was sure that beneath that brave face her sister was understandably deeply wounded by her run of bad luck. She didn't want Beatrice to become a recluse because of two gentlemen who'd proved they weren't worthy of her.

It saddened Elise that Hugh's upturn in fortune seemed to have turned him into a heartless Lothario. She felt a fool for having cherished a hope that Hugh might honourably pursue her sister. But now another problem had gone into the mixing pot: their father had received a lengthy missive from his sister.

Aunt Dolly had reported that tongues were wagging following publication of the doctor's engagement notice. Inquisitive people had been asking why Sir Colin Burnett favoured a bold hussy, half his age, over her niece. Dolly had made it clear she'd given short shrift to anybody suggesting Beatrice must be distraught by his defection. Dolly had further written that she strongly advised Walter to send Bea to town to scotch such damaging rumours once and for all or his elder girl would be forever pitied and avoided.

'Aunt Dolly is right, you know.' Elise pushed the letter across the table so her sister could not help but look at it. Their father had insisted they both read it and discuss if action needed to be taken. 'Are you going to quash these rumours that you're hiding away, desolate? Come to Mayfair with me and hold your head high at the best places. That will show them all!'

'You have not even discussed with your husband about inviting me to stay with you,' Bea pointed out mildly.

'Alex always loves to see you, and besides he is quite furious with that rakish—' Elise bit her tongue. In her enthusiasm to get Bea to London she had almost let slip that her husband's rage was directed at his best friend rather than Sir Colin Burnett.

Bea frowned. Her sister was now keen to escape her gaze and she could guess why that might be. 'Oh, please say you haven't told the viscount that Hugh propositioned me.' After a tiny silence Bea angrily threw onto the table a half-folded pillowcase.

'Really, Elise! She pushed to her feet. 'You promised you would not—'

'I swear I did not betray you!' Elise interrupted anxiously. 'Alex could tell I was dreadfully upset after you went home following the funeral and he kept on and on at me for a reason. He thought I might have lost the babe, and that made me even more tearful, so I admitted I was fretting about you. I swear I did not mention Hugh's name, or the nature of your problem...but Alex guessed in the end, and I confirmed it for I could not lie to him.'

Beatrice pivoted about, white fingers flying to cover her gasp. '*That's* why Alex went off to London without waiting for you to accompany him!' she breathed. 'He's gone to challenge Hugh over it.' She could tell from her sister's forlorn expression that she'd hit on the truth.

'I honestly did not ask him to, Bea; in fact I tried to make Alex see the sense in calming down before setting off.'

Bea thrust two hands into her silky hair, cupping her scalp. 'He will think that I acted like a whining child, running to my brother-in-law to complain about him.'

'Do you care what he thinks?' Elise asked pithily.

'Of course not!' Bea fumed beneath her sister's arch expression. 'Well...naturally I do not want him to think me incapable of putting pen to paper to tell him my opinion of him. Neither do I want him believing me cowed. I intended to give the impression that his offer of *carte blanche* was not worthy of any further attention.'

'Well, if you don't want Alex to stand up for you it only remains for you to tell Hugh yourself that his pursuit is most unwelcome and in vain.' Elise crossed her arms over her middle and sighed. 'It'll be sad if Alex and Hugh have fallen out. Hugh can't be an *incorrigible* rogue or Alex wouldn't have been friends with him for so long.'

Bea felt guilty that her brother-in-law might have suffered an unpleasant argument because of her, but she was also exasperated because she'd not asked Alex to champion her.

'Hugh is probably embarrassed to have overstepped the mark with you, yet won't admit it. I'll wager he's already lined up a more suitable candidate.'

'If that is supposed to make me feel better, Elise...' Bea was torn between laughter and annoyance.

'It is supposed to make you feel like damning the lot of them!' Elise fell silent as their father entered the room.

'For a lady, you cuss like a navvy.' Walter was not averse to chastising his daughters, no matter their ages or the fact that the younger outranked him.

'Sorry, Papa,' Viscountess Blackthorne said meekly.

Walter pointed to his sister's letter, a gleeful smile spreading across his face. 'So, this woman Sir Colin must marry is a cheap flirt! Hah! Just what he deserves! I've a mind to go to town and tell him so!'

'Why do you not, Papa?' Elise suggested. She had not thought her father would undertake the journey, but he seemed fired up enough to do it.

'I might...yes, I might...and while I'm at it I'll ask the skinflint where my compensation has got to.'

'Colin has not returned the money you spent on our wedding arrangements?' Beatrice sat down on the chair opposite her father, looking shocked and concerned.

'Not all of it,' Walter confirmed. 'I would remind the fellow of his promise face to face, as he has ignored my letter.'

'So she told you, then...?' Having voiced this sour response to being hit in the mouth, Hugh touched his bleeding lip. As he picked himself up off his hallway floor he sent his assailant a baleful look

'She? Are you talking about my wife?' It was an icy demand.

'I wasn't...no...I was talking about Beatrice.'

Alex Blackthorne stalked closer, flexing his sore

fingers. He halted on seeing Hugh's stance altering: his friend was balancing aggressively, preparing to defend himself. Alex might have got in one lucky punch and sent his opponent reeling, but he was certain he wouldn't manage another. The two men were evenly matched in combat skills and had sparred, fenced and shot at targets together since the age of about twelve.

'I haven't seen Beatrice since she went home after the funeral. Elise told me what you'd done. You said you'd leave my sister-in-law alone.'

'I can't...'

'You damn well will!' Alex thundered. 'If her father finds out you've propositioned her he'll crawl to town, if necessary, just to shoot you.'

Hugh used the back of his thumb to smear away the blood trickling towards his chin. 'Don't tell him, then,' he said bluntly.

'That's it, is it? Don't tell him?' Alex mimicked in disgust. He strode to and fro over the marble slabs in Hugh's palatial hallway. 'What in damnation's up with you? You've got two willing women set up in London; you've got attachments in India you're not willing to forgo. Still you're not satisfied!' Alex roared. 'How dare you treat Beatrice as though she's some cheap strumpet—?'

'I've not,' Hugh coolly interrupted. 'She can have everything she wants—including all the discretion money can buy.'

'She can have everything from you but a wedding ring?'

Hugh displayed even white teeth in a soundless laugh. 'She doesn't want one.'

That took the wind out of Alex's sails. He stopped prowling and shot Hugh a dark look. 'What do you mean by that?'

'She told me she'd sooner be Burnett's mistress than my wife.'

Alex continued glaring at Hugh but inwardly his attitude altered. If what Hugh had just said were true it put a whole different light on things. Ruining a virgin spinster was one thing; bidding against somebody else for a self-confessed paramour was another matter entirely. He'd done so himself on many occasions before he'd met Elise.

Alex thrust his fingers through his hair in exasperation, unsure now how to proceed. It was none of his business if Beatrice and the doctor had been lovers, or indeed if she'd succumbed to Hugh all those years ago when they'd been besotted with one another. His sister-in-law had made no complaint of having been ravished at any time.

Alex realised he probably owed his friend an apology, and beneath his breath he groaned at the mess of it all.

'Actually, if we're going to come to blows over grievances…' Hugh approached in a single athletic stride and knocked Alex onto his back with an efficient jab. 'It was *my* job to tell Beatrice about Rani. How much does she know about my time in India?'

Alex levered himself up onto an elbow. 'I haven't

even told my wife about that damned web of deceit!' he bawled out in his defence.

'If it wasn't you or Elise who mentioned a foreign liaison—'

'It's bound to have got out,' Alex interrupted harshly. Your brother knows, after all, and so does Lord Mornington.' Alex dragged himself upright. 'You got yourself into the confounded mess so you'll have to suffer the consequences of being so blasted noble…'

'Drink?' Hugh invited acidly. A thumb pointing over his shoulder indicated his study, situated along the corridor. He knew they were both feeling foolish for having swung first and asked questions second.

Hugh knew he was wrong for wanting Beatrice in his bed, but if necessary he'd fight his best friend to have her—because just a single memory of her silky lips slipping beneath his, and her moaning response to his ardour, was enough to send tormenting heat to his loins.

'Promise me you'll stay away from my sister-in-law and I'll take a drink with you.' Alex feared his terms and his olive branch would be rejected.

'I can't do that.' Hugh turned away from his best friend, calling over his shoulder to a footman, who'd remained stoically seated in a shadowy alcove during the fracas, 'The viscount's leaving; show him out.'

Chapter Eleven

Elise had hoped that the hostility between her husband and his friend might ease in a day or two, but she was disappointed on that score.

Raising herself up on an elbow and resting her rumpled blonde head into a cupped palm, she watched Alex pulling on his clothes. He'd welcomed her back to his side as he always did, by taking her to bed to make love to her at the earliest opportunity. As soon as his son had been settled in the nursery and his in-laws were safely occupied in unpacking and resting in their chambers Elise had been scooped into his arms and the stairs mounted two at a time.

Following their leisurely pleasure Elise had tried to question Alex about recent upsets, but he'd refused to have Hugh Kendrick's name mentioned and had stopped her words with a hungry kiss before springing out of bed.

'I'm off to see Adam in the nursery before going out. What will you and Bea get up to for the rest of the day while I pore over dusty old files with my solicitor?'

'Mischief…' Elise rolled onto her back, feeling languid, a smile tilting her mouth as she twirled a finger into the dangling golden fringe of the bed canopy.

'That I can believe…' Alex approached the enormous four-poster and leaned over his wife, planting a fist either side of her lissom body. 'And your intended victim, sweet?'

'Hugh Kend—'

A finger was placed on her lips, silencing her.

'We must speak of him, Alex,' Elise said crossly, sliding free. 'Papa likes him and is bound to ask after him. How are we to explain away your argument with him?' She sat up, using both arms to draw her knees beneath her chin. 'Also, Papa is going after Colin Burnett for the money he owes him.'

Alex sat down on the edge of the bed, sensing his wife's anxiety. 'I was unaware of any shortfall. Walter's not mentioned the debt or asked me to help in the matter.'

Elise sighed. 'He probably did not want his son-in-law to think him incapable of sorting out his own affairs. You know how independent he is.' She frowned. 'I know it wasn't long ago that my father could not abide Hugh because of the way he'd treated Beatrice. But Papa has his whims, and he thinks that Burnett is now the foe and Kendrick, as he calls him, is his knight errant.'

'If Walter knew what that gentleman had planned for Beatrice he'd call him out—and me too, for introducing Hugh to his daughters in the first place.'

'It wasn't strictly you who was responsible…it was Hugh's Aunt Edith who made the introduction.'

Alex smiled sourly. 'I don't think your father would quibble over details, sweet, he'd just reach for his choice of weapon…'

'Stay with me a while longer…please…'

Gwen Sharpe stretched out a hand to the lean contours of a naked male buttock just within reach of a fingertip caress. Her husky plea went unheeded and a pair of buff breeches sheathed the muscled flesh from her touch.

'Hugh! I want you to get back in bed!'

If Gwen had hoped an authoritative tone might work better than a seductive one she was wrong, but not surprised. She was aware that her hold on this charismatic man was slipping, and whereas once she might have blamed that doxy he kept on the other side of town now she wasn't so sure that Sophia Sweetman was to blame. Gwen flopped down onto silk sheets, pondering on the identity of the woman who'd caught her lover's eye.

She knew that a silly little debutante was flirting with him at every opportunity. She'd heard reports of Stella Rawlings even before she'd bumped into the redheaded wench in Oxford Street. Gwen had persuaded Hugh to take her shopping and had looked on, amused, as the chit negotiated several drapery counters to bring herself directly into Hugh's path. Gwen had seen genuine boredom in Hugh's face at the unexpected meeting. But he'd courteously exchanged a few words with Stella and her aunt before moving on.

It certainly wasn't Miss Rawlings stealing him away. He'd an impatient nature and no desire for novices, however willing they were to learn the sensual arts. Gwen rolled onto her stomach, watching as he shrugged his powerful shoulders into a tailcoat then straightened his shirt-cuffs.

Aware of his mistress's gaze, Hugh turned about and gave her a smile. 'Do you want to go to the opera later in the week?'

'Will you have more time to devote to me that evening?' Gwen asked ruefully.

'Perhaps…' Hugh walked back towards the bed, glad that Gwen was coming to accept, without too much recrimination, that their relationship was coming to an end. Of course ordinarily he'd have enjoyed her charms for longer than six months. Gwen was a competent mistress: shapely, skilful, passionate…the list of her attributes was almost as long as that of the reasons why he was a confounded idiot for considering forgoing them.

'I was surprised to see that your friend's wife has returned to town,' Gwen mentioned idly, sliding a long fingernail to and fro on Hugh's breeched thigh, inches from her face. Her eyes slid sideways, watching for his renewed arousal and her victory, but he seemed impervious to her teasing even when she replaced the digit with her moist lips.

'Why were you surprised? The funeral is over and the viscountess resides mainly in London.' Hugh strolled to a chair and picked up his gloves.

'The scandal concerning her poor sister is very absorbing.' Gwen clutched the sheet to her bosom, sitting up. 'It's bizarre that a fellow like Sir Colin would jilt a refined lady to marry that silly girl, don't you think?'

'Burnett's affairs are of no interest to me…' Hugh raked tidying fingers through his thick hair in front of the pier glass.

'*He* is of scant interest to anybody; it is the combatant ladies who will now be gleefully observed at all times.'

'Ladies?' Hugh selected the word that interested him, pivoting on a heel towards Gwen.

'I saw the viscountess in her landau in Hyde Park. With her were an elderly gentleman and a pretty blonde who very much looks like her, although not in the first flush of youth—older, I'd say, by a year or two. Methinks the spinster and her father have come to do battle with the minx and her aunt.' Gwen felt her breath catching in her throat at a subtle fleeting intensity in his expression. 'If the viscountess has brought her sister to town do you think sparks might fly when the rivals meet?'

'Possibly,' Hugh said, staring sightlessly at his paramour, a mirthless laugh grazing his throat. 'But not in a way anybody might expect.'

Hugh clattered down the stairs from Gwen's apartment and out into the street, unheeding of his paramour at the window, watching his dawn departure. He sprang aboard his phaeton, setting the greys to a trot. His mouth twisted in a bitter smile as he brooded that as far as he was concerned the rivals in this game were men, not women.

He was sure Gwen had correctly described seeing the Dewey family out for a drive in the park. If he were arrogant and conceited, as Bea had accused him of being he mocked himself, he'd believe she had followed him to London to become his mistress. But it was closer to the truth to suppose Mr Dewey had come after the doctor for compensation of some sort. Burnett was sure to refuse ceding his birthright for Beatrice, so perhaps the less formal role she'd stated she'd be willing to undertake might be arranged between them.

Hugh knew he could outplay the doctor at every turn at the negotiating table and he was determined to have Beatrice at any cost…

And damn any man who tried to stand in his way.

'The old biddies will do their best to extract from you an account of Sir Colin's betrayal simply to be feted as the first to pass it on. You must refrain from calling him a swine, though he deserves it.'

Beatrice received that blunt advice from Fiona Chapman while the two of them were ascending the magnificent stairway of Lord and Lady Whitley's townhouse on Devonshire Square. Outwardly Beatrice remained exquisitely cool and calm. Inwardly her heart was racing, while her mouth felt arid and her palms clammy. She moved them inconspicuously against the skirt of her sister's blue silk gown, borrowed for the occasion.

Elise had stayed at home; her morning sickness had lasted so long she'd finally given up hope of leaving the house, saying she felt too queasy to socialise. Nevertheless she'd insisted Beatrice attend with Aunt Dolly and their friends. The sisters had spent some time—in between spells of Beatrice rubbing the expectant mother's back while Elise used a china bowl—in selecting a perfect ensemble for Bea's first social outing since Colin jilted her.

The idea of facing down the stares and whispers had been daunting, but there was undeniable good sense in the advice to thwart the gossips and boost her pride and reputation. So, following her father's declaration that he'd like to go to London before his aching legs put him in a Bath chair, Beatrice had agreed to the trip.

Earlier that evening, during the ride over to Devonshire Square in the viscount's coach, her Aunt Dolly had bluntly stated that the wretched doctor might have dreadfully humiliated Beatrice, but it was her niece's duty not to show it bothered her in the slightest. Bea could not but agree.

Glancing over a shoulder, Bea received a bright smile and a little wave from Aunt Dolly, coming up the stairs just behind them. Despite a tilting stomach that Bea was sure made her feel as sick as her poor sister, she inched up her chin and went with Fiona towards the hum of conversation issuing from the assembly.

'It is a shame Elise is not with us,' Fiona whispered. 'She has perfected the art of batting back a snide remark.'

Bea choked a giggle and put a silk-gloved finger to her lips to hush such talk in case it was overheard.

'That's the spirit!' Fiona hissed. 'Keep smiling—it will confound them all.'

On entering the brightly lit drawing room Lady Groves and Mrs Woodley sailed immediately in their direction.

'How very nice to see you again, my dear. We heard

you had come to town and hoped you might attend this evening.' Lady Groves glanced over Bea's shoulder. 'Is the viscountess not with you?'

'My sister is indisposed, ma'am,' Bea replied.

'Ah…so I was right…' Gloria gave her companion a nod. 'The viscountess looks to be blooming because she is increasing again, Mary.'

Bea started to attention and gulped down a spontaneous denial. Only very close friends and family were aware of the good news. 'I…I beg you will not say that, madam, as it is not…um…' Bea fell short of telling an outright lie, yet neither could she hint at the truth before her sister and brother-in-law thought it the right time to make an announcement. 'Elise is in mourning for her mother-in-law…' Bea blurted, having just remembered the recent funeral.

Lady Groves patted Bea's fingers. 'Of course…I understand; that was naughty of me.'

'Ah…I see that Mr Kendrick has just arrived,' Fiona burst out, keen to change the subject lest Beatrice tried to flee after such an inauspicious start.

Though feeling compelled to do so, Bea didn't turn about. She knew her first glimpse of him would increase the weakness in her knees and make her insides again lurch painfully. She'd come here with Elise's assurances that Hugh wouldn't be interested in such tame entertainment. A meeting with the fiancé who'd abandoned her she was prepared for…but a run-in with the dangerous philanderer who wanted to sleep with her was too much…

'Gracious! Whatever has brought him here tonight?'

Gloria Groves gushed behind her fan, endorsing Elise's idea that Hugh was likely to shun the Whitleys' invitation. 'My...but doesn't he look handsome?'

'He always does, Gloria.' Mary sounded resigned to admiring him. 'Perhaps he is here to take advantage of the viscount's absence now they no longer like one another,' she suggested.

Lady Groves frowned at her companion. It was well known that the two gentlemen had fallen out, but the cause of the argument had yet to break surface. 'That was not kind, Mary. Miss Dewey is present and she is the viscount's relative.'

Mary looked suitably chastened and blinked behind her fan's ivory sticks.

'There is that little madam with her future husband.' Lady Groves had been distracted just as she'd been about to probe Miss Dewey for a hint as to why the viscount and Mr Kendrick had taken exception to one another. Elevating her hooked nose, Gloria peered down it at the new arrivals, then deliberately turned back to Beatrice. 'Don't worry, my dear. We are your friends. Disgraceful conduct. Don't know how Sir Colin has got the nerve to flaunt that hussy.'

'You are kind...' Bea rattled off, feeling light-headed with suppressed hysteria. 'Oh, I see Jago and Verity are here.' She indicated Fiona's sister and brother-in-law, some distance away. 'Shall we join them?'

As the two young women walked away Bea tried to still her racing heart, but gave an involuntary little gulp of dismay.

'You're trembling, Bea.' Fiona immediately linked

arms with her in concern. 'You must not let him unsettle you so! I could throttle the brute,' she muttered with asperity.

'Which one?' Bea returned on a sob of a laugh.

'Burnett, of course,' Fiona said, glancing at Bea. 'Did you have another man in mind?'

'Shall we just take a breath of air on the terrace before joining your sister?' Bea asked, glad when Fiona immediately complied and steered her in the direction of the breeze.

Once on the flags, Bea approached the railings and curled her warm fingers on cold iron, closing her eyes and breathing deeply to still her panic.

'It is as well he *has* turned up,' Fiona said gently. 'I know it is dreadfully hard for you, my dear, especially when he has Miss Rawlings with him. But you can show once and for all that neither of them has the better of you.'

Bea nodded, despite her friend having got the wrong end of the stick. She couldn't blame Fiona for misunderstanding the root cause of her agitation. She'd not realised herself until a moment ago just how she'd be affected when again in Hugh Kendrick's vicinity.

The memory of his dark silhouette against the storm-washed sky was behind her eyelids. His final words to her again spun in her mind: *'My offer of carte blanche still stands...perhaps in the circumstances you should consider it...'*

And she'd told him to go to hell…

But Fiona knew none of this and believed Hugh Kendrick was just a mutual friend of the family—as had

Bea until a short while ago, when he'd turned up out of the blue, heightening the turmoil in her life.

'Ah, there you both are!' Verity Clemence emerged through the curtains. 'I was wondering where you had disappeared to.' She approached Bea and took her hands. 'It is very brave of you, Bea, to turn out like this. But quite the right thing to do.' She added, 'Never fear, you have plenty of good friends here tonight and Colin Burnett and Miss Rawlings have very few—if any.'

'That seems rather pitiable…' Bea said, stepping away from the balustrade to link arms with her friends. 'Well, I'm ready to join the fray…are you?'

Chapter Twelve

'Ah…Jago's over there with Hugh.' Having spotted her husband in the throng, Verity set off to join him.

Instinctively Bea dug in her heels, then covered her cowardly lapse by needlessly adjusting her satin slipper. Smiling, she allowed her friends to lead her on, having bought a few seconds to boost her courage.

'I've not seen you in an age, Bea!' Jago Clemence was glancing appreciatively at his wife's friend. 'You look exceedingly well—and how is your father? Did he not fancy a game of Faro tonight?' Jago diplomatically avoided mentioning anything sensitive in his welcome.

'Papa is well, thank you, but he rarely socialises now as he is not very sprightly.' Bea felt relieved to have kept her voice level, despite the blood pounding in her ears.

'I doubt Mr Dewey would have wanted to be in the same room as that odious man!' Fiona's eyes targeted the doctor, stationed some yards away.

'We must all show Sir Colin that Bea has our support and he has our disgust.' Verity gave her verdict.

'The man is a fool!' She admired the sleek blue gown swathing Beatrice's figure, emphasising her tiny waist and creamy décolletage. 'Bea looks exceedingly young and beautiful this evening, don't you think, Hugh?'

'Indeed…she always does…' Hugh replied, far too seriously. 'And Burnett already has my opinion of him.'

Beatrice felt a tingle of heat in the profile she'd presented to him. She knew without glancing up to find out that the faint irony in his voice would be mirrored in his eyes. She bit back a spontaneous reminder that she'd no interest in his opinion of her looks and she'd sooner he didn't meddle in her affairs.

'Hugh took Burnett to task before anybody else knew of his hateful behaviour,' Fiona praised. 'He did you a service, Bea, on the evening he sent Sir Colin packing from Verity's *soirée*.'

Beatrice realised the ensuing quiet was to allow her to thank her gallant. 'I've told Mr Kendrick my thoughts on it,' she said huskily. 'I'm hoping he's heeded them…'

'I always listen to what you say, Beatrice.'

'Good…' Bea breathed. 'Because I meant every word…'

'As did I,' Hugh returned silkily. 'And will repeat it all if necessary.'

Verity cleared her throat, aware—as were the others—of a tense atmosphere developing. They were all saddened that Hugh and Alex had fallen out over some unknown matter, fearing it might result in divided loyalties. 'Shall we mingle, then play cards?' Verity slipped a hand onto Jago's elbow, urging him forward.

Fiona took Hugh's arm a fraction before a dark sleeve

appeared in Bea's line of vision. Wordlessly Hugh had offered her his escort and she raised solemn blue eyes to him, looking at him properly for the first time that evening. Lady Groves had commented on his distinguished appearance not one hour ago, yet Bea was unprepared for the full effect of his raw masculine appeal.

He turned away first, but behind his lazy glance had been an emotion that momentarily stopped her heart. If she'd harboured a tiny hope that he might signal remorse for having treated her like one of his doxies, she was to be disappointed. She feared that his veiled threat, issued moments ago, referred to his readiness to again insult her with a proposition rather than to renew his attack on Colin Burnett.

Not wanting to draw further attention to them, Bea allowed her hand to skim his fine suiting as they followed Jago and Verity through the throng.

'Isn't that Sir Toby over there, Hugh?' Fiona tapped Hugh's arm to draw his attention. 'I've not seen your brother in an age.'

'You're fortunate, then,' Hugh returned dryly, barely glancing at Toby. 'I wish I could say the same.'

'I'm sure he's not as bad as you would have us believe,' Fiona reproved, chuckling. 'I see that Toby has his fiancée with him for a change. Katherine rarely accompanies him anywhere.'

'She's a sensible girl and probably escapes him when she can.'

'Hugh! How can you be so mean? The poor thing would not agree to marry a man she dislikes.'

'Quite so...'

'Have you heard the wedding might be off?' Fiona whispered, aghast, as she flicked a glance at the couple.

'I couldn't possibly make a comment,' Hugh muttered.

He'd been told yesterday in White's that Katherine's father had had enough of his future son-in-law's ways. Toby was indiscreet with his paramours, but Hugh reckoned it was more likely to be his brother's wheedling for money that had finally made Mr Lowell reconsider the wisdom of allying his family with such a character. Hugh sympathised with the man's predicament and only wished he could just as easily make a break with his brother.

'Another failed engagement…' Fiona murmured, then glanced apologetically at Bea for her thoughtless remark.

Bea had been aware of their conversation flowing back and forth and was feeling rather ambivalent. Once upon a time she'd been able to enjoy Hugh's company, and had laughed and joked with him in the way her friend was now doing.

The fingers she'd placed on his arm curled against her palm as she realised she envied the easy intimacy the couple shared. Hugh had courted Fiona for longer than he had her, and Bea wondered if her friend had yearned for his teasingly tender kisses and caresses never to end, as she had…

'I see my aunt Dolly is beckoning me.' Bea hastily stepped away, hoping that putting distance between them would drive such maddening thoughts from her head.

She'd not lied; Dolly had been gesturing, trying to catch her eye.

'I shall keep my aunt company for a while or she will sulk.'

Weaving a path towards Dolly, Bea was aware of many pairs of eyes following her progress. On coming level with groups of people she heard the whispering fade, only to resume the moment she had passed by.

'Take no heed,' Dolly said, glaring at a woman who seemed particularly intent on gawping at her niece. 'You are doing very well indeed. Hugh Kendrick does not give his attention to many young ladies in the way he does to you.' Her eyes bolted to one side. 'See—the doctor and his fiancée are looking quite forlorn, all alone over there.' She clucked her tongue in disgust. 'Of course Lord Whitley hovers around, but we all know why that is!'

'I don't…' Bea replied, genuinely puzzled.

'The little wanton is always making eyes at him, even if he is old enough to be her grandfather and his wife is close by.'

Beatrice glanced over to see that indeed Colin and his female companions did appear to have been abandoned by all but an elderly fellow she now knew to be their host.

'Oh, *she* is the girl's aunt.' Dolly anticipated Bea's query about the middle-aged woman by Stella's side.

'Miss Rawlings is pretty,' Bea said quietly, having made a quick assessment of her child-like successor. 'Her hair is an unusual colour.'

'Nothing like as fair and glossy as yours, that's for sure,' Dolly sniffed.

Beatrice felt compelled to once more peek at those tumbling red locks…until she noticed Colin watching her. She dragged her eyes away, unexpectedly pitying him. He looked miserable, yet she'd expected him to seem proud of his new status and his young bride-to-be.

Lord Whitley had ambled away, leaving the trio quite isolated, and on impulse Bea started towards Colin, hesitantly at first but then with increasing confidence. She didn't falter even when her Aunt Dolly guessed her purpose and followed her for a few steps, hissing at her to halt. Neither did she waver on becoming aware that the hum of conversation in the room was receding.

Everybody present was watching her, Bea realised. Still she carried on, till her steady, graceful pace brought her to stand in front of the newly betrothed couple.

'Hello, Sir Colin.' It was a level greeting, if lacking in warmth. 'I hope you have been well since we last spoke.'

Colin ran a finger inside his tightening collar. 'I've been very well, Miss Dewey, thank you,' he croaked. 'And you have been well?'

Beatrice inclined her head in answer, smiling at him to put him at ease as his eyes darted hither and thither like a trapped animal. Bea turned her attention to the women, noticing that the younger appeared careless of her arrival. Bea guessed that Stella hadn't been told the whole story…or perhaps she felt secure enough of her hold over her future husband not to care that a short while ago he had professed to love and want to marry another.

'Are you not going to introduce me to your fiancée?'

'Of course... Stella, this is Miss Dewey. We were once...' Colin's words tailed away, confirming Bea's idea that Stella had been ignorant of her existence.

Bea held out a hand and Stella took it, rather lazily, with the hand that sported a garnet engagement ring. Bea wondered if Miss Rawlings had done it deliberately, to flaunt in her face that she now possessed the gem that her predecessor once had proudly worn. But Bea got the impression that the girl's attitude was prompted by boredom and a lack of breeding rather than rivalry.

'Margaret Monk is my name.' The middle-aged woman spoke before Colin had time to make an introduction, and barely touched Bea's fingers before dropping them.

'The weather is changeable today, don't you think?' The formalities over, Bea made conversation to cover the ensuing awkwardness.

They remained under observation, although a rumble of voices had now lightened the depressing silence. Enduring a few more minutes with her ex-fiancé and his future wife would achieve her purpose. The worst of the excruciating exercise was over and quiet contentment bathed Bea, because this meeting with Colin had stirred little emotion other than her sympathy for him.

She could tell from the intensity of his gaze that he would like to speak privately to her, and indeed she would like to speak to him, too. He owed her father an amount of money that he had promised to repay. Beatrice thought it mean of him to hold on to it now he had bettered himself, and at the first opportunity she would tell him so.

'We were saying it might storm,' Colin burst out, when it seemed neither of his companions was going to bother herself with chitchat. Reassured that she had not approached to make trouble, but rather the reverse, Colin gazed at Bea with eyes glowing with gratitude.

'There'll be a storm… Oh, indeed there will…' The look passing between Stella's future husband and his past love had made Maggie Monk's blood boil. Stella might not know that Miss Dewey had almost got Sir Colin to the altar, but she did. She gave Beatrice a frosty smile. 'I think a lady is trying to catch your eye, my dear.'

'Ah…my aunt…Mrs Pearson…is accompanying me this evening.' Beatrice stepped away, aware that Mrs Monk had dismissed her and that Colin had allowed it. Stella, on the other hand, seemed as uninterested in her farewell as she had in her greeting. The young woman was sliding coy peeks at her elderly admirer, observing the scene from a distance.

'Well? What did he say? What did *you* say?'

A barrage of garbled questions met Beatrice when she was once more at her aunt's side.

'I…I think our meeting went well,' Bea answered, smiling slightly on realising she'd spoken the truth. 'At least the expectancy is over for everybody. Miss Dewey and Miss Rawlings have come face to face and then civilly parted without attempting to scratch out each other's eyes.'

'Very disappointing for one and all, I'm sure,' Dolly

sniffed. 'Never mind that; what did the doctor say? He could not take his eyes from you, Beatrice…puppy dog eyes they were too.'

'I'm sure Colin was pleased I'd attempted to clear the air…once he'd got over the shock of me confronting them like that.'

'He looked more than pleased to me!' Dolly smoothed her neck with restless fingers, peering askance to ascertain whether the doctor was still watching Bea. 'He looks like a man who knows he's just lost a sovereign and found a shilling.'

She was a bold chit—Hugh had to give her that. He had been aware of Stella Rawlings behind him from the moment he'd stepped into the Whitleys' gaming room. In fact, if he'd not dismissed the notion as being unworthy of consideration, he'd have believed her dogging his footsteps. She'd shaken off Lord Whitley and her fiancé, and seemed irked that her aunt was sticking close to her as she sashayed to and fro, tossing her red curls.

Hugh despised Colin Burnett, but in his estimation the fellow at least deserved some moral support from this young woman, considering he was taking criticism on her account. Stella Rawlings was obviously thick-skinned; she'd observed him eject Colin from the Clemences' house so knew they were at loggerheads, yet it didn't seem to bother her. She was attempting to flirt with him, although Hugh had shown no interest in her that night or this.

Hugh had no intention of being hounded into a duel by her enraged fiancé should he be tempted to take up the offer in her saucy gaze. In Hugh's opinion young ladies should be taught about the dangers of coquetry along with their music and French lessons. He dearly wished his sister had had such schooling, saving him the cost of rescuing her reputation.

Hugh knew that his roving eye was being jaundiced by the memory of Beatrice. Frustratingly, he found that her honeyed taste and fragrance were always infiltrating his mind, overriding his desire for other women. His mistresses had enthusiastically welcomed him back to town when he'd returned from the dowager's funeral, yet even with Gwen's sinuous body writhing beneath his he hadn't been able to banish Beatrice's image from the backs of his eyelids. He wanted her and he wasn't about to give up after one setback…or a hundred…he reminded himself with savage humour.

Bea was likely to be a virgin, and he could no longer deny that acknowledging her inexperience made him a first-rate hypocrite. His long-held beliefs that untried spinsters weren't fair game for artful seducers like him had so far been pushed back in his mind where she was concerned.

That morning by the stream, when he'd offered her *carte blanche,* it had suited him to think her Burnett's mistress. He despised men who took advantage of chaste women…yet he was tempted to do exactly that with Beatrice. He was in danger of losing his best friend and his own self-respect, yet still a gnawing obsession to possess the only woman he had ever loved pervaded his being…

A few moments ago Hugh had been tempted to drag

Bea to his side, and then out of the house, when he'd seen her approach Burnett. Within minutes of observing the meeting he had felt admiration and respect for her salve the jealousy knifing his side. He'd realised that rather than wanting to irritate her rival, or win back the doctor, she'd hoped to put an end to the speculation that she was bitter over her fiancé's defection. The trouble was Hugh couldn't be absolutely certain that Bea wasn't acting aloof with Burnett just for her audience. If the love she'd felt for the doctor were rekindled she might succumb to an offer of informal protection before Hugh could win her for himself…

'Are you not going to join the gentlemen having a smoke on the terrace?' Fiona had seen Hugh standing quite alone, watching a game of Faro, while Miss Rawlings prowled very obviously in his vicinity.

Sensing he was about to go, Stella quickly moved so close to Hugh that he felt a movement of air on his profile caused by her fluttering fan.

'Considering she is spoken for, I don't know what game Miss Rawlings thinks she's playing.' Fiona gave the redhead a glare as she steered Hugh away. 'The shameless baggage was most definitely flirting with you and needs to be taught a lesson in propriety.'

'I didn't notice,' Hugh lied glibly. He saw no sense in stirring up trouble; he was determined to leave and visit Gwen, so she could attempt to soothe his restlessness.

'A hand of cards, Hugh?' Jago suggested, having returned from the terrace.

'I'm leaving in a moment…'

'Oh, do stay for a while yet,' Verity bubbled. 'Never

mind tedious gaming, the rug is being pulled back and soon there will be dancing.'

On a raised dais a few musicians were tuning up and, in front of it, two footmen were rolling back an Aubusson carpet to reveal the polished wood beneath.

'You're likely to frighten him off even sooner with such talk.' Fiona consolingly patted Hugh's sleeve. 'Never fear, I will protect you from being frogmarched into a quadrille.'

Fiona liked Hugh, despite the fact he'd once made an effort to woo her and been gently rebuffed. She'd known all along that he'd approached her on the rebound. He had still been in love with Beatrice and would have returned to his first choice in an instant if he had managed to raise the money to enable him to propose.

Hugh gazed again in Bea's direction, feeling a frustrated desire to stride over and take her somewhere quiet and secluded. The hope of talking privately to her had brought him here in the first place, although it wasn't fair to run the risk of embarrassing not only her but also her aunt and their mutual friends. He cursed beneath his breath, acknowledging the insanity in his behaviour; he should have avoided this genteel party and attended one of his usual haunts. There would have been a better time to approach her again… The trouble was he was too impatient to wait for it to crop up…

Having said goodbye to his friends, Hugh had nearly reached the exit when Colin Burnett appeared in front of him, blocking his path.

'I believe you owe me an apology, sir.' Colin had had ample time to brood on his dressing down by this man.

The opportunity to salve his wounded pride and subdue his bubbling resentment had presented itself this evening and he'd been unable to ignore it.

'I owe you nothing, Burnett. However, if you would like to take this up with me somewhere more appropriate do call round to Grosvenor Square tomorrow. I'll be pleased to see you.' Hugh made to pass, a curl to his lips.

'You may address me by my title if you speak to me or about me,' Colin enunciated. 'I have taken my birthright and am Sir Colin Burnett.'

Hugh's mouth slanted in a mirthless smile. 'Yes…I realise you've improved your lot.' His tawny stare slewed to Stella, now watching them from beneath her lashes. 'Or have you…?'

Colin understood the sarcastic remark. He'd noticed that his future wife had been shadowing Hugh Kendrick's movements. It was bad enough watching her flatter and tease other gentlemen with her batting lashes and soppy smiles, but to have her take such an interest in this fellow was galling. Contrarily, Colin also felt injured because Kendrick seemed to find Stella contemptible rather than alluring.

'Perhaps I *will* call on you,' he snarled beneath his breath. 'I don't like you paying such attention to my fiancée.'

Hugh grinned, genuinely amused. 'I've not a shred of interest in the girl and I find it pitiable that you do…'

Jago had observed the exchange between the two men from a distance. Seeing he might kill two birds with one stone—defuse the situation between two of

Miss Dewey's past loves and keep some interesting male company for a while longer—he strolled up.

'Lord Whitley would like you to roll dice with him, Hugh. You'll oblige the old fellow, won't you? A couple of games won't delay you by more than fifteen minutes or so.'

With a muted oath Hugh allowed himself to be once again steered towards the centre of the drawing room.

Chapter Thirteen

The sound of Mrs Monk's voice close to his ear transformed Colin's moodiness to annoyance. He had guessed what had prompted Maggie to suggest they leave even before he'd glanced in his fiancée's direction. He realised that in polite society it was considered *de trop* for a gentleman to object to his lady's circle of admirers so up to now he had bitten his tongue—apart from earlier, when confronting Hugh Kendrick. But Colin's patience with Stella's behaviour was almost expired. She had four fawning gallants dancing attendance on her, and from her aunt's stern expression it was obvious Maggie was also at the end of her tether where the girl was concerned.

Two of Stella's lapdogs were army officers in redcoats—eager and fresh-faced, perhaps not yet turned twenty-one. The other two gentlemen were older but apparently equally ensnared.

Colin cursed beneath his breath. If only his damnable uncle hadn't meddled in his life he'd have married the woman he wanted. He had been observing Bea since he'd arrived, and before the evening was out he hoped to have a proper conversation with her. She was everything a man could want in a genteel wife, whereas Stella…was not.

He had noticed the way Kendrick circled Bea and suspected his nemesis had come to a similar conclusion about Beatrice's charms and was about to take advantage of her availability. To his shame, Colin knew that Stella fired his blood in a way that Bea had never done. The flame-haired vixen made his hands itch to rip off her clothes. But he'd come to understand that Stella purposely teased other fellows in the same way she did him. His fiancée was making a fool of him, prompting people to snigger that he'd be a cuckold before he'd taken his vows.

Maggie Monk had been nagging at him to name the day but, having got to know the woman's niece better, Colin was no longer in a rush to do so. Why should he? He had his birthright, and as long as he wed no other but Stella he would keep it. He had a feeling that the little wanton would lie with him for a few baubles whether he walked her down the aisle or not…

So he wasn't about to leave this party early. He hadn't given up on the idea of having a talk with Beatrice and perhaps confiding his feelings on all sorts of matters… They might never be able to marry, because of his dratted uncle, but Colin was confident Bea might appreciate an invitation to come back into his life in a less formal role than that of wife…

* * *

'I'm so proud of you...'

The moment Lady Groves drew Dolly Pearson away for a chat Fiona snatched the opportunity to speak privately to Beatrice.

'Verity was worried when you approached the doctor, thinking you might be rudely rebuffed, but I knew you'd be fine. It was very brave, and quite the right thing to do,' she enthusiastically praised.

'I'm glad it is over with.' Bea gave a heartfelt sigh.

'Stella Rawlings has been flirting outrageously. Was she impolite to you?'

'Nothing unpleasant occurred,' Bea answered. 'It was just a bit awkward, that's all.' She chuckled. 'Now it is done, and I have escaped my aunt's beady eye too, by the looks of things.' She glanced at Dolly, in animated conversation with her cronies. 'I think I deserve to enjoy myself for an hour or so before going home.' She squeezed her friend's fingers. 'Shall we play cards? I have brought some money for a little flutter.'

'Jago has lost five pounds already.' Fiona grimaced a caution.

A pile of cash littered the green baize of the Faro table. Jago was seated beside his wife and looking rather glum. Verity was smiling, perhaps because she appeared to be doing rather better, judging by her stack of coins.

'I think I might try my luck.' Bea felt quite carefree now the burden of her meeting with Colin had been lifted. 'Papa says I'm good at Faro, although I suspect when he's banker he lets me win.'

'My allowance is already overspent.' Fiona glanced about. 'I wonder where Hugh is? He was throwing dice earlier with our host. I hope he has not already gone…'

Bea frowned, her eyes darting to and fro for a glimpse of him. She too hoped he hadn't left yet, which was odd considering she'd been dismayed when he'd turned up.

As a fellow threw in his hand and vacated the table Bea sat down opposite her friends.

Some time later she realised that the fellow slouched in a chair, with his chin sunk low on his chest, was Sir Toby Kendrick. Of his fiancée there was no sign. Bea had never before met Toby, but recalled Fiona pointing him out earlier. Hugh's caustic remarks about his older brother were also still in Bea's mind. She hadn't noticed the two men exchange even the briefest of greetings during the evening.

In her buoyant mood she decided that Fiona had spoken wisely when observing that Sir Toby might not be as bad as Hugh would have them all believe. Sibling rivalry was often to blame for such animosity, she decided, having unexpectedly received a smile from Hugh's brother.

'You're doing rather well, Miss Dewey.'

Beatrice smiled, flushed with pleasure and excitement. Her three shillings had won her over four pounds so far. Only a few gamesters remained at the table, the others had folded their hands on hearing the orchestra start up. Jago still toyed with a few chips, and a Hussar in splendidly brocaded uniform was staring intently at the cards in his hand.

It had been Toby Kendrick who'd congratulated Bea a moment ago. As the banker pushed her winnings her way Bea again considered that Hugh had been unfair about his brother; Sir Toby had been unfailingly pleasant. Perhaps Hugh had a tendency to deliberately rub Toby up the wrong way…just as he did her…

Despite his elevated status Sir Toby was not as charismatic or as handsome as his younger brother. Nevertheless his light brown hair and regular features were attractive, if somewhat marred by a complexion that was turning florid from the effects of the brandy he was steadily consuming.

'If I had your luck I'd be tempted to up the ante.' Toby placed his bet.

'I must not!' Bea lightly remonstrated. 'I will be jinxed if I do and might lose my winnings.'

'Superstition.' Toby made a dismissive gesture. 'Only the faint-hearted would hold back on such a run of luck—and you, Miss Dewey, are not a coward, are you?' He held Bea's gaze with a stare that mingled admiration and challenge.

'Miss Dewey can make up her own mind on the state of play,' Jago said, with an undercurrent to his voice.

Bea sensed Jago was warning her against betting heavily. She knew he was doing it kindly, to protect her, but she felt quite drunk with exhilaration, and flattered that Sir Toby had faith in her ability. Besides, if she netted a tidy amount she'd be able to reimburse her father for her wedding expenses. Not that Colin Burnett should be let off the hook; when an opportunity arose she would remind the doctor of the solemn promise he'd made to honour his debts on the day he jilted her.

It was the sense of a hand pressing on the rail of her chair that alerted Beatrice to Hugh's presence… that and a faint familiar redolence of cigar smoke and sandalwood. If she had not been in shock at what she'd done she might also have guessed at someone being directly behind from people's reactions: they were no longer pitying her with sly eyes but gawping over the top of her head.

Sir Toby Kendrick had a particularly malicious glint beneath his dropped lashes. But Beatrice was no longer surprised at his meanness. That gentleman had minutes ago transformed from kindly advisor to debt collector.

'Ah…my dear brother…come to rescue the fair lady,' Toby drawled. 'Indeed she needs *somebody's* help as she now owes me…let me see…' He made a show of counting on his fingers. 'One hundred and fifteen pounds.' He tapped a hand on baize. 'Too late to be a hero, I'm afraid.'

Beatrice felt as though a knife had stabbed at her heart, making her physically wince. 'No…it cannot be as much as that!'

She made to rise, but a cool hand on her shoulder stayed her, then withdrew slowly in a way only she might recognise as a subtle caress. She glanced up, her lovely face bloodless with strain. Following an infinitesimal wordless reassurance Hugh's eyes were once more on his brother, his jaw tense with controlled fury.

'Miss Dewey is retiring from the game and I'm taking her place,' Hugh announced quietly. 'Does anybody object?' His gaze swept the remaining players at the Faro table, lingering for a moment on Jago, making his friend squirm beneath a blaze of wrathful accusation. Jago's attempt at gesturing in explanation was ignored; Hugh's attention had gone.

'I object,' Toby purred, smugly sprawling in his chair.

'You're outvoted,' Hugh said.

'Those aren't the rules I play by,' Toby returned defiantly.

'They are now.' Hugh stared at the banker, who in turn peeked at Lord Whitley, standing amidst the audience to this spectacle.

Their host inclined his head rather reluctantly, because the old fellow enjoyed a scandal and a scuffle and he thought that both were in the offing this evening. The fact that a newly jilted spinster now had two brothers fighting over her was quite piquant, and an air of horrified excitement was electrifying the atmosphere.

With a nod the banker indicated that Hugh could join the game in Miss Dewey's stead.

'In that case I shall withdraw my person and my winnings…and my IOUs stand.' Toby knew that to act in such a callous way and prevent the young lady having a chance of cancelling a debt he'd deliberately led her into would brand him a cad. But he didn't care what people thought; he was obsessed with feeding the envy and enmity he had for his brother.

Toby had always known that Hugh wanted Beatrice Dewey. He'd known it years ago when the couple had been inseparable for weeks. His suspicions that his brother still lusted after the blonde had been confirmed when Hugh had unexpectedly strolled into the Whitleys' drawing room earlier. Miss Dewey had quite quickly distanced herself from his brother, enlightening Toby, if nobody else present, to the nature of the rift between Viscount Blackthorne and Hugh. Toby hadn't imagined an opportunity would arise this evening to torment his brother, but the moment it had he'd happily made use of it.

He surged out of his chair as steadily as his inebriated state allowed, grabbing his cash and sneering as a murmur of disapproval grew in volume. Pushing his way through the hushed spectators, Sir Toby Kendrick quit the room, then the house. He chuckled as he sauntered along the pavement. He might have lost his fiancée tonight—Mr Lowell had taken his daughter off home a moment after Toby had asked the miser for a few sovereigns to use as stake money. But luckily, he'd had some pocket change with him, and he'd cleverly turned those few coins into a tidy sum…

'Come…stand up, Beatrice…it's time to go…'

Beatrice heard the quiet baritone commanding her, felt gentle fingers touching her arm to coax her out of her seat. But she was unable to move. Tears were burning her eyes, but she managed to keep them at bay until a shrill voice heralded her aunt's approach.

'What have you done?' Dolly cried, thrusting her panic-stricken face close to the miscreant's blurry vision.

When her niece seemed incapable of explaining herself she pulled out a chair next to Bea and collapsed into it. Just minutes ago Fiona had sidled up to warn her that Bea might be in a spot of trouble, interrupting Dolly mid-flow in singing her niece's praises to her friends. *A spot of trouble* hardly did justice, in Dolly's mind, to this latest disaster threatening the Dewey family.

'My poor brother!' Dolly whimpered. 'How is he to repay the odious fellow that amount of cash? What were you thinking of, playing so freely, you stupid girl?' Dolly clapped her hands in frustration.

It was the trigger that Beatrice had been dreading. She stiffened, attempting to control her inner quaking at her aunt's fully deserved reprimand.

'What is to be done?' Dolly turned to Hugh for support as Bea dropped her forehead into a hand and used a thumb to smear away the moisture on her lashes.

'The matter can be rectified,' Hugh soothed.

He sat down on the opposite side of Bea and immediately she raised her glistening eyes to him. 'You think your brother is lying? I don't really owe him that much, do I?'

'Yes…you do…' Hugh disabused her. He'd had a muttered confirmation from the banker that the sum was correct. Sir Toby had encouraged Beatrice to engage in cocking—her whole pot of money had been risked on the turn of a card—and then, when she'd had nothing left and had panicked, his fiend of a brother had pretended to help her recoup her losses by loaning her more cash to stake.

'Papa shall not know of this,' Bea whispered.

'Indeed he must!' Dolly spluttered. 'However are

you to save yourself from ruin if your father does not settle with Sir Toby—?'

'He shall not know!' Beatrice interrupted, so forcefully that her aunt shrank back in her seat.

'You are overwrought, Beatrice, to speak so.' Dolly sounded miffed and glanced about.

Thankfully most people had had the good manners to exit the room while the crisis was debated by kith and kin. But Dolly knew that by tomorrow every breakfast table would be alive with gossip about Miss Dewey. Beatrice's good deed in being nice to Miss Rawlings would be overlooked and only the gory details of her misbehaviour picked over.

'I shall go home now.' Beatrice slowly gained her feet, but with a strengthening determination shaping her features. Drawing in a deep, inspiriting breath she elevated her chin. 'If I must run the gauntlet I'd sooner do it right away.' She felt ashamed that Hugh had witnessed her stupidity. She'd gone against him in trusting his brother when he'd made it clear Sir Toby was a bad character. 'Thank you for trying to save me by taking my place,' she whispered.

'My pleasure…' He inclined his head.

'Will you leave with us now?' Fiona had arrived with them in the viscount's coach and Beatrice realised she might like a lift home.

'Indeed I shall not!' Fiona replied with asperity. 'I'm going to stay here with Verity and Jago and defend your reputation by telling everybody what a vile monster Sir Toby is!' Fiona's cheeks were flushed with anger at what Hugh's brother had done. 'I can get a ride home with my family later.'

Verity murmured full-hearted agreement to her sister's plan. 'Jago has told me that he feared Sir Toby was playing a dastardly game with you…'

'It's a shame he didn't think to come and tell me,' Hugh pointed out, in a tone of voice that caused Verity to squirm on her spouse's behalf.

The little party exited the gaming room, Bea and Dolly escorted by Hugh, and the sisters marching right behind them.

Feeling light-headed with embarrassment, Bea involuntarily gripped tighter to the muscled flesh beneath her fingers, causing Hugh to smile encouragement at her. She snapped her head higher, her eyes steadily on the exit…until she came level with Colin and their gazes merged. His brows were drawn together, making him seem puzzled rather than disapproving. However, Bea noticed that Stella and her aunt looked to be relishing her disgrace.

'Is this evening's blasted bad luck never to end?' Dolly cried, hands jigging in distress. She peered up and down the road, seeking any sign of a coach bearing the Blackthorne coat of arms.

'It doesn't matter that the coach has disappeared,' Hugh said mildly, flicking his fingers to attract his servant's attention. Immediately a sleek vehicle stationed at the opposite kerb was steered to a halt in front of them.

'It doesn't matter? I think the viscount might disagree on that!' Dolly shrilled, already tottering gratefully towards the open door of Hugh's transport.

A moment ago they had descended the stone steps from the Whitleys' townhouse to find that Viscount Blackthorne's carriage was nowhere to be seen. On questioning one of the footmen stationed at the base of the steps, Hugh had ascertained that the vehicle had left almost as soon as it had dropped off its occupants. The servant had guessed why that was, and so had Hugh: the driver had had an assignation to keep and had believed he'd time to see his sweetheart before returning. The unlucky swain had been caught out because his passengers were departing far earlier than expected.

'You are good to us, sir, to help like this!' Dolly's belated thanks were heartfelt and thrown over a shoulder as a groom sprang from his perch at the back of the coach to assist her boarding.

Dolly had felt appalled at the idea of calling a Hackney, with no money to pay for it—and of course her niece now had not a penny on her either. All in all, Dolly deemed it a very bad ending to what had started as an enjoyable affair.

Wordlessly, Hugh extended a palm to Beatrice. For a moment their eyes tangled, and he could tell from her reticence in accepting his help that she suspected he might have an ulterior motive in offering her and her aunt a ride home. As indeed he did.

'Do you want to walk back to Upper Brook Street?' he suggested softly.

Beatrice nibbled her lower lip but finally placed her fingers in his. As she settled into the luxurious seat she kept her eyes averted from the man who'd leapt in and slammed the door then lounged opposite. She was alarmed by the thought that she was now unsure which Kendrick brother intended doing her reputation the most harm.

Chapter Fourteen

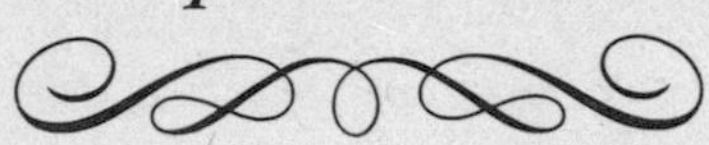

'It is a bit late to make a fuss about etiquette, miss!' Dolly snapped. 'Your reputation has been patched up too many times for that. You are now beyond the pale and fortunate Mr Kendrick is willing to put himself out for you.'

Scooting forward on the seat, she profusely thanked Hugh for his assistance in helping her alight from his coach.

Turning to her niece, Dolly poked her head into the vehicle's interior. 'Don't think your father shall remain in ignorance of this latest mischief. If you will not tell him that you have again added to his woes, then I shall.'

Beatrice had guessed her aunt had been simmering on the night's shocking events on the way home to Marylebone. The journey had passed in virtual silence and every time Bea had tried to make a little conversation her aunt had barked at her. Even Bea's quiet, stuttered apologies had been angrily flicked away by Dolly. As for the man ensconced opposite… Bea had tried to avoid looking his way, acutely conscious as she was of his powerful presence.

A few moments ago, when it had become clear from passing landmarks that Hugh had instructed his driver to head to her aunt's house first, Bea had urgently whispered to Dolly that it would be seemly if she were the first to quit their Good Samaritan's company. In response, her aunt had snappily overruled her.

'Mrs Pearson is over-anxious; she'll see things differently in the morning.'

Bea glanced at the pair of broad shoulders easing into the squabs as the coach once more set off. 'I think you are being over-optimistic, sir,' she murmured.

'Do you? Why?'

'Because in the morning things will be worse, not better, than they are now,' Bea answered unsteadily. 'And well you know it. So if you are trying to kindly make light of my folly...please do not bother. I must face the consequences of my actions. I am not a child.'

'I know you're not a child, Beatrice...far from it...'

There was an insinuation in his husky reply that put Bea on her guard as she peeked at him from beneath thick lashes. Ever since he'd helped her into his coach an idea had been circling her mind that he might try to take advantage of her predicament. He'd told her weeks ago to consider his offer of protection. Then she had been a jilted spinster, living with an ageing parent. Now her position—and her father's—was even more precarious, due to her foolhardiness.

Bea hated the idea of her father taking on the burden of her debt; neither did she want to seek help from

Viscount Blackthorne. Walter would be mortified to discover that money had been borrowed from his son-in-law to pay off his dependant daughter's gambling debts.

Queasiness in her stomach—part excitement, part dread—made Beatrice fidget on the seat. She had a feeling that she'd given Hugh Kendrick an opportunity to remind her why she should become his mistress. And many women of her age and unfortunate position might listen to such a rich and charismatic man's persuasion…

'When we last spoke you seemed determined not to come to town. What changed your mind?'

The unexpected question jolted Bea from her reflection into stuttering a reply. 'My father…well, both of us, actually…decided we would after all like to stay with Elise for a week or two.'

'Did the fact that Burnett was in London have a bearing on that decision?'

'I'm not sure it is any of your business either way,' Bea returned stiltedly, her indignation rising as a flash of white teeth in the dusk demonstrated that her tartness hadn't bothered him.

Hugh hauled his back from the upholstery to lean towards her. His eyes slanted up at her mutinous profile. 'Are you expecting the good doctor to sort out this evening's mess for you, Beatrice?' he suggested.

Bea swung an astonished face towards him. 'No, of course not. What on earth made you think he'd offer to do so?'

Hugh shrugged, brushed a speck from a dark sleeve. 'It's what a gentleman does for a woman he cares for.'

Bea moistened her lips, trying to fathom his meaning. 'Sir Colin now cares for Miss Rawlings, as you know.'

'So he does…' Hugh dulcetly concurred, straightening on the seat. 'But perhaps he cares for you too. *Does* he?' His lazy tone had turned demanding.

'If you think that just because I went out of my way to speak to him this evening that I am trying to wriggle back into Colin's life, then you are mistaken, sir.' Bea's fists were planted either side of her on the seat as though she might shoot upright at any moment.

'You're to be commended for treating the couple civilly. Burnett seemed pleased you had, and might approach you next time rather than the other way around. Will you encourage him?'

Finally understanding his hints, Bea gave him an icy glare. She had nobody to blame but herself for him thinking what he did. That particular seed had been sown in Hugh's mind when she'd declared she'd sooner be Colin's mistress than his wife. Stupidly she'd flung at Hugh intentionally wounding words, uttered thoughtlessly, and they'd returned to haunt her.

'If you believe that Sir Colin Burnett might pay your brother off for me if I sleep with him then you are utterly wrong,' she breathed. 'You should not apply your own lax morals to others. *He* is a respectful gentleman, and besides he has not yet settled his own account with my father…' Beatrice's small teeth were suddenly clamped on her lower lip. She regretted that she'd disclosed details of Colin's meanness.

'Burnett owes your father money?'

'It is none of your concern.' Beatrice turned her head, watching the darkling street scene. She wished to be quickly home, to avoid any more awkward interrogation, yet part of her craved to continue savouring the dangerous thrill of Hugh Kendrick's company.

'No matter, if you'd rather not say…' His voice was again as smooth as honey. 'I'm sure Walter will be happy to oblige me with an answer.'

'You will not speak to him about it!'

Her father might with alacrity take up any offer Hugh made to act as debt collector, especially once he discovered that his financial position had considerably worsened following her recklessness. There was already bad blood between Hugh and Colin. She had no intention of heightening their feud, and with it the damage to her reputation.

'It's likely everything is now resolved and resurrecting the matter will upset Papa.' Bea hoped her blurted argument was effective.

'I think you know it is not resolved,' Hugh countered. 'I think you intended giving your father your winnings to mitigate his losses. Am I right?'

It seemed pointless fibbing. She gave a single nod, glad the gloom concealed her chagrined blush. 'Instead I have stupidly made things much worse.'

'It was good of you to think of your father's gains rather than your own.'

'I owed it to him to try to help. My wedding expenses have left him out of pocket—' Bea knew it was silly continuing to pretend her father had been paid up.

'It's Burnett's duty to make amends, not yours,' Hugh interrupted mildly.

'I know…' Bea sighed, staring at her clasped hands. 'And he said he would.'

'Perhaps you of all people should know that his promises are not worth the paper they are written on.'

Again Bea felt her face heating beneath his soft sarcasm. But she couldn't deny that his criticism of Colin was accurate and well-deserved.

'There is a solution.'

Again Hugh closed the gap between them so their heads were mere inches apart.

Bea felt her heart cease pounding, then resume with breathtaking speed. Eyes that gleamed like black diamonds in the coach's interior had entrapped her and she steeled herself not to flinch when a long cool finger circled with seductive slowness on her burning cheek.

'I know we've had our differences. I know you don't trust me because I've let you down in the past.' Hugh took one of her hands, raising it and touching his lips to her fingertips. 'I admit I pursued you, told you I wanted to marry you, all to no end. But I didn't lie and I withdrew from your life the moment I realised I could not raise enough cash to take a wife.'

Hugh paused, angled his head to watch her averted profile.

'Throughout our friendship we were always very compatible indeed…in one way. I believe we still are, and I want to prove it to you.' His hand opened, forked on her narrow chin as he turned her towards him. 'Forget Burnett. He's not worthy of you; he never was. I can protect you and easily deal with my brother's spite.' Without warning his mouth covered hers, expertly parting her lips, daring her to deny his next brutally honest words. 'Where's the shame in mutual pleasure, or in letting me care for you and your father?'

Bea couldn't deny it…or him… Her mouth softened beneath his renewed wooing and when he lifted her onto his lap with a groan of frustration her instinctive resistance was easily overcome.

Hugh's hands plunged beneath her cloak, caressing her midriff, his thumbs thrusting upwards to tease the hardening nubs beneath her bodice. Bea continued a token struggle and yet her back began arching so she might have more of his rapacious touch. It was all the permission Hugh needed to sweep his mouth down the slender column of her throat to the undulation of her bosom, tempting him closer with every panted inhalation.

'Tell me you don't want this and I'll leave you be,' Hugh growled, his breath steaming against her milky skin.

He raised his head from her naked throat to read her expression but Bea moaned, tightening her fingers on his nape, wanting more of the tantalising magic of his cool, clever mouth soothing her fever.

Hugh smiled. 'Is that a yes to my offer of *carte blanche*, sweetheart?' he murmured as some of his long fingers disappeared into her cleavage, curving beneath a warm breast so he might feast on the satiny flesh with eyes and mouth.

Bea gasped at the exquisite delight of cold air and

hot tongue on her sensitive nipples and when he began to draw upwards the silk of her skirts her protest was lost in an instant beneath the onslaught of an erotically demanding kiss.

His stroking fingers slipped to the smooth skin of an inner thigh, just one insinuating itself beneath the lawn of her undergarments to fondle her a fraction away from the core of her femininity.

Bea writhed against him, parted her limbs in wonderment as a tingle streaked through her veins. No man had ever before touched her so intimately, and as he fractionally entered her with a fingertip a jolt of untasted pleasure made her panic and ram together her knees. Hugh groaned a chuckle, dipping his head to skilfully suckle a taut nipple, drawing her back into his web of desire.

Bea squirmed on his lap, and when his hand again slipped beneath her skirt she made no effort to stop him knuckling the sensitive dewy bud hidden in crisp curls. She bucked her hips to nudge the instrument of her delight, allowing him to reposition her so she was straddling his body, then pressing her pelvis willingly against his solid torso. The rocking motion of the coach was tormenting her, as was Hugh's long, drugging kiss. His tongue thrust little by little into her in time with the fingers he was moving between her legs. Bea's whimpering gasps became louder, her body more tense as inner friction mounted towards an unknown crescendo.

'I promise I'll never leave you,' Hugh whispered against the febrile heat of her shoulder. 'Should I marry to get an heir I swear I'll still want you in my life. I won't abandon you, Beatrice…'

It seemed to Beatrice that his vow of loyalty came from a long way off and was intended to lull her; yet it instantly stole away her bliss. When his mouth swooped again to hers she shook her head, freeing her lips, and two small fists were jammed between them, holding him at bay.

Struggling to keep her footing in the swaying coach, she slapped away hands that would have dragged her back and stumbled against the opposite seat, skimming over the hide to huddle in the furthest corner. Tugging down her clothes, she whipped aside her face, closing her stinging eyes.

'Your future wife need fear no rival in me,' she croaked, feeling desperately ashamed of what she'd let him do to her. She knew just seconds ago she had been close to crying out in rapture and was thankful she'd called a halt before losing all control. Trapped in his seductive net a moment longer she might have ended up pinned beneath him on the seat, a willing party to her thorough ruination.

'And your future husband—whoever he may be—has no rival in me,' Hugh returned quietly. 'So long as we adhere to the accepted rules, my dear, where would be the harm in carrying on enjoying each other's company?

'The harm would be in the deceit and the hurt to other people, and it is telling that you do not understand that. *If* I should marry, my husband will know he can trust me when I pledge to love and lie with only him. In return I would expect to be equally honoured.'

Hugh laughed soundlessly. 'You are holding out for a love-match, are you, and a faithful spouse?'

'Don't you dare mock me,' Bea cried. 'You might intend seeking a wife to improve your status but such mercenary plans are abhorrent to me.'

'I'm not mocking you, my dear. I'm impressed...but dubious you'll get what you want. Most married couples of my acquaintance have...other attachments...'

'Is my brother-in-law being unfaithful to Elise?' Bea whispered. She had always admired her sister's seemingly perfect relationship with Alex Blackthorne, and would be devastated to know it was a sham because he kept a mistress.

'There's always an exception to prove the rule,' Hugh replied gently. 'To my knowledge Alex is enviably content in every way with your sister.'

Bea expelled a pent-up breath.

'It would sadden you to know otherwise, wouldn't it?' Hugh murmured.

'Of course...Elise would be devastated. Alex is the love of her life.'

'And Burnett...was he the love of *your* life?' Hugh asked in a voice devoid of emotion.

'I have given up on love...' Bea prevaricated, gazing through the coach window.

'You just said you would marry for love...'

Bea choked a bitter little laugh. 'So I did, and thus will need to remain a spinster—for the likelihood of finding somebody suitable is remote.'

'Spinsters are entitled to get pleasure from life, Beatrice…discreetly, perhaps, and with no hurt caused to anybody else.'

'Apart from your wife…'

'Alas…like you, I fear I might be doomed to a single life,' he returned solemnly.

'I have said do not mock me,' Beatrice answered levelly while continuing to watch the stars. Her anger and embarrassment seemed to have drained away, leaving her calmer.

'I wasn't. I was telling the truth. Why do you feel you must deny yourself the comfort I offer?'

Hugh stretched out a hand but Bea knocked away his fingers.

'Are you going to tell me you didn't like what we just did?' he taunted.

'I'm going to tell you never to touch me again,' Bea said. 'Keep your empty promises and your payments for services rendered for your courtesans. They are sure to appreciate them, whereas I do not.' She met his gaze squarely, unflinchingly. 'You will not degrade me with your lust any more than will your brother with his malice.'

Bea glanced away from the flinty glitter in black eyes. She knew she'd angered him by thwarting him, and by comparing him to Sir Toby.

With a sigh of sheer thankfulness she glimpsed the top of Upper Brook Street and knew she was finally able to escape. One of her hands darted to the door, but she hesitated before jumping out of the coach. 'I trust in the future you will keep to your word and leave me alone as I've asked you to. I know you are entitled to visit the Blackthornes because you are the viscount's friend...'

'Not any more...' Hugh said smoothly over her words.

There had been no hint of accusation in his reply and yet still Bea felt suddenly guilty that the two men, companions since childhood, had fallen out over her.

'I did not complain to Alex that you had propositioned me and I regret that he went after you, resulting in a bad argument.' She paused before adding, 'I told Elise what had occurred in confidence and she...' Bea tailed off, not wanting to blame Elise.

'Did you think your sister would not confide in...*the love of her life*?' Hugh asked ironically.

'It's not Elise's fault. She didn't betray my trust; Alex badgered her till she hinted at what was troubling her.'

'Have I been troubling you too, Bea?'

'Not at all...you are never in my mind...' She blurted out the lie while studying the sliver of moon in the navy blue heavens. 'And I would not have you and Alex becoming worst enemies over me.'

'You're the viscount's sister-in-law and it's right he protects you; in his position I would have done the same,' Hugh admitted tonelessly. At her questioning glance, he shrugged. 'I'd risk that friendship again for your sake. Nothing has changed...I want you...' He repeated it with emphasis. '*Nothing* has changed, Beatrice.'

'Nothing has changed for me either,' Beatrice echoed in a voice that had lost a little composure. 'I have told you to stay away and hope, as a gentleman, you will accept my wishes.'

She noticed a corner of his mouth tilt upwards. 'I'll do whatever you want, sweet…' He moved towards her, his narrowed, gleaming eyes steady on her. 'How about a wager?' he suggested. 'I'll bet the money you lost tonight that within a week you come to me.'

Bea shrank back against the side of the coach, alarmed by his indolent confidence and the reason for it. Her eyes were drawn to his thin mouth…the lips that had so recently soothed and excited her and no doubt could savage equally efficiently…

'All you need stake in return is one night spent with me.' Hugh captured her chin with a masterful hand as she tried to avoid his eyes. 'Come…you're adamant you don't want me…never think of me…what's to fear? Take the wager and clear your debts in one fell swoop.'

His fingers fell away from her skin and were held out for her to shake. Beatrice stared at those outstretched digits, then impetuously she grabbed at them, before flinging away his hand as though she'd been scalded. Without a word of farewell she hurtled out of the carriage and up to the Blackthornes' house, breathless by the time she'd reached the top step.

When the butler opened the door to Bea's agitated rap she darted past and immediately dropped her face into her shaking palms, making the fellow glance at her in concern.

Chapter Fifteen

'Please accept my sincere apologies for having called so early.' The impatient visitor shoved his hat beneath an armpit as he jerked a bow. Behind him hurried a housekeeper, who'd been barged aside by the fellow so he might waste no time in securing an audience with her employer. 'I must let you know that papers requiring your urgent attention have just come to light, Sir Colin.'

In fact Percy Withers Esquire had known for over a week that a severe discrepancy had occurred. In the interim he had been frantically trying to discover how to mitigate his grave error in order to preserve his reputation as an attorney gentlemen might rely on to efficiently manage their business affairs. Having rallied his courage that morning, Mr Withers had set out without delay, praying he might deflect the barrage of criticism he was sure to face.

Colin Burnett rose to his feet, intrigued and yet also exasperated at this intrusion before he'd even dressed for the day. He tossed his napkin onto the breakfast table, tightening the belt on his dressing gown.

'Well, come in, Withers,' he invited, a touch sarcastically. He dismissed his hovering red-faced servant with a curt nod.

Colin had been renting this modest townhouse since he'd turned up in the city, and had pondered whether to invest some of his inheritance in buying the freehold. The staff would have to go, of course. He found them all—cook, housemaid and manservant—far too lax in manners and industry.

Confronted with the task of commencing his report, the lawyer seemed momentarily unable to do so. He coughed, jutting his chin twice in quick succession, his Adam's apple bobbing nervously.

'These urgent documents?' Colin prompted, feeling in no mood for bad news.

He'd risen late, having spent a restless night brooding on the events at the Whitleys'. On the journey home Stella had nestled into him in the carriage while Mrs Monk turned a blind eye to her niece's canoodling. But despite the heat in his loins caused by memories of his betrothed's teasing touches Stella had faded from his mind when his head had touched the pillow, leaving just his former fiancée dominating his thoughts.

Colin regretted many things where Beatrice was concerned. Mostly he was sorry she had got herself into a bad scrape by listening to Sir Toby Kendrick's poor advice. Previously Colin had harboured no opinion of Hugh's elder brother; now he disliked the two men equally. Again and again throughout the night Colin had cursed his damnable uncle for altering the terms of his bequest and denying him the chance of contentment with Beatrice. Instead he had to contend with being shackled to a coquette and to receiving his solicitor at an ungodly hour of the morning.

Irritably Colin cleared a useable space on the cloth by rattling crockery sideways, then indicated Withers take a chair at the table.

Percy remained where he was but did bring forth a scroll from the cavernous inside pocket of his coat. 'You might recall, Sir Colin, that shortly after your uncle's will was read, and certain unpalatable clauses were found to be contained therein, you asked me to examine the document for loopholes to allow you to have a bride of your own choosing.'

About to reseat himself, Colin instead unwound, pivoting slowly on a heel, his features a frozen mask. For a long moment he said nothing, simply staring as the fellow's complexion alternated between sickly pallor and bright pink.

'Are you about to tell me that finally you have found something...when it is too late?'

'I examined the text minutely, Sir Colin, as indeed I told you at the time,' Percy lied robustly.

'You did say as much...' Colin remained unmoving, his expression perilously quizzical. 'Yet I sense you are about to add that something vital was overlooked.' He watched his visitor shift uneasily. 'What was overlooked?' It was a deceptively dulcet enquiry.

'The authentic document.' Mr Withers raised the roll of parchment gripped in his hand. 'The other is a forgery, sir...'

Colin took a single stride towards the fellow, mouth

agape. 'A forgery?' he bellowed. 'Where in damnation did you get a forgery?'

'From you, sir,' Percy croaked, shrinking back.

Pulling out a chair from the table, Colin slumped into it. He gazed up at Withers, casting his mind back to the critical time and inwardly dissecting what had occurred just prior to his predecessor's death.

'Mrs Monk gave me the will. She had nursed Sir Donald during his last days and told me he had ordered her to hand his personal papers to me and no other.'

'Indeed...' Percy said in a commiserating tone.

'What are you implying?' Colin barked. 'Mrs Monk was Sir Donald's sister-in-law. When his brother died and Maggie was remarried to Peter Monk they remained friendly. The woman has nothing to gain from meddling.' Colin jumped to his feet, pacing to and fro. 'Donald provided her with an allowance when she was widowed for a second time. The amount did not increase or decline after my uncle expired.' He ceased prowling. 'The only person to improve their lot, if she considers marrying me to be a positive step,' Colin muttered bitterly, 'is my cousin Stella.'

He gestured away the idea. Colin believed his fiancée to be an ambitious chit but innocent of criminality. He'd noticed that at times Stella seemed careless of his presence, and she never pressed him for a date to be set for their wedding. Only Maggie did that. Stella might cosy up to him when worried she'd angered him with her flirting, but it was absurd to suppose her guilty of falsifying the will to trap him and he told Percy Withers so.

'Indeed, Sir Colin, neither do I think the girl had a hand in it. I believe we must look to her mother...'

'Her mother is dead!' Colin exclaimed testily. 'My uncle became Stella's guardian when her parents sadly died. Of course I know we are not natural cousins, and previously I had not met Stella, but she grew up calling her benefactor "uncle", and Mrs Monk has been an honorary aunt to her.'

He paused, gesturing wildly as though exasperated by his own explanation.

'Over the years information filtered down through the family that Sir Donald had formed a friendship with Stella's birth father when they served together under Nelson. So, despite being a bachelor, my uncle stepped in to help when at ten years old the girl was orphaned following a fire at her home.'

'A fiction, I believe, concocted for propriety's sake,' Withers sighed out.

'By whom?' Colin demanded, forcing his fists against his hips.

'By the child's true mother under direction from the reluctant sire, I imagine.

'How can you possibly know that?' Colin spluttered.

'I have lately attempted to trace the girls' parents—a Mr and Mrs Rawlings of Pontefract, who perished in the fire—and have found that no such people ever existed.'

Percy twisted his hat between his hands, anticipating that once his client had conquered his obvious amazement he would furiously demand to know why such diligence had not been applied sooner. Withers was unwilling to admit that he had allowed a junior clerk to peruse Sir Donald's will because business accounts for a more prestigious client had occupied him personally. Mr Kendrick paid handsomely, and on time, and never quibbled over necessary expenses as Sir Colin did. Thus the solicitor had considered the wealthy mine owner worthier of his attention.

But he was regretting his lack of vigilance now that he had finally compared the signature on the document Sir Colin had given him with the earlier version held in his office. The fraudster had made a fair effort to mimic the deceased's wandering scrawl, but it could not fool the man who had dealt with Sir Donald's papers for over two decades. And the only difference from the original document was the insertion of a clause that stated Colin Burnett must promise to wed Stella Rawlings in order to take his birthright.

Deeming it prudent to use his ace before Sir Colin had mustered his thoughts and threatened to sue, Percy confidently resumed. 'During my investigation I turned up the fact that Mrs Monk's maiden name was Rawlings. It is my belief that she has deliberately deceived you; furthermore I believe she is Stella's mother and Sir Donald fathered the girl…'

Hugh Kendrick had enjoyed no better sleep than had Colin Burnett, and for the same reason: Beatrice had been on his mind the night through. Whereas Colin had tossed and turned, rueing that a sweet, decorous woman had slipped through his fingers, Hugh's thoughts about her had been reprehensibly torrid. To Hugh, Beatrice was no poised goddess worthy of a pedestal; she was a maddeningly sensual temptress whose silky limbs had entwined perfectly with his while she'd panted sweet breath against his lips.

Till dawn light he'd lain with his hands pillowing his head, scowling at the ceiling, with the scent of her skin teasing his nostrils. So aroused had he felt following their passionate encounter in his coach that he'd almost flung off the silk sheets and got dressed. But he hadn't set off for Gwen's or Sophia's, despite being charged with sexual frustration, because he knew it would have been pointless. Neither woman had the power to heal an ache that had started years ago in his loins and then spread to enclose his heart.

Bea was the one he desired above all others; she was also the woman with whom he wanted to grow old. He wanted her in his bed and at his table; he wanted to host parties with her by his side, dressed in satins and sumptuous jewels, then watch her blush in pleasure beneath his adoring gaze. He wanted her to mother his children…

Hugh knew that he loved Beatrice and wanted to marry her, and but for his damnable pride getting in the way he would by now have told her so—although he'd have some explaining to do about his time in India. But he trusted Bea to understand; she had an empathetic and kind and loving nature… He grimaced ruefulness. Obviously she'd held back on bestowing it on him recently…and with just cause.

He could have proposed last night and vowed to protect her as his wife from his foul brother. Instead he'd come very close to losing control and taking advantage of her while she was at a low ebb. From her startled response to his increasingly intimate seduction he'd learned that the doctor hadn't bedded her. Hugh knew he'd come close to taking her virginity on the seat of the coach, and had he done so he would have deserved her loathing and disgust. He would certainly have had his own.

What point had there been in coercing her into a stupid wager? He could not remember taking more than a couple of shots of whisky at the *soirée* and yet he now believed he must have been drunk to act in such a way. Whether he won the wager or not, forcing Bea to surrender and come to him, he'd deal with Toby. He'd make certain his brother never again dared hurt Beatrice because he was too cowardly to pick a fight with *him.*

Hugh pushed away his coffee cup and stood up. He'd stop acting like a sulky youth and declare his feelings and his honourable intentions. If she refused him… He tossed back his head, frowning at the ceiling. What would he do if she refused him? Revert to trying to make her his mistress? Or would he give up gracefully? A mirthless laugh grazed his throat. He knew he couldn't give her up…

'Your brother is in the hallway, sir…'

Hugh snapped his face to the servant hovering on the threshold and his features, shaped by agonised indecision, began displaying his aversion to the imminent meeting. He had not been expecting Toby quite so soon, yet had guessed he'd be confronted by his gleeful brother, keen to rub salt into his wounds, at some point during the day.

'Bring him in.' Hugh resisted the urge to ask the footman to fetch him a brandy decanter at the same time. Instead he poured himself another cup of coffee from a silver pot.

'I thought you'd be partaking of something stronger this morning.' Toby swaggered over the threshold.

'Why is that?'

'Come...are we to pretend that you are not furious with me for putting Miss Dewey in a bad light?'

'You showed yourself up more than you did her,' Hugh responded contemptuously. 'Could you not see that, you fool?'

Toby coloured as that barb hit home. He'd never been popular, but the few friends he did have had probably now deserted him...just as his fiancée had. He'd received a note from Katherine's father that morning, advising him that he intended cancelling the marriage contract. Toby was incensed that an alternative source of income had been cut off and he must rely solely on his brother for hand-outs. He knew he had to tread carefully...yet press home his advantage.

'I'm not fretting, but I think you are. You want the chit—you always have done. I know you don't like seeing her at the gossips' mercy...or at mine.' Toby's expression became calculating. 'As you know, I'm not a callous chap. I've kept my mouth shut about your *commitments* in India, haven't I?' He sniggered as his comment strengthened Hugh's acerbic smile. 'But needs must when the devil drives, dear brother. You keep threatening to tighten your fist against me, so what am I to do but find another way to make a shilling?'

Toby sounded confident but in fact felt dubious. The amount he'd won from Miss Dewey would hardly keep him in women and cigars for a year, let alone keep a roof over his head. He pulled out the fistful of IOUs.

'Would you like these?'

'Are you giving them to me?' Hugh asked, barely glancing at Beatrice's debts.

'For a price...'

'And that is?'

'A thousand pounds.'

Hugh's answering grimace was unfathomable.

'She's worth that and more to you.' Toby slyly eyed his brother while fingering his fleshy lower lip. 'Of course I could go and see her father...or I might approach the young lady herself. How do you think she'll take knowing of your lust for exotic harlots? Perhaps she might not want you then and I might think of a way she could repay me. I reckon she'd taste sweet as honey...*does* she?'

Toby's intentional provocation received an immediate response.

Simmering with pent-up rage and frustration, Hugh delivered a single punch that sent Toby reeling to the ground.

'Fifteen hundred pounds is the price now.' Toby wiped his bloodied lips with the back of a hand, chuckling contentedly. 'I seriously underestimated just how enslaved by her you are, dear brother.' He struggled to a seated position, wrapping his arms around his knees. 'In which case you might like to throw in Gwen Sharpe for me, too. I've always fancied that vixen.'

Hugh turned his back on his brother. He understood that once it became known he'd protected Beatrice financially the purity of his motives, and her virtue, would be questioned.

'I'll think it over and let you know.' Hugh made for the door before the temptation became too great to again remove the smirk from Toby's face with his fist.

'Well, don't think about it for too long.' Toby scrambled to his feet, incensed that his brother would take himself off before an agreement had been reached.

Chapter Sixteen

'Now do you understand, you stupid girl, why I wanted you married as soon as maybe?' Maggie Monk raised a hand as though to slap some sense into her daughter.

'It is all your fault everything is lost!' Stella cried hysterically, scrubbing at her eyes with a hanky. 'You should have told me sooner all about it. Why keep it secret? I cannot be *your* offspring…I cannot.'

She sent her mother a look of utter distaste. In Stella's opinion such a drab-looking woman could not be so closely related to her; she deserved parents who were charming and glamorous. Since childhood Stella had imagined her father to be a tragic gallant who'd perished in a fire while bravely attempting to rescue his wife and baby girl from an inferno. She'd been brought up thinking she'd been safely dropped from a bedroom window into the trusty arms of a servant, then her poor parents had succumbed to the flames, lost to her for ever…

Stella had now learned that no such heroics had occurred and that she'd been brought into the world following a sordid affair between an old miser and a plain-faced adulteress.

'I cannot be *yours*.' Stella gave a pitiful sniff.

'Well, you are, my girl!' Maggie boomed. 'You're mine and Sir Donald's and you're entitled to his protection from beyond the grave.' Maggie wrathfully wrung her hands. 'The tight-fist left no provision for you in his will and he left me nothing more than I'd already got, despite me tending to him till he'd expelled his dying breath.'

Her mouth knotted in bitterness.

'So I did what I had to do to keep us comfortable. My meagre pension would never run to fine gowns for you so you might socialise with the Quality and find a good husband.' Maggie strode up to her daughter and pinched her chin in cruel fingers. 'Did you fancy a yokel touching you with his callused hands?' She gave a grim smile as Stella flinched from the idea of marrying a labourer. 'Sir Donald's name and his wealth are yours by right and I did my utmost to get them for you.' She shook Stella's shoulder in emphasis. 'You should thank me for what I did. Once vows had been taken Sir Colin would never have admitted to being hoodwinked; neither would he have wanted the scandal of a divorce.'

'But he's not bothered about abandoning his fiancée!' Stella screeched, again dabbing her watering eyes. She'd not cared much for Sir Colin, but she'd loved the life and the people to which he'd introduced her. She'd been determined to keep him hooked while she cast about for a better catch. Her circle of admirers would disperse once those fellows discovered she was a bastard and her mother a fraudster.

'You're not the first Colin's jilted; he'll be known as a fickle rogue.'

The only crumb of comfort Maggie had was that Sir Colin Burnett's reputation might suffer following his breaking off another engagement. Maggie was banking on him keeping the matter to himself as far as he was able. She'd forged Sir Donald's signature on a replica will when bubbling with rancour because the man to whom she'd devoted her life had treated her and their daughter shabbily. Maggie had cuckolded her mild-mannered first husband for almost a decade with his brother, then carried on sleeping with Donald for the duration of her second marriage. After her lover's death she'd finally realised that she, and their child, had meant little to the man she'd adored. He'd left everything to a nephew he barely knew and nothing to his own flesh and blood.

At noon that day Sir Colin Burnett had turned up, thunder-faced. Stella had still been abed and Maggie had been relieved that her daughter had missed most of the argument that had taken place. At first Maggie had denied everything. Once Sir Colin had produced the authentic will she had known the game was up and taken refuge in bluster. Their raised voices had eventually drawn Stella downstairs and Sir Colin had tarried only long enough to demand back his engagement ring before storming off.

Maggie was anxious to know how Burnett might retaliate. If she were mistaken in thinking he'd wish to smooth over the matter to protect his credibility she must prepare to flee to avoid arrest. If she were imprisoned her beloved Stella would be at the mercy of rough sorts in need of a wife but with nothing to give her but coarse manners and backbreaking work.

'Damn that solicitor and his eagle eyes,' Maggie spat resentfully.

Stella knuckled her wet eyes. 'Are we in bad trouble, Mama?'

'No…' Maggie stroked her daughter's fiery tresses, pleased to hear the girl call her Mama. 'Sir Colin will not want this all played out in court because of the risk to his reputation. It will blow over.'

'What of *my* reputation?' Stella wailed. 'Lord Whitley will never again have me in his house if he knows I'm a bastard…'

'Never mind that old man!'

'But I like him…'

Maggie sighed, eyeing her daughter shrewdly. 'I reckon Lord Whitley likes you, too, my dear.'

Once the old lecher found out her wedding was off he might proposition Stella. It was no perfect solution, but Maggie believed her daughter would be better off protected as a rich man's mistress than a poor man's wife…

'You must allow me to pay off Toby Kendrick…prior to knocking his teeth down his throat.'

'You may knock the blackguard's teeth down his throat with my blessing, but paying my daughter's debts is my responsibility.' Stubbornly Mr Dewey turned from his son-in-law to cast a censorious look in Beatrice's direction. 'Would that she had a husband to keep her in check,' he muttered darkly, 'For I am fast running out of cash and patience with her.'

'Papa! It is not wholly Bea's fault! The vile wretch tricked her into thinking he was offering sound advice during that game of Faro.' Elise attempted to soothe her father's agitation.

Beatrice's sorrowful shake of the head indicated to her sister that she deserved their father's wrath, and would bear it if it eased his mind. Approaching Walter, Bea took one of his withered hands. She hated seeing him overwrought.

Walter shook off her comfort, limping to an armchair to flop down. 'You have overstepped the mark this time, miss, with your impetuousness.'

Alex shrugged, wordlessly enquiring from his wife how else he might persuade Walter to sensibly allow him to take control of the matter.

'Papa, listen to me. It is best that the odious man is quickly paid off or he might charge interest on the debt, you know,' Elise warned briskly.

'Hah! He can try! I'll broadcast far and wide that he is a dastardly money-grabber.'

'I think most people have already come to that conclusion,' the viscount commented dryly. 'What's more, Toby Kendrick gives the impression he's too thick-skinned to care about vilification.'

'He was not liked before this blew up; now people roundly despise him,' Elise chipped in. 'Why would he go out of his way to make a target of Bea?'

Alex had his own ideas on that, but realised he'd

better not air them or his father-in-law might have apoplexy. He and Hugh had been close for decades, and Alex was sorely missing his friend's companionship. He knew Hugh almost as well as he knew himself. In Alex's opinion Hugh had never stopped loving Beatrice and desired her with a passion bordering on obsession. Alex also knew that Sir Toby Kendrick was bitterly resentful of his younger brother's success. If Toby had discovered Hugh's Achilles' Heel he would jab mercilessly at it and enjoy watching his brother squirm.

'Your sister had it from Kendrick that his brother was no good.' Walter wagged a finger at Elise. 'Beatrice told me that herself; yet she ignored the good fellow and heeded the bad character.'

Again Beatrice winced beneath her father's rebuke, clapping her hands over her ears as the debate over Sir Toby's hatefulness and her stupidity continued batting to and fro.

Two days had passed since the evening she'd gambled so heavily. Early the following morning she had told her father and sister what she'd done. Under chaotic interrogation, when questions had been fired at her from every direction, she had admitted that Hugh Kendrick had said he didn't consider his brother a trustworthy individual. Bea was glad she'd owned up straight away that a scandal was brewing, before her family learned gory details from gossip.

Aunt Dolly had arrived in high dudgeon just after luncheon, to complain to her brother that his elder daughter had learned nothing from her past mistakes and had cast a shadow over them all once more.

Beatrice hadn't ducked any criticism, and simply wished to put matters right…but how? She dared not tell her father that the gentleman he lauded had made her an indecent proposal in order to clear her debt.

The idea of carrying out the forfeit both excited and appalled Bea. At the time, the wager had seemed too good to be true. As, of course, it was. Once the anxiety fogging her mind had lifted Beatrice had realised that she had shaken hands on a deal that she could never win. In the eyes of the *ton* she'd be damned if she did go to Hugh Kendrick and damned if she did not.

There was only one reason a gentleman would pay a young lady's debts if she were unrelated to him, and everybody knew what it was. Toby Kendrick would reveal that his brother had paid off Miss Dewey's IOUs and revel in seeing her suffer the dreadful consequences.

But what right had she to feel outraged? She had already come close to becoming Hugh's paramour. The memory of the exquisite pleasure Hugh had aroused in her was preventing her focussing on finding a solution to this latest crisis. Even now she was conscious of the low throb in her belly caused by a need to see him. She felt restless enough to want to leave the house—even if it meant enduring stares and whispers—so she might meet Hugh by chance rather than by design.

'I have some insurance policies that can be sold to pay off the rogue…'

Mr Dewey's sighed declaration pierced Bea's consciousness. 'But…but those policies provide your pension, Papa,' she stammered. 'You cannot sell them and leave yourself without an income.' Bea was coming to accept there was little option but to let her brother-in-law salvage her reputation by dealing with the matter.

'So what else do you suggest I do, miss?' Walter bellowed.

'A gentleman caller, my lord,' a liveried footman announced.

Viscount Blackthorne quirked an eyebrow at his manservant.

'Sir Colin Burnett, my lord.' The footman answered his master's wordless enquiry.

'Show him to my study.'

'What in God's name can *he* want?' Walter muttered testily once the footman had withdrawn. 'Mayhap he's come to crow over our worsening misfortune. And he set the ball rolling, damn him!'

'I'm sure he has not.' Beatrice spoke up for the man who'd jilted her. Her father rarely used expletives with his daughters present so she knew how angry he was feeling. 'Colin was pleasant to me at the Whitleys'.'

'Was he, now? Well, perhaps he'll be nice enough to hand over my expenses so I can put the cash towards those other costs you have dumped at my door.'

'What do you think he wants?' Elise whispered to Bea as they sat together on the sofa.

Alex had gone to meet his visitor and the two sisters had settled down, allowing their father to brood moodily in his armchair. Every so often Walter would thump down his stick on the rug as some private thought vexed him. But he'd directed no further reprimands at Beatrice.

'I hope his purpose is to belatedly open his purse

and hand over what he owes,' Beatrice replied in an undertone. 'Papa might then calm down while we sort out the other mess I've caused.'

Elise knew Bea was feeling very guilty indeed. 'Perhaps Colin will ask to see you, if you are again friends,' she suggested, giving her sister's hand a comforting pat.

'I wouldn't go so far as to say we're *friends*.' Bea sounded rueful. 'I've nothing more to say to him. Papa is quite able to speak for himself about his expenses.' She slipped a glance at their father, glowering into space. 'He seems ready to do so, too.'

Bea cast her eyes heavenwards, acutely regretting having spoiled what might be her father's final outing to town.

'It is lovely staying with you, Elise, but I wish now I had remained in Hertfordshire. Every time I come to London I seem to bring problems with me.'

'Indeed you do not!' Elise again attempted to buck up her morose sister. 'You don't deserve the bad luck you get, Bea…'

'Sir Colin would like to speak privately to Beatrice.' Alex had re-entered the morning room and closed the door before making his announcement.

'Would he, now?' Walter used his stick to assist him to his feet. 'Well, you can tell the turncoat that *I* am the one he ought to visit, and you can also tell him that my daughter sees no gentleman privately without my permission.'

'Papa!' Beatrice sounded mildly irritated. 'I am twenty-five years old and have been alone with Colin many times before.'

'That was when you were his future wife,' Walter

retorted. He turned to his son-in-law. 'What reason did he give for asking to see Beatrice?'

'He said there had been developments, but wouldn't disclose more to me. He seemed prepared to leave if his request was denied. I've had him shown to the small salon to await his answer.'

Her father's high-handedness had made Bea feel contrary; she was also becoming increasingly curious to know what Colin wanted to talk about. She remembered Colin's bemused expression as she quit the Whitleys' house in disgrace. If he'd brought news concerning that calamity it would be best to have the gossip sooner rather than later, and she told her father so.

'Very well, you may have a few minutes with him.' Walter backed down because he was also keen to find out why Colin had called; they had all parted company under a very black cloud. Therefore he reasoned it had to be a matter of some magnitude that would bring the doctor, cap in hand, to see the woman he had jilted while she was in the bosom of her family.

Chapter Seventeen

'Would you like some refreshment, sir? I can ask for some tea to be brought to us.' Beatrice made her polite offer on entering the small salon and closing the door behind her. Her arrival had interrupted Colin pacing and, remembering him as a staid character, she found it remarkable that he appeared so restless.

'No…nothing…thank you…' Colin immediately approached, grasping her hands and then raising them as though he might kiss her fingertips.

Flustered by such an eager and inappropriate greeting, Beatrice speedily freed herself from his clasp. She didn't want him to believe they were now friends just because they had exchanged a few courtesies at the Whitleys'.

'I have made a dreadful error, Beatrice, and would beg you to hear me out,' Colin erupted. 'I know you have every right to hate me but I'm optimistic you do not. You were kind enough to come and talk to me the other evening, and you have agreed to see me today.'

He raked back from his forehead an untidy fringe of auburn hair.

'I am hoping that your natural grace and goodness will allow you to forgive me. Indeed, I pray you will, and that you'll take pity on me when you hear of the injury I have suffered.'

'The injury *you* have suffered?' Beatrice echoed, rather tartly. If her memory served her correctly she had been the wounded party.

'I have been duped, Beatrice!' Colin exclaimed, a whirling hand and furrowed brow emphasising the gravity of his situation. 'My uncle's will did not after all contain a stipulation that I must marry Stella Rawlings.'

Beatrice blinked, momentarily rendered speechless. 'You have only just thought to check on it?' Despite her astonishment Bea realised there was no immediate relief at having Colin's news. In fact, as an inkling of his reason for visiting her pricked her mind, she inwardly mustered a rebuff.

'Oh, I ordered it all to be checked thoroughly.' He tutted. 'There is no point in picking over upsetting details now, because what is done is done. I shall sue my solicitor, of course, and am confident of eventual success...but enough of that.' He gazed pleadingly at Bea. 'One vital aspect must be remedied straight away. There was never any need for our engagement to be broken, my dear.'

Once more, Colin captured her small hands in his sturdy digits.

'I cannot reveal all to you at this stage, but suffice to say that a crime has been committed and Miss Rawlings and I are no longer engaged. I am free to marry you, and would do so this very moment if I could.' Her crushed fingers were taken to his heart and held there, miming his devotion. 'We must set a date before the end of the month…next week if you like. Your father will not need to spend a farthing more than he already has, I swear.'

Delving into his pocket, Colin drew out the garnet ring he had just hours ago demanded Stella return to him. In finger and thumb he held it out to Beatrice, anticipating her joy at the sight of it.

'It gives me immense satisfaction to return this to its rightful owner. I have never stopped loving you, Bea…'

'But I have stopped loving you.' Beatrice jerked her hand back to her side as Colin would have forced the ring on her finger. 'I'm very sorry to be blunt, and to hear that you and Miss Rawlings are not to be married, but I refuse to be drawn into your problems or substitute myself for her.'

Colin smiled softly. 'You must not be indignant that I have come back to you; I wanted you as my wife all along, Beatrice. You are not second fiddle, and I have not rushed here on the rebound from her.'

Bea coughed a startled laugh. 'I do not think of myself as second fiddle, and I am not indulging in a fit of the sulks because of wounded pride.'

She stepped to a sofa, using its back as support as the magnitude of what she'd heard sank in. She knew her family—waiting patiently in another room to hear the outcome of this meeting—would be shocked to learn that there had been no reason after all for Colin to jilt her. And yet, in a way, it had been right that the wedding had been cancelled, Bea realised. She'd since come to accept that her feelings for Hugh Kendrick had never completely died, and now had rekindled to a passion that threatened to overwhelm her. Every waking moment and every restless night were disturbed by thoughts of him. When she tried to force her mind to other, pressing matters she could not concentrate on them for longer than a minute before his dark sardonic features were before her eyes.

'I'm not sure you understand all the advantages to be had from marrying me, Beatrice.'

Colin's stern words startled Bea into focussing on him. He looked taken aback at her rejection.

'I'm sure you will again admit to loving me in time.' In renewed agitation he strode to and fro before the chimneypiece. 'I'm prepared to make you my wife as soon as possible and would naturally accept the responsibility of your debts.' He grimaced. 'I know that Sir Toby Kendrick took advantage of your trust and innocence during that card game. It is being bandied about that he did so more to spite his brother than to spite you, but your reputation will be salvaged when you take my name—'

'What do you mean by that?' Beatrice interrupted. It had never occurred to her that she might be a pawn in a battle of egos between the two Kendrick brothers.

'Hugh Kendrick's interest in you had been noted even before his inappropriate intervention during that card game. The two brothers are at loggerheads, and what better way for the elder to get at the younger than through a matter of the heart?' Colin's eyes narrowed on her. 'Is it a matter of the heart for you, also, Beatrice?'

'I...I think it is none of your business, sir, and impertinent of you to ask.'

Tilting his head, Colin assessed Beatrice's flushed countenance and blazing blue eyes. 'When I say Sir Toby might attack his brother through *a matter of the heart* of course I am assuming that Hugh Kendrick is capable of finer feelings where the fairer sex is concerned. I have no liking for the arrogance of the fellow, and I've heard rumours he is a callous suitor.'

'And I have heard similar things said about you,' Beatrice spontaneously retorted.

'You champion him...' Colin swung away angrily from Beatrice. 'Kendrick might flirt with you but he will not protect you in the way your father would want. I'm optimistic his calculated flattery has not turned your head...am I to be disappointed in that, Beatrice?'

Blood prickled beneath Beatrice's cheeks. She should have guarded her tongue when Hugh's name cropped up rather than readily betray herself.

'Has he proposed? I mean marriage rather than an informal arrangement.' Colin smiled sourly at the telling reaction he got. 'I vow to be a steadfast husband to you. If you choose him you must be prepared to face disgrace and share him with his other women.' Colin barked a laugh. 'It is common knowledge that Kendrick has a mistress set up either end of town; where he might position another paramour is anybody's guess.'

'I think you should go now, sir,' Bea said icily, though burning with ire. 'There is nothing more to discuss. I'm sorry for your problems and wish them quickly resolved.' She moved towards the door and held it open in a significant way.

'I shall speak to your father before leaving and have his opinion on the matter.' Colin jerked a bow, then strode past into the hallway.

'He will be pleased to grant you an audience, sir,' Bea returned with admirable aplomb to his retreating back. 'Some time has elapsed since our aborted wedding. There will be no marriage between us, therefore it is high time my father received all the repayment he was promised.'

Colin spun about, his ruddy complexion white about the mouth. 'I imagine your father might sooner I took you off his hands than reimbursed him.' His expression was as severe as his voice as he continued. 'I came to know Mr Dewey as his physician and his future son-in-law during my time in Hertfordshire. I am certain he regrets that a child of his has acted in the manner you have. A gentleman's daughter of your age should know better, and act with some decency and decorum.'

Before Bea could conquer her indignation and summon up an appropriate response Colin had turned on his heel.

Stella had been surprised and delighted by her mother's attitude to securing her future since Colin Burnett had abandoned her. Shrewd by nature, Stella understood that she must capitalise on her youth and virginity before both were gone. She had no more liking for the idea of being tied to a middling gentleman than she had for being a farmer's wife. Socialising with the cream of society was vital to Stella, and for that she needed to inflame a rich man's desire. So, with the hurdle of her mother's objection cleared, Stella had allowed her excited thoughts free rein on the subject of being a kept woman.

Snaring Lord Whitley was no trouble. But he was old enough to be her grandfather and, though nice enough, he might pop off at any minute and leave her in the lurch. Stella also knew she did not fancy him in the way a woman should if she were to lie with a man. Again and again her mind returned to the person she'd wanted from the first moment she'd spotted him in London.

Hugh Kendrick was everything a girl might dream about: a wonderfully handsome bachelor in the prime of life who had fabulous wealth. If rumours were to be believed he was also, and most importantly, ridiculously generous to the women with whom he consorted. Stella believed that to be no exaggeration. She'd seen him with his mistress when out shopping and had immediately coveted the role of the pretty brunette decked in expensive finery and sparkling gems. The woman's air of smugness had simply heightened Stella's longing to take her place.

Maggie had told her that the woman was Gwen Sharpe, currently Hugh Kendrick's preferred paramour. Stella guessed Gwen to be a few years her senior, and was hoping that a man as jaded as Hugh Kendrick was sure to be lured away with the promise of her maidenhead. Stella knew if she kept him interested for a year it would be enough, so long as she did not fall in love with him. But the rumour that he always discarded a mistress giving her a plump pension pot was sure to mend her broken heart…

'You've got a look of mischief about you.' Maggie caught Stella's crafty eyes in the dressing mirror while hanging up the clothes her daughter had discarded on the bed. Picking up a hairbrush, Maggie began drawing it through her daughter's Titian hair. 'Come, tell Mama what you are thinking,' she teased fondly. 'Are you hoping to flatter old Lord Whitley into buying you a pretty trinket next time you meet? If he does, you'll have hooked him.'

'I wasn't thinking of him at all,' Stella answered airily. She twisted about on the stool, raising an animated face to her mother. 'I'm after more than pretty trinkets and old codgers. I want diamonds and…and a handsome man—' She broke off, giggling, without naming her quarry.

'So you're after Mr Kendrick, are you?' Maggie guessed, bringing a sulky thrust to her daughter's mouth. 'Well, that one won't be as easy to twist about your finger.' Maggie dropped the hairbrush on the bed. 'If your heart's set on him you'll need your wits about you.' Maggie's smile turned calculating. 'One thing I have learned along the way is that a gentleman loves to have what another fellow covets—especially when the two of them are at loggerheads.'

Stella perked up; she believed that Colin desired her, even if he didn't want her as his wife. She also knew he and Hugh Kendrick intensely disliked one another. 'You think that if Sir Colin shows an interest in me as his mistress Mr Kendrick might then want me too?'

'Pah!' Maggie swept away the notion with a flick of her hand. 'Hugh Kendrick would waste no energy on *him*! The one beneath his skin is that brother of his. Mark my words: he would do much to ease that particular itch…'

'Are you certain you've not too quickly turned Colin down?'

'I no longer want to marry him…I'm surprised I ever did.'

Bea had not long ago broken the news to her family that Sir Colin had reissued his proposal. Oddly, none of them had seemed as astonished as she'd imagined they would be. Her father had gone off, muttering, to speak to Colin before he left the house. Alex had tactfully withdrawn to allow his wife to speak privately to her sister, as Bea now seemed under siege on all sides.

Beatrice turned from the window, where she had been gazing over the rose gardens, and gave Elise a wry smile. 'When I was first introduced to Dr Burnett I recall you warned me that I might fall for him on the rebound. Had we gone ahead and married all those weeks ago I would have done my best to be a good wife to him, although I have discovered I still have feelings for…'

Elise had been holding her son by his tiny hands, helping Adam take a shaky step on the carpet. As her sister's voice faded away she sent Beatrice an astute glance. 'I'm guessing that the person who years ago propelled you towards Colin has now drawn you away.'

Beatrice's head swayed back on her shoulders in despair, but it was answer enough for Elise. Lifting Adam to sit on the sofa, she came quickly to her sister's side. 'I like Hugh—you know I do, Bea—but he is…different from the charming gentleman we knew all those years ago. I'm not saying his good fortune has spoiled his character…' she began diplomatically.

'Well, if you won't say it, I will,' Bea quietly replied. 'But it doesn't matter…I love him anyway. I think I knew it that first time when he came to Hertfordshire with the news about the dowager's illness.' Bea turned to face Elise. 'It frightened me that he could turn up out of the blue like that and turn my world upside down…'

'Does Hugh know how you feel about him?' Elise asked hoarsely.

Bea shook her head. 'As you say, he is very different now. I wouldn't embarrass myself, or him, with a declaration of love. Oh…he desires me—he has made that clear too—but what future is there in being taken into his harem?' Bea stifled a mournful chuckle with the back of a hand. 'Colin took pains to tell me that if I chose Hugh over him I would disgrace myself and my family and should expect to have several rivals for his time and affection.'

'You need not heed Burnett's opinion!' Elise had spoken dismissively, yet she feared the doctor was right in his forecast of her sister's prospects. Hugh was a rogue where women were concerned. 'Shall I ask Alex to visit Hugh and discover if he might be persuaded to propose marriage?' Elise asked anxiously. 'Alex is moping since he fell out with his best friend. I know he's keen to make up with Hugh, so he'd probably appreciate the opportunity to talk to him…'

'No!' Beatrice emphasised the single word with a deep frown. 'Promise me you will not mention any of our conversation, Elise, even to Alex.'

Bea didn't want Hugh to believe she'd again sent her brother-in-law to sort out personal matters because she lacked the courage to do so herself. If Hugh were ever to know she loved and wanted him, she'd sooner be the one to tell him.

'You are not seriously considering Hugh's proposition of *carte blanche*...are you?' Elise asked. She could see why her sister might be tempted by such an offer from a handsome and generous man. Bea had every right to be heartily fed up with regular romance when in the past three gentlemen pursuing her as a wife had let her down. But she could see nothing but heartache ahead for Bea if her sister drifted into a liaison with a man as jaded and cynical as Hugh.

'Of course not,' Bea said breathily, pushing back a blonde curl from her forehead. She wished she'd sounded more convincing. Objectionable as many would deem the idea, Bea had found herself wondering whether a discreet, informal arrangement with a man she truly loved and desired would be preferable to an arid marriage to suit convention. When younger she had desperately wanted to be a wife and have a family of her own, but always her dream had eluded her. Constant disappointment had eroded the yearning till she no longer knew what she wanted...other than Hugh. If she could not have a wedding ring from him, would it be so bad to accept the gift of his passion instead?

'Burnett's just gone.'

The sisters turned in unison as Alex entered the parlour. He scooped up his gurgling son from the sofa, chucking him beneath the chin. 'I think your father might like to speak to you, Beatrice.'

With a fierce look for Elise that threatened dire consequences should she tell Alex what they'd talked about, Bea quit the room.

'I don't blame you one bit, my dear, for turning Burnett down this time. Bumptious fellow!'

Walter's abrupt exclamation met Bea on entering the room. 'Sir Colin tried to bully me into persuading you to have him back, you know.' He sighed deeply. 'That fellow has changed since he inherited his money…and not for the better…'

'It seems to be the way of things…' Bea gave a hollow laugh.

'He made it plain that your gambling debt would be cleared the moment the marriage contract was signed. I made it plain that I'd like him to clear his own debts and mind his business about yours. He said he would send me a bank draft this afternoon. I'll believe it when I see it,' Walter concluded pessimistically.

'I'm sorry that I'm such a trouble to you, Papa,' Bea said softly.

'Oh…don't take any notice of my huffing and puffing, my dear,' Walter patted the delicate fingers his daughter had laid on his arm. 'I didn't mean what I said earlier about wanting you wed and out of my hair. You're a good girl, if far too rash at times. Let's forget about Burnett and that blackguard Toby Kendrick.'

'You will not sell your pension policy, Papa, will you?' Bea asked in concern.

Walter gestured wearily. 'An old man like me needs little money to live on, and one day soon a good man will come along for you and keep you in a far better manner than I can. I know your luck will change for the better.' Walter gave a final comforting pat to Bea's hand, then sank down into a chair, lying his head back against the upholstery. 'Don't let's speak of money any longer…I'm sick of hearing about debts and bills.' He sighed. 'It will be nice to go home. I feel tired out by all this frantic business in London. Shall we pack up tomorrow, ready to leave at the weekend?'

Bea nodded, watching her father's eyes flutter shut. She felt a pang of deep affection and regret that they would not be leaving town unburdened but with problems of her making hanging over them. 'Yes…let's go home, Papa,' she murmured, settling a cushion beneath her snoozing father's drooping head.

She stepped back, gazing at him as he settled into sleep. A fierce determination rose in Bea to cure the ills she'd caused. She would make sure her father enjoyed his twilight years, and the independence that was so important to him, buffered by his modest pension income. He would not sell the policy and live in penury to get Toby Kendrick off their backs! She could not allow it…

Chapter Eighteen

Maggie Monk nipped behind a large shrub protruding from a railing. Then, from her vantage point, she watched her quarry hurtling down the steps of Viscount Blackthorne's mansion. Having noted Sir Colin's rigid bearing and black expression, she felt her spirits lift.

Earlier that afternoon she'd been on her way to the bakery when she'd spotted her daughter's former fiancé. Ever conscious of their dwindling fortunes, Maggie had been hoping to haggle over a stale pie to share with Stella for their dinner. Burnett might have bought her daughter little gifts but he'd kept his fist tightly closed when it came to helping out with their household bills. Maggie had come to town with a little pot of savings gleaned from her small pension from Sir Donald. However, with Stella wanting every pretty frippery her eyes landed on in shop windows, the money was almost run through.

On spotting Burnett all thought of food had fled. Sir Colin had been striding purposefully along on the other side of the street. His air of urgency had prompted Maggie to follow him, curious to know where he was heading. When she'd seen him charging up the steps of a house on Upper Brook Street she'd easily guessed why Burnett might pay a call there. Boiling with resentment, Maggie had waited for him to reappear. She was glad she had tarried, for she now felt cheered up. If she'd been correct in thinking he'd just proposed again to Beatrice, his demeanour proclaimed him as having been roundly rejected.

It seemed that Miss Dewey now had bigger fish to fry than Sir Colin. Gossip was rife that the spinster must be under Hugh Kendrick's protection since he'd championed her at the Whitleys'. It stuck in Maggie's craw that the two eligible bachelors who should have been competing for Stella's favours were instead under an older woman's spell.

Before emerging from her hiding place Maggie watched Colin stride across the road and turn the corner. She sent a grim scowl at the house he had quit. Miss Dewey was beautiful but past her prime, and couldn't match Stella for youthful freshness in Maggie's opinion. If Stella were hungry for Hugh Kendrick's protection, Maggie would do her utmost to bring about her wish.

Since Stella's birth Maggie had had to idolise her daughter from afar, in case suspicions were aroused about their true relationship. Now there was no secret to keep and the floodgates of her maternal affection were wide open. If Stella couldn't have Hugh, then neither should Beatrice get him.

But all was not yet lost; she still had a hand to play,

and had noticed when they'd passed Sir Toby Kendrick on Regent Street that he readily responded to Stella's coy glance with an eager grin. Hugh and Toby Kendrick loathed one another, and Maggie knew there was always a profit to be had when love or hate skewed the odds. As far as she was concerned there remained a chance to win the game.

'I'm intrigued, madam, to know what vital news you have that could not have been conveyed in the note that summoned me here.'

As he looked Maggie Monk over an expression of disdain shaped Toby Kendrick's features. He had pitied Colin Burnett, having a future shackled to a shameless hussy like Stella Rawlings. Though of course, in common with other red-blooded fellows, he'd jump at a chance to take up the offer in those impish eyes of hers. It was that hope that had drawn Toby here to meet Mrs Monk by Marble Arch at the appointed hour.

Maggie licked her lips. She'd heard rumours that Sir Toby was a profligate on his own account but a tight-fist where others were concerned. She had no real desire for him to take up with Stella for, baronet or no, she feared he'd turn her daughter into a skivvy to get his money's worth out of her. But so far Hugh Kendrick had ignored Stella. Maggie was praying she could change that by enabling him to spite his older brother by snatching her daughter away from Toby.

'Come, woman…what is it?' Toby demanded testily. 'I've not all afternoon to tarry with such as you.'

'Your brother has been showing an undue interest

in my sweet Stella,' Maggie rattled off. 'I thought you should know of his pursuit.'

Toby shouted a laugh. 'What do you expect me to do about it? The chit plays up to every man she meets.'

Maggie resented his scoffing criticism. What he'd said might be true, but she didn't want her nose rubbed in it.

'She's a vivacious beauty, I'll give you that,' Maggie said, struggling for levity. 'But she has her...*preferences* in gentlemen, and appreciates a fellow's breeding. Now that rogue Sir Colin has done the dirty and left my dear girl to her fate she is keen to meet a fellow of similar status...such as your good self.'

'Got cold feet, has he?' Toby purred. It was news to him that the engagement was off, and suddenly the carrot the woman was dangling was looking exceedingly tasty. He guessed that for all the girl's sauce she was still intact, and taking maidenheads was a sport Toby enjoyed above all else. 'If you think I'll wed the chit now she's been cast off—'

'Mayhap you will, sir, given time,' Maggie hastily interrupted. 'But that brother of yours might come up to scratch for my Stella first. Mr Kendrick is smitten, and will naturally want to have children for that fortune of his...'

'He might get her increasing but he won't marry her,' Toby chortled. 'He's produced a boy already and left it abroad.'

Toby suddenly realised how very stupid and indiscreet he'd been. His lust for Stella had overridden his sense and he'd risked losing his valuable hold over

Hugh. If his brother found out he'd broadcast his secret he'd cut off his money…maybe knock him senseless into the bargain. He groaned inwardly on noticing the gleam in Maggie Monk's eyes as she digested this confidential information.

'A bastard, has he?' Maggie grunted a coarse laugh, turning away satisfied. She'd got far more than she'd bargained for and might no longer need to manipulate Toby after all. She left him gawping after her and hurried away, muttering gleefully, 'Well, well…I wonder if the spinster knows about *that*…'

Bea could not risk being spotted in a clandestine tryst with Hugh. She had reasoned that a rendezvous in the open, as though they had bumped into one another by chance, would be the only option if she were to avoid heaping more embarrassment on her family.

Following her talk with her father earlier, Bea had acted before her courage fled, despatching a note to request that Hugh meet her at Oxford Street in the environs of Meredew's haberdashery. Far too impetuous, her father had called her, just a few hours ago, and indeed she was, she realised, frowning at her pale reflection in a shop window. She feigned an interest in a feathered hat behind the glass, not wanting to appear to be aimlessly dawdling.

Glancing at the clock inside the premises, Bea noticed that the appointed hour was nearly upon her. She took a deep calming breath as her heartbeat accelerated, sending blood to pound deafeningly in her ears. Of course her note might have gone unheeded: Hugh might either be out of town or otherwise engaged and unable to respond to her summons.

Unsure whether that possibility gave greater relief than disappointment, she reminded herself that she didn't want it all to be a squandered effort.

The street scene behind her was reflected in the pane and she began scouring the crowds. She longed to see Hugh approaching, yet confusingly also dreaded a first sight of his powerful presence. What would she say? What would *he* say? Would he laugh in that infuriating way of his that mingled lust and mockery? She feared he might unwittingly shrivel her determination to bare her soul and admit that she wanted him in the same way he desired her. If he were unable to say he loved her but promised instead his affection and respect it would surely be enough…

'Bea!'

A familiar voice startled Bea from her tortured thoughts. At any other time she would have been delighted to see Fiona Chapman flying towards her on Oxford Street, but a rather strained smile was all she could manage as her friend closed the gap between them.

'Is Elise out shopping with you today?' Fiona came to a gasping halt by Bea's side.

Bea shook her head. 'Are you on your own too?'

'I am now…' Fiona answered flatly. 'I was with Verity and her mother-in-law. Mrs Clemence is driving my poor sister mad, going on about arrangements for a christening before the babe is yet born.' Fiona pulled a face. 'I've escaped with the excuse that I must go home because of a headache. Now I've run into you

I won't have a completely spoiled afternoon.' With a cheeky grin, Fiona linked arms with Bea, urging her to stroll on. 'I'll come window-shopping with you; you deserve to be cheered up after that hateful episode at the Whitleys'.'

Bea's faint smile disappeared at that reminder.

'You must not worry that people blame you!' Fiona reassured her. 'Everybody is saying what a weasel Toby Kendrick is to have manipulated you in the way he did...'

Suddenly she began waving frantically.

'Now, over there is a Kendrick I *do* like—very much!'

The driver of a sleek curricle appeared unaware of Fiona's enthusiastic welcome as he steered towards the kerb.

'What a lucky coincidence to run into Hugh,' Fiona announced, glancing at Bea. Having taken a closer look at her friend's rosy complexion, she murmured conspiratorially, 'Ah... I see...' Fiona's lips curved. 'Not such a coincidence after all, is it?' She tugged on Bea's arm. 'I've always thought the pair of you were a perfect match. This is no time to turn shy. Let's go over and say hello now he's arrived.' She chuckled. 'He's looking for you already and seems rather stern; perhaps he thinks you've stood him up.'

Bea watched as Hugh vaulted from his seat and immediately frowned at the vacant spot by Meredew's shop window. He did seem severe, she realised with a sense of womanly satisfaction, that she hadn't been where he expected her to be, meekly awaiting his arrival.

'Well…it's a lovely day for a drive,' Fiona piped up, causing Hugh to turn around. 'Are you going to be kind and offer to take us for a spin around the park, Hugh?' When he seemed more interested in gazing at Beatrice than answering, Fiona prodded his arm. 'Oh, say you will. I can act as chaperon.'

Hugh's narrowed gaze slid from Bea's beautifully bashful expression to settle on Fiona. 'You are extremely forward, not to mention bossy at times, Miss Chapman.'

'Yes, I know, but there's no point in waiting for you two to dither over how to escape prying eyes so you might talk privately.'

Fiona's warning was called for; she moved a gloved hand, acknowledging Lady Groves and her friend, who had seen them.

'We must all go off together for propriety's sake,' she whispered. 'Then you may lose me along the way.'

'I imagine you're prepared to take a drive with me, Miss Dewey, as you've brought suitable company?'

Hugh's smooth confidence heightened Bea's blush.

'Of course she is, or she wouldn't be here at all, would she?' Fiona declared, thrusting a hand at Hugh so he could help her aboard his curricle.

With a despairing look and a tiny head-shake Bea hoped to convey that she'd not sought her friend's moral support because she was afraid to be alone with him. Hugh's expression remained darkly quizzical and, conscious of Lady Groves bearing down on them, Bea accepted Hugh's assistance in alighting.

'Thank you,' she murmured, settling back next to

Fiona and withdrawing her hand from long fingers that seemed reluctant to release her.

Bea slid a glance at her companions, wondering why she'd ever felt jealous of Fiona's relationship with Hugh. The way they sniped so good-naturedly made them more suited to being brother and sister than lovers. But there were other faceless women who stirred that new and unpleasant emotion in her. Ever since Colin had taunted her about Hugh's mistresses Bea had felt curious: were they blonde or brunette, younger or older than she was? His Indian lover…lovers—how many were there?—would be dusky-limbed with jet-black hair. Of course all her rivals were bound to be exceptionally pretty…

The horses were set to a brisk trot and Bea tipped back her head, relaxing a little beneath the cooling air on her flushed face. The respite was short lived. Hugh suddenly captured her eyes with a stare of such intensity that she was jolted back to the night he'd taken her home in his coach. The memory of what they'd done in the dark, while the vehicle swayed through the deserted streets, grazing together their bodies, sent fiery heat rippling through her. The piquant excitement she'd experienced had been unforgettable, as had the sensation of his artful hands tormenting her bare flesh.

Involuntarily Bea's eyes travelled to his dark fingers, tangled in leather as they capably mastered the sinuous greys to a pace he liked.

'Goodness! I have a migraine.' Fiona put the back of her hand to her head in a theatrical pose, drawing glances from both her companions.

'I'll take you home,' Hugh said easily, and turned right at the next crossroads.

Beatrice was sure Fiona gave her a wink…or perhaps a genuine headache was making her squint…

'I should return home too.' The words tumbled out of Bea.

Colin Burnett's criticism of her had suddenly refused to cease thudding at the forefront of her mind. A gentleman's daughter should indeed, at her age, act with some decency and decorum. What was she thinking of, running after a notorious womaniser to tell him she'd chosen to lose the wager they'd made and become one of his mistresses? Being in thrall to unrequited love was no excuse for acting like a dullard or a doxy…

Fiona's elbow dug Bea's side and her friend gave her a fiercely encouraging look. A moment later Hugh handed Fiona down from the carriage and she set off towards her front door with a cheery wave.

In an easy leap Hugh was again aboard, taking the reins. In quick succession Beatrice darted several anxious glances at his shady concave cheek, hoping he'd sense she wanted him to talk to her. Any chitchat would do, she thought wistfully. But he remained uncommunicative as he wove in and out of traffic, then gave the horses their head on a clear stretch of road.

'Are you feeling pleased with yourself?' Bea burst out, unable to stand the silence any longer.

'Should I be?' There was no hint of either lust or mockery roughening his tone.

'You've won our wager, as you said you would.' A tremor had crept into her voice.

'Forget about that stupid game.'

Hugh's words were so quiet that Bea had to strain to hear them. 'It was a game to you?' she demanded in a suffocated voice.

He ejected a low expletive that was more unsettling to Bea than hearing him acknowledge his victory. But he said no more and set the greys to a faster pace.

'Will you take me home, please?' Bea's hand flew to her bonnet as the breeze lifted it from her shimmering fair hair to droop at her nape.

'Eventually.'

It was difficult for Beatrice to discern his mood from his abrupt conversation. 'What does that mean?' She strove for composure while removing the bonnet and laying it on her lap.

'It means I'm not yet ready to do so.'

Hugh turned in through the park gates and within a few moments had brought the curricle to a halt beneath a canopy of undulating tree branches. He rested back into the seat, easing a muscular leg out in front of him.

Bea again forced her eyes to meet his, moistening her mouth. She saw he was watching from under long black lashes as her tongue trailed to and fro, so sank small teeth on her lower lip to still its quiver.

'I sent that note to you on the spur of the moment,' she blurted.

'Do you regret doing so?'

'I'm not sure,' she answered honestly. 'I've been told time and again that I am far too impetuous, and I admit it's true.'

'It sounds as though your sister has been dispensing pearls of wisdom.'

'It wasn't Elise…although she always does try to set me straight on such things.'

'I recall she tried to talk sense into you years ago, when we first met. She told you not to waste your time on me, didn't she?'

'Indeed she did…' Bea's mouth slanted wryly. 'And after all this time it has still not sunk in.'

Hugh barked a short laugh, frowning into the distance. 'I'll admit I'm glad of that, sweetheart, even if you are not.'

'My papa called me impetuous today.' Beatrice avoided his eyes.

'And did he warn you to stay away from me too?' Hugh asked quietly.

Bea noticed his thick dark brows drawing together in a wordless demand for some details. But she wasn't prepared to be distracted into telling him about Colin Burnett's visit. There were far more pressing matters to deal with.

'Any number of people, concerned for my reputation, might advise me to avoid a notorious rake—as well you know.'

'Notorious rakes can reform,' Hugh pointed out with dulcet mockery. 'Your sister could vouch for that…'

'Alex told Elise that he grew up when he fell in love with her,' Bea remarked, sounding wistfully reflective.

'Are you hinting I'm immature?' Vague amusement modulated his voice to a velvety huskiness.

'If the cap fits…' Bea started sourly, before biting

back the rest of the phrase. But there was never likely to be a better moment to condemn his philandering. And he had asked for it! 'Actually…I do think that in certain ways your behaviour is immature,' she said.

'In what ways?'

'I think you can guess at them.' Hungry as Bea was to know more about his other women, she backed away from letting him glimpse her jealousy.

'If my memory serves…you've called me disgusting and a degenerate in the past, and now you've added being immature to the list of my faults… Yet still you wanted to meet me today. Why was that?'

'I had little choice but to contact you,' Bea retorted. 'If I've been drawn into a feud between you and your brother and suffered for it then I think you owe me an apology and your assistance.'

'I gave you assistance when I made plain my opinion of my brother, yet still you trusted him, gambled with him and accepted his loan.'

Bea felt her cheeks burn. The comment had been idly made, yet she recognised the reprimand and the truth in it.

'Why did you do that, Beatrice? To annoy me?'

'Perhaps.' Her mouth slanted mutinously

'And your reason for wanting to annoy me…?'

'Do I need a reason other than that you constantly annoy me and insult me and…?' She gestured impatiently.

'Such an explanation makes *you* sound immature,' he said, straight-faced.

'Oh…this was a mistake!' Beatrice fumed. 'I might have known we would do nothing but bicker.'

'We could go somewhere private and do something far more pleasant.' Hugh's suggestion was coupled with a sultry look before he turned his head, watching the paths becoming more populated as the fashionable hour approached, bringing strollers and carriages into Hyde Park.

'As you seem to want to make light of it all,' Beatrice hissed, blushing furiously, 'I'm sorry I wasted my time and asked you to meet me. Would you take me home?'

'I wasn't making light of it, sweetheart,' Hugh said quietly. 'I was being very serious.' His eyes swept over her, burning like coal embers.

'In that case,' Bea whispered, 'you have your answer on why I think you immature; simply reflect on what you have just said and your obsession with—'

'Please carry on,' Hugh invited with studied gravity.

'Your obsession with womanising…' Bea rattled off.

'There's only one woman I'm obsessed with, Beatrice.' He paused. 'If wanting you, thinking about you day and night, makes me immature, then I admit to the fault.'

Bea blinked, then her large luminous eyes began searching his face for signs of irony. But she could see none. He returned her stare quite openly and calmly.

'When have I insulted you?'

'What?' Beatrice breathed.

'You said a moment ago that I had insulted you.'

'I think you know very well the answer to that.'

'You think that offering you anything your heart desires is an insult?'

'My heart desires more than I think you are able to give, sir,' Bea murmured poignantly.

'Ah…you are still pining for the good doctor, are you?'

'No! I am not! And I have today impressed the fact on him too.' Bea had spoken hotly, without due consideration for the interrogation that was sure to follow such a declaration.

'Have you seen Burnett?'

There was no reason not to recount that Sir Colin had called on her and reissued his proposal but Bea twisted together her fingers in her lap in indecision. Such information would beg the question of why she had rebuffed a man she had recently been sure she loved and wanted as her husband.

'He paid us a visit earlier.'

'And his reason for that…?'

'He came to tell me that he had been tricked into believing he must marry Miss Rawlings to get his inheritance. He said he'd broken their engagement and wanted to marry me instead.'

Bea watched the surprise in Hugh's eyes being overtaken by another darker emotion.

'As you're here with me, I am guessing that you turned him down?'

'I did…'

'Why?'

'My reason is none of your concern.'

'You know that's not true.' Hugh unfolded an arm

along the back of the seat. 'I thought Burnett was the love of your life.'

'So did I…' Bea stifled a mournful giggle.

'What has changed your mind?'

'Sir Colin aired some unpleasant views and now my father and I have seen him in a different light.'

'What did he say?' There was an abrupt hardening in Hugh's tone.

'He told me that a gentleman's daughter of my age should act with some decency and decorum.' The admission trickled out of Bea as she gazed at the leaves fluttering overhead. In her opinion her former fiancé was a hypocrite to voice his disapproval when—whether in error or not—he'd abandoned her to better himself.

'Was he criticising your behaviour with my brother?'

'No…he was criticising my behaviour with you…'

Chapter Nineteen

'As I've been named in Burnett's slander I think I should be told more about it.'

Bea hesitated before blurting, 'In short, Colin told me to avoid your company or suffer the consequences.'

Hugh laughed soundlessly. 'It sounds as though you championed me, Miss Dewey. Did you?'

Bea fidgeted beneath his warm, humorous regard. 'I didn't find his lecture necessary. Neither did I like being told who I might choose as a friend.'

'Am I your friend?'

'I'm not sure any more,' Bea said with bittersweet honesty. 'Despite our squabbling, I'd like to think we were friends at least…if only for Elise and Alex's sake. I know they'd like everybody to be harmonious.'

'As I would, too,' Hugh said. 'But I'm aiming higher than harmony between us, Bea.'

Bea turned doubtful blue eyes his way, remaining still as he raised a hand, smoothing the backs of his fingers over the silky dip beneath her cheekbone.

His wooing touch was gone too soon; Hugh's clenched fist dropped to his lap as a carriage rattled closer at quite a pace, its female occupants gawping inquisitively at them.

'It's getting too crowded,' Hugh muttered. 'I should have taken you somewhere else…just to talk, that's all, I swear.' He grimaced in self-mockery. 'I know you think me a lecherous reprobate, and perhaps I have been. But I do understand it's vital to sort out certain matters between us.'

Bea gave him a small grateful smile and for the first time felt hopeful that things could come right between them.

'I'm determined to kiss you…if nothing more…' he groaned.

I want you to... The unspoken response keened in Bea's mind, making her dusky lashes droop over her soulful sapphire eyes.

'I will before the day's out,' Hugh vowed, as though sensing her need. He stared moodily after the disappearing carriage, then suddenly jumped from the curricle and came round to open the door. 'We'll arouse less interest if we walk for a while.'

Bea allowed him to hand her down, glad to stretch her legs but conscious of time passing. 'I must go back soon. I said I wouldn't be out shopping for long. I don't want my papa to fret over my absence.'

'How is your father?'

'Tired and depressed…and it's my fault,' Bea admitted through a lump forming in her throat. 'He wants to go home to Hertfordshire.'

Hugh drew Bea's hand through his arm as they strolled, his large palm warming her delicate fingers. 'He'll cheer up soon and perhaps choose to stay…'

'No…he wants to go, and so do I.'

'When are you planning to leave?' he asked distantly.

'In a few days' time.' She sensed his stare heating the top of her head.

'In that case we've not much time.'

'I know…' Bea murmured, lowering her eyes and marshalling her thoughts. 'I don't want my papa to live out his days in straitened circumstances,' she confided quietly. 'Alex, being the good fellow he is, has naturally offered to set everything straight, but my father is too proud to let him. He is intending to sell his pension policy to settle my debts rather than accept help.' She sighed. 'You said you would deal with your brother, so I wrote that note to you. I can't bear that Papa must suffer the consequences of my folly.'

Having expressed her private heartache, Bea glanced at Hugh for a comment, but he remained worryingly quiet while escorting her to a bench. While she perched on the edge he remained standing, one foot raised and braced against the planks, his expression inscrutable.

'And you? Can you bear to suffer the consequences of your folly?' he asked solemnly, his eyes drifting away as though he were more interested in the verdant scenery than in having her answer.

Very conscious of the breeched thigh close to her cheek, Bea darted her eyes from its muscular contours to his saturnine profile. She wanted him to look at her now they'd finally reached the purpose of this meeting:

the wager she'd lost… But he remained aloof, giving no encouragement or comfort.

It was only pride, she told herself as she tried to force words past the ache in her throat. Why could she not tell him that she craved his kisses and caresses? Why make it seem that he had her backed into a corner and she would acquiesce only reluctantly to his lovemaking?

Hugh plunged a hand into a pocket and pulled forth some crumpled papers. He let them fall, one at a time, onto the seat.

Bea glanced at her IOUs, then raised wide blue eyes to his preying gaze. 'You have already paid Toby?' she whispered. 'You were very certain of your victory, then.'

'I bought those days ago—long before I received your note.'

Bea imagined that with such animosity between them Sir Toby would have extracted the best possible price for her markers.

'How much did you pay him?' she breathed.

'It doesn't matter. Take them.' He swooped on the notes, held them out, smiling sardonically when her fingers clasped together in her lap.

'Are we not friends, then, Beatrice?' Hugh gently taunted.

Bea knew if she accepted the notes she would have tacitly agreed to their becoming lovers. When she'd left the house earlier she'd persuaded herself that having his promise of respect and affection was enough for her. Yet now…now the scene was real—not in an imaginary theatre in which she played the part of a tragic heroine.

With those IOUs in her possession she must lie naked with a man…*this* man…for the first time, and allow him licence to do whatever he wanted…whatever she wanted… So he'd promised her weeks ago, when coarsely propositioning her.

A sweet shiver raced through Bea but she flicked aside her face, forcing her mind to examine the dark side to her ruinous pleasure. Her ostracism from society was a mere breath away; so was her father's despair. Discreet as she and Hugh might endeavour to be when they rendezvoused to make love, gossip would eventually reach Walter's ears and break his heart.

But there was more firing her indecision than the effects of her disgrace: she couldn't bear to toss and turn jealously, wondering whose bed Hugh shared when he was absent from hers. He might say she was the woman with whom he was obsessed, but what about when the chase was done and he'd had his novice mistress? Would he grow restless and desire a new hunt? Or again visit paramours well versed in ways of pleasing him?

Suddenly, and very bleakly, Bea realised that crumbs of his affection would never be enough when she was greedy for so much more. She wanted him to tell her that, like his friend before him, he too had given up carousing because he'd finally found a woman he could cherish and adore—the only one with whom he wanted to live his life and rear his children…

'Nothing…' Hugh said gruffly, having watched raw emotion flitting over Bea's profile.

His single word penetrated her mind and Bea raised

an expression of wonderment to his face. 'Toby gave up my IOUs for *nothing*?'

'No… Toby wanted to be paid…' Hugh removed his boot from the wooden bench and strode off a few paces. 'Whereas I don't. I'm not expecting a thing from you.'

'Why is that?' Bea finally touched a finger to the IOUs, shifting them to and fro on the timber.

'It's what a gentleman does for a woman he cares about.'

She'd heard that from him before, spoken with the same caustic inflection.

Hugh glanced sideways at her, ramming his hands into his pockets. 'Don't look so scared, Beatrice,' he said. 'Stupid game, maybe, but you've won…hands down.' He gazed across the park towards the water glistening in the afternoon sun. 'I was going to have a servant deliver them to you tomorrow. I'd have brought them myself, but I know Alex might not want me darkening his doorstep.'

'He is pining for your company. Elise said so.' Bea collected the papers and put them in her pocket, then rose from the bench, joyous optimism unfurling in her breast. She had just glimpsed the gentleman Hugh had once been, before his good fortune turned him into a sophisticate.

'Why would a rogue act with such chivalry and kindness?' she asked with a hint of teasing.

'I've been asking myself the same question,' Hugh muttered, a cynical slant to his thin lips. But he avoided her eyes as she glided closer to him. 'I owe it to you and your father. I let you down before, years ago, leading you into thinking I was in a position to propose.' He gestured roughly. 'I was a fool to ever want what I couldn't afford.'

'And now?' The question sighed unbidden out of Beatrice.

'And now I can afford whatever I damn well like…' He turned ferocious golden eyes on her. 'But some things can't be bought, can they…?'

'No…they can't…'

'Did Burnett offer to pay off your debts?'

'He did…'

'So why did you come to me?'

'Colin said I must marry him. That was the deal he offered.'

A mirthless sound scratched Hugh's throat. 'Trumps mine, I think,' he muttered sourly.

'Ask me why I could not accept him.' Boldly Bea touched his abrasive chin with a finger to make him look at her when he would have turned away.

'Are you again about to tell me that you'd sooner be Burnett's mistress than my wife?'

'Of course not! I regret that I ever made such a daft and dishonest statement.' With dawning enlightenment she choked out, 'Did you really believe I meant what I said?'

Hugh stared at her, then stepped forward purposefully, as though intending to take her in his arms. Instead he gripped her wrist, tugging her behind a stout tree trunk. Before they were completely out of sight his mouth swooped on hers, brutally passionate, soothingly wooing. His fingers cradled her skull, protecting it from the rough bark as the pressure of his mouth forced back her head. The texture of timber was at her back, and his hard muscular body moulded about her softly curving silhouette, keeping her trapped to him. Inside her cloak, a hand stroked her hip…and Bea could sense the tremor in his caress…

Hugh suddenly spun away from her and Bea, sensually dazed, clutched behind her at the bole of the tree to steady herself. The second time a cultured baritone boomed Hugh's name Bea heard it through the blood pounding in her ears. Hastily she stepped into view, her heart in her mouth.

Cursing beneath his breath, Hugh began to prowl casually over the grass, his raging frustration masked by an indolent expression.

The approaching barouche slowed to a halt and Lord Whitley affably doffed his hat. The two women seated in the vehicle made no attempt to inject sincerity into their smiles.

Maggie Monk resented Lord Whitley for having alerted the couple to their having been spotted. Another moment and she reckoned that refined Miss Dewey might have allowed the gentleman to sully her virtue beyond repair. Of course once the spinster knew about Hugh Kendrick's brat she might no longer want to be taken down the aisle—or to bed—by him. Maggie was still determined her daughter would get the diamond magnate, but Whitley was first reserve so she was keen to keep him sweet.

'Mr Kendrick…and Miss Dewey too! What a surprise to see you…*together* like that…' Maggie slyly exchanged a knowing look with her daughter. Despite his mild manner Maggie could tell Hugh was enraged, and his conquest was rosy with embarrassment.

'Fancy a nip of brandy, Kendrick?' Lord Whitley held out his silver flask, hoping to lighten the heavy atmosphere. 'Getting chilly now at this time of the day…'

A lazy hand-flick was Hugh's response. Unconcerned that his hospitality had been rejected, Lord Whitley took a swallow himself. Ordinarily he might have been on better behaviour in mixed company; but recently he'd had confirmed his idea that his female passengers were no ladies. And his suspicions about Miss Dewey's character were growing.

Yesterday Maggie Monk had accosted him as he emerged from his club. Whitley had not been surprised at her audacity, nor to learn that Burnett had jumped ship on marrying Miss Rawlings. It was plain that the girl was fashioned in looks and character to be a wench rather than a wife. Whitley was still mulling over Mrs Monk's list of requirements. Before getting down to serious negotiation with the bawd he had brought the chit out to test her enthusiasm for it all.

It seemed he'd interrupted Hugh Kendrick auditioning Beatrice Dewey for a similar role. Whitley was surprised such a proficient philanderer hadn't headed to a more secluded spot for the seduction.

Not long ago people had speculated about the reason for the animosity between Hugh Kendrick and Alex Blackthorne, but they no longer did so. All had become clear when Kendrick had rescued the viscount's sister-in-law in that card game.

Little wonder that Blackthorne was livid with his best chum for sullying Beatrice before she had a husband's name to shield her reputation. It was the girl's father that Whitley felt sorry for. The poor old fellow would be distraught if he heard that the wanton had been spotted kissing Kendrick behind a tree in Hyde Park.

'Would you help me down, sir?' Stella imperiously extended a hand to Hugh, eyes flashing challengingly at Beatrice. 'I should like to rest on that pretty bench.' Angry colour lit her cheeks when he appeared not to have heard her demand, and continued strolling to and fro, frowning into the distance.

Having regained composure, Bea stepped forward, a wavering smile curving lips that still pulsed from being kissed. 'I'm sure Mr Kendrick will escort you.' She hoped Hugh would conquer his exasperation and play his part in smoothing over the situation. 'You are quite right, Lord Whitley, the weather is cooler now.' Bea rubbed together her gloved palms.

Hugh had complied with her signal to help Stella onto the grass, but Bea knew she was in grave trouble if this excruciating episode wasn't properly defused. She couldn't be sure what the trio had witnessed, but was praying they'd seen no more than a couple standing close together in the shade of a tree.

Stella dimpled up at Hugh. She'd yearned to bump into him by chance but had not wanted to see him embracing another woman. Her mother had made an attempt yesterday to waylay him and hint at her willingness to be his mistress. Stella had peeked from behind the window blind of a Hackney, but Hugh had barely stopped to talk to Maggie before striding impatiently on towards his house. Her mother had been grumpy on her return, insisting they waste no time in transferring their efforts to Lord Whitley as their little kitty was almost run through. Then today her mother had bucked up and, intriguingly, said she might have found a way to hook Hugh. But Maggie would give no more details of her plan to snare the gentleman Stella wanted above all others.

'I'll stretch my legs too, I think.' Lord Whitley alighted in quite a sprightly hop, then offered to help Mrs Monk down.

'I was saying to Mr Kendrick that I should love a drive in his racing curricle.' Stella turned excitedly to her mother.

'I'm sure the charming gentleman will oblige you with your wish, my dear.' Maggie's lips knotted in satisfaction. Her daughter was playing her part well, with no rehearsal.

'Unfortunately I have no time,' Hugh began coldly, removing Stella's clutch from his elbow. 'We were just leaving as Miss Dewey is expected home shortly.'

'Oh...I can run that errand for you, Kendrick. Why not take Miss Rawlings for a spin? Do you object, my dear, to me taking you home?' Lord Whitley turned gleaming eyes on Beatrice, confident she'd snatch at his proposal to avoid further embarrassment. Beatrice might be older than Stella, but she had a rare classic beauty and a figure that Whitley would pay handsomely to see naked. If Kendrick tired of her, Whitley would, with alacrity, take his cast-off.

'It would be kind of you to drop me off, my lord.'

Bea ignored her sinking heart; she and Hugh had no option but to appear nonchalant on parting but there was so much left to say to him, she thought wistfully as she allowed her elderly escort to help her climb aboard the barouche. With a wave they set off, and she noticed that neither Hugh nor Stella glanced at the departing vehicle.

But Mrs Monk did, and it seemed to Beatrice that there was something vilely triumphant in her smile.

Chapter Twenty

'I told you Kendrick was a good fellow.' Walter beamed at his daughter, picking over the IOUs spread on his lap. 'It's my lucky day…I received Burnett's bank draft while you were out.'

Bea smiled on hearing that Colin had eventually paid her father. 'You don't mind that a gentleman has settled my gambling debts, Papa?'

On reaching home, Bea had immediately gone to see her father to ease his worries—and hers. She wanted his reassurance that he had not yet brokered his pension but had kept it safe.

'Kendrick isn't *any* gentleman—is he, my dear? He's the scoundrel's brother, so his family's honour is at stake. I shouldn't like kin of mine to act in such a despicable way. I'll wager he gave Sir Toby a cracking facer before parting with his cash.' Walter chortled, neatening the notes into a stack. 'Of course Kendrick should have dealt with me when handing them over… but that's a minor peccadillo compared to all those that have gone before.'

That bald fact brought a remorseful blush to his daughter's wan cheeks so he gave her a smile.

'I shall write and thank him, but not too enthusiastically.' Walter rifled in a desk drawer for a parchment and dipped his quill in ink.

Beatrice rose from her kneeling position by Walter's armchair, her relief at his attitude slightly dampened by twinges of guilt. Her father was unaware there was yet another misdeed, committed that afternoon, and she hoped he would remain in blissful ignorance of it.

It was early evening, and Elise was still out at an afternoon salon with her friends. Alex was no doubt ensconced at one of his clubs. The house seemed unusually quiet, and the family would not dine for over an hour, but Bea didn't have any appetite for company or food. She felt exhausted from the day's events, and from constantly reflecting on what might have passed between them if she and Hugh had not been interrupted in the park. For one bittersweet moment earlier that afternoon she'd sensed that her wounded heart was finally healing…

'I'm going to rest in my room for a while, Papa.'

Walter raised a hand to his daughter while continuing to scratch on parchment.

Bea was sure she'd never settle into a snooze with her mind so muddled, but she drifted off almost immediately. When she woke over an hour later the brightness at the window had dimmed and just a hint of strawberry sunset streaked the ceiling.

Rubbing her eyes, she swung her toes to the floor, then pattered to the sash to peer at the sky. The vividly painted horizon was a wonderful sight and, sighing, Bea rested her warm forehead against the cool glass as fraught memories of the day caught up with her.

Glancing down into the street, Bea blinked, her eyes bolting back to a familiar figure huddled on the opposite pavement. Mrs Monk stared back at her, then nodded slowly in such a significant way that Bea's lips parted in surprise. A moment later the woman repeated the signal.

Frowning, Bea let the curtain drop into place. Daft as it was to suppose that Mrs Monk had been awaiting an opportunity to accost her, Bea could see no other reason for Mrs Monk's loitering outside. If the woman desired an audience it seemed odd she'd not knocked at the door…unless her news was too sensitive to be conveyed other than very privately…

Bea twitched the curtain an inch and peeped down; she was still there, chin lowered into her collar as she fidgeted around a lamppost, glancing, at intervals, at her window. With a sense of foreboding Bea wondered whether Mrs Monk's presence had something to do with their meeting that afternoon in Hyde Park. Bea realised it was highly probable she *had* been observed kissing Hugh in broad daylight.

With a tingle of alarm hurrying her, Bea straightened her clothes, grabbed her cloak, then went downstairs.

'Have you something to say to me, Mrs Monk?' Bea kept her voice level despite the butterflies in her stomach.

'Indeed I have, my dear.'

The woman's friendly tone increased rather than lessened Bea's uneasiness.

Maggie gestured at the street corner. 'Shall we take a walk?

'If you wish…'

'No point in beating about the bush,' Maggie announced abruptly as they set off. 'I saw you disgrace yourself with Mr Kendrick, and I know Lord Whitley's eyes aren't blind either.'

Beatrice's complexion grew hot but she gave no other outward sign that the woman's accusation disturbed her. If Mrs Monk had come to blackmail her in some way let her voice her threat rather than hide behind innuendo.

'Don't fret. I'm not about to gossip and cause trouble for you…unless I have to.' Maggie's piercing dark eyes assessed Beatrice. 'I reckon a lady of quality like yourself will choose to be sensible. If such a tale got out it would put you beyond the pale, and your poor papa with you. Quite a risk you took, letting Mr Kendrick do that to you out in the open—but then he's an irresistible charmer, isn't he? My Stella could vouch for that.'

'Is there a point to this?' Beatrice demanded coldly, although she'd already guessed the gist of it. Now that Colin had dropped Stella like a stone Maggie Monk had turned her sights on Hugh, but she was concerned about her charge having an interfering rival.

And indeed the woman was right to be worried!

Bea wasn't about to be intimidated by other females' jealousies and ambitions. Had they not been driven apart earlier that day, she believed that Hugh would have told her his feelings for her ran deeper than mere lust.

'I know what you're thinking, my dear,' Maggie purred. 'You're thinking he wants you, not Stella. Hugh

Kendrick is a fellow who wants lots of girls. The one he wants in particular, though, is my Stella. Do you know why that is?'

Instead of telling the woman she was talking rot, Beatrice heard herself murmur, 'No…tell me…'

'Sir Toby's after Stella too. When warring brothers clash heads the victor takes all the spoils, even those he might once have overlooked.' She grinned at Bea's involuntary intake of breath. 'My Stella wants Hugh and he wants her—that's plain to see.'

'I don't believe you,' Bea whispered, abruptly turning for home.

'So you thought you were the only one worth kissing, did you, Miss High and Mighty?' Maggie chuckled coarsely, hurrying after Bea. 'You'll never match up to my girl and get a Kendrick diamond on your finger; you're too old, my dear, and sullied by scandal. Why not take Sir Colin after all?'

'What do you know about Sir Colin and me?' Bea demanded on swinging around.

'I know he abandoned you for Stella and she broke his heart because she wanted more than he could offer. Burnett came back to you with his tail between his legs, didn't he? Hugh Kendrick told us all about it. We had a fine time once you'd gone. Of course I had to leave the lovebirds alone for a while,' Maggie lied slickly, without a hint of conscience.

Bea took a backward pace, her heart drumming in consternation. Nobody knew about Colin recently reissuing his proposal to her other than her close family… and Hugh. The idea that he might have discussed her private business with this vulgar woman was making her feel nauseated.

'You think about what I've said,' Maggie warned, grim-faced. 'Stella's like a honeypot where those brothers are concerned. You keep away, I'm warning you, or you'll get stung.'

'You're lying!' Bea said in a shaky exhalation of breath.

'Am I, now? I'm giving you a friendly warning, but if you upset me I'll have a chat with Stella in Oxford Street about what Miss Dewey was up to with Mr Kendrick behind a tree. If society ladies eavesdrop on our conversation you'll suffer the consequences, my dear—not us or him.'

'Say what you like about me. I'll never bow to blackmail!' Bea gritted through her teeth with a confidence she was far from feeling.

'Perhaps you'll think differently about your lover when he tells you *his* secrets.' Maggie was ready to use her trump card, because Miss Dewey was made of tougher metal than she'd anticipated.

'Mr Kendrick makes no secret of his affairs…'

'You didn't deny that you're lovers!' Maggie pounced.

'Good day to you, madam,' Bea said icily, turning away.

'Has Mr Kendrick told you about his bastard son in India?'

Bea felt frozen to the spot, then pivoted about very slowly. The smirk on Maggie's face was gleefully triumphant and Bea needed no further proof that the woman was speaking the truth. The memory of Lady Groves implying there was an overseas scandal in Hugh's background sprang to Bea's mind. She had assumed Lady Groves's hint concerned an Indian mistress, but would never have guessed a child might also be involved.

Despite a thickening in her throat Bea whispered in desperation, 'You're lying again…'

'Ask him, if you dare.'

Maggie swung away. She'd hoped to keep that ace up her sleeve in case she got a chance to play it another day. She knew Stella would have to settle for Whitley's protection after all. Hugh would never soften towards her daughter once Miss Dewey threw her knowledge of his son in his face and revealed her source. But Maggie was confident there'd be no happy ending for the diamond magnate and Miss Dewey either, and she realised that consolation would have to suffice…

Bea didn't run back the way she'd come, though she was tempted to when she heard Maggie let rip a raucous chuckle. Tilting her chin, she straightened her shoulders, glad her tormentor couldn't see her blinking back the tears scorching her eyes.

Halfway up the steps to her door, Bea clutched double-handed at the iron railing to support her shaky legs. She knew Mrs Monk hadn't followed her because she'd looked back over a shoulder, just once, and seen the older woman disappearing in the opposite direction. Bea sank down to sit on a step, aware of curious glances from passers-by. She couldn't make herself go inside the house because she knew she'd fidget and fret; neither could she share this latest appalling news with her family. She had burdened them far too much already with her woes.

There was only one person capable of soothing her torment. Only he could tell her whether he'd fathered a child and then abandoned the boy overseas. Whatever Hugh admitted to, his carousing in India might excite a furore but it would eventually die down. Wealthy men and their bastards were nothing new, even if the woman seduced was a foreigner.

Of course being spotted kissing a gentleman behind a tree in Hyde Park would secure lifelong ostracism for a genteel spinster. And if she were discovered visiting Hugh at home it would simply add to her infamy. But what did it matter if she committed one final, vital sin and went to his house to demand an explanation?

She was right to have been worried, Bea realised as a regal-looking butler stood, appalled, at the sight of her.

A few minutes ago Beatrice had paid the Hackney cab driver and gazed up at the dauntingly imposing façade of Hugh's townhouse on Grosvenor Square. The sunset had faded to twilight and she'd quickly ascended a flight of stone steps before her courage evaporated and she turned tail. As she tilted her chin up to squarely meet the butler's eyes she cocooned herself in her anger and jealousy, though realised she had little to gain from either.

Hugh had not professed to love her or to want to marry her. He had not offered to remain faithful to her. He had promised her nothing that might make her entitled to have his past exposed to her scrutiny or forgiveness. Yet deep within Bea felt she deserved every possible explanation and apology from him…

Having conquered his outrage, the butler politely asked for her name and her business.

'My name is Miss Dewey and I should like to speak to your master, if you please,' Bea said firmly.

As she stepped unsteadily over the threshold into a vast cool hallway Bea noticed the manservant's eyes dart to the street, as though checking whether her lone arrival at a bachelor's house was under observation.

Having led her to a huge hallway chair, the fellow disappeared. Bea sat rigid-backed, unaware she had been holding her breath until the sound of her sighing exhalation echoed eerily in the silence of her opulent surroundings. A moment later she spotted the butler marching back towards her. He threw her a flustered frown before diverting to the stairs and scooting up them.

When two housemaids appeared and gawped at her from behind a marble pillar Bea's awkwardness increased to such a degree that she was tempted to leap up and leave. She clasped her hands, then untangled her fingers as minutes passed and other servants crept up to congregate and whisper about her.

Bea could stand it no longer. She was on the point of announcing that she would return another time when the butler flew down the stairs. This time he ignored her, glaring instead at his inferiors, who melted away into the shadowy corridors.

'Mr Kendrick will be here directly. He has invited

you to wait in the blue salon.' He held out a gloved hand, his demeanour once more phlegmatic as he led the way.

They had got no further than the first set of ornate doorways when Bea heard a familiar baritone voice.

'You may leave us.'

Hugh had addressed his manservant from the top of the wide curving treads. Now he approached, hands plunged in pockets, a towel draped negligently about his shoulders.

Following a stiff bow the butler backed away, then turned towards the vestibule.

Bea raised her eyes, overwhelmed with embarrassment as Hugh came closer to her. No wonder his staff had acted as though she were a nuisance and a spectacle to behold. Nobody, let alone an unaccompanied young woman, should interrupt a gentleman in the middle of bathing. Why had he not just sent her away? she wailed inwardly as another wave of heat deepened her blush.

Hugh raised the cloth to his slick dark hair, drying it, and the more casually he took her intrusion the more acutely awkward Beatrice felt. He appeared to have dressed in a hurry, and his ruffled linen shirt was damp and clinging to his broad torso, exposing an expanse of tanned skin at his throat.

'I'm so sorry…' Bea croaked, finally forcing words past strangling embarrassment. 'I shouldn't have come. I'll go…and leave you to finish your…umm…' She turned to bolt towards the door.

Hugh had caught hold of her before she'd made it more than a yard or so.

'No, you don't,' he said softly, turning her about.

'You've found the courage to come here to see me so it must be on an urgent matter. I want to know what it is.'

'It *is* an urgent matter...' Bea blurted, finally forcing her gaze to his face.

His lashes were still heavy with water, fringing caramel-coloured eyes, and slick ribbons of jet hair adorned his temples. If he still hadn't got a penny to his name Bea knew he could enslave her with his breathtaking good looks as easily as he had three years ago.

Then he hadn't been able to afford even one residence to call his own. Now Hugh Kendrick, diamond magnate, had the wherewithal to support households and dependants at home and overseas. Bea knew there was so much more to discover than whether he'd revealed Colin's renewed marriage proposal to Mrs Monk and Stella. But with startling clarity she realised that answer was more important to her than any other. If it transpired that he had done so then those other questions crowding her mind about his life in India would no longer be important. Love him maybe she would, till the day she died, but she could never see him again after tonight if he'd betrayed her trust to the vile Mrs Monk.

'Come with me...' Hugh extended a hand to her. 'Let's find somewhere comfortable to talk.

'There's no need for me to tarry.' Bea ignored his beckoning fingers, pleased that her composure was strengthening and the wobble had gone from her voice. 'It's very wrong of me to be here, and I apologise for coming, but...but I have an important question to ask.'

'Go ahead...' Hugh's mouth skewed as he sensed he was about to be accused of something. He could hazard a guess at what it was. But how Beatrice had found out that Mrs Monk had tried to solicit his protection for Stella Rawlings he could only guess. The woman was a mischief-maker and the girl was made in her image.

The vision he wanted to keep lodged in his mind was that of a tantalising temptress sharing his bath, her golden tresses floating on soapy water, her limbs entwined with his… A dry chuckle rasped in Hugh's throat as his phantom lover brusquely interrupted his fantasy.

'Did you tell Mrs Monk that Colin had again proposed to me?'

'No.'

Bea moistened her mouth. She hadn't anticipated such a concise response, nor that he would follow the single word with a steady, low-lashed stare. She waited for him to elaborate, but he didn't.

'I see…' she blurted. 'And did you kiss Stella this afternoon?'

'No.'

Again Beatrice shifted beneath his ruthless regard as the silence lengthened.

'Are you accusing me of such behaviour?'

Bea hesitated just a moment too long before shaking her head so vigorously that her bonnet loosened on its ribbons, hanging at her nape on flaxen waves. Before she could carry on her interrogation masterful fingers manacled her wrist. Hugh forced her with him towards the nearest doorway, propelling her inside when she seemed unwilling to step over the threshold.

'Sit down,' he growled, standing with his back against the door.

'Please don't order me about,' Bea returned haughtily. Nevertheless she perched obediently on the edge of a fireside chair in what appeared to be a small reading room. Newspapers were on a table and ceiling-high bookshelves flanked one wall.

'Now I have some questions to ask,' Hugh dulcetly drawled as he strolled to ram a foot against the fender. 'Did you have a *tête-à-tête* with Mrs Monk or Stella after you left me?'

'Not by choice!' Bea answered hotly, shooting to her feet. She could tell from his attitude that he thought she'd been secretly checking up on him. 'I've no wish for anything to do with either woman.'

'No more have I.'

'That's not what Mrs Monk says!' Bea retorted frostily.

'So...tell me what Mrs Monk says...' Hugh quit the fireplace, stationing himself in front of her. 'Come, I answered you a moment ago—I'd like the courtesy returned, Beatrice,' he needled her, his expression impenetrable. 'If I'm to be charged with something at least provide your evidence.'

'Mrs Monk loitered outside the viscount's house till I went out to speak to her.'

Bea nibbled her lower lip, sensing that behind Hugh's cool exterior lay a simmering fury...directed at *her*. Of the two of them, Bea judged she had more right to feel angry and ill-used. Fearing she was within a hair's breadth of shouting that opinion at him, she took a deep, calming breath.

'Mrs Monk said you'd told her that Colin had returned to me with his tail between his legs after Stella jilted him.' She glanced up to find a pair of tawny eyes preying on her face. 'The woman warned me to stay away from you because you and your brother were competing for Stella's favours and Stella had chosen you. She said if I didn't heed her she'd broadcast that I'd been caught kissing you in broad daylight.'

'That's it?' Hugh asked with an amount of ennui.

'No…indeed it is not!' Bea exploded. She'd not expected a fulsome denial, but had anticipated more of a reaction than she'd just got. 'Mrs Monk added that you'd all had a fine time this afternoon and hinted that you and Stella had flirted and kissed.'

'Was anything else mentioned about my lecherous intentions towards that damned minx?'

'What more might have been said?' Bea stormed, dreading to hear the answer, yet desperate to have it too.

'The meddlesome witch might have told you that I took them home immediately and declined an invitation to take refreshment; she might have told you that I refused the girl's services as a paramour when they were offered to me…for the second time,' Hugh clipped out.

'What?' Bea asked faintly. She'd imagined that Mrs Monk was after a husband for Stella.

'So have you anything else to say to me?' Hugh asked, taking her chin in strong fingers and tilting her face up to his so she couldn't avoid his black-eyed stare.

Bea felt the words jumbling in her mind before clogging her throat. During the journey to his house she had rehearsed how she'd demand to know if he'd fathered a child with an Indian woman and then left them both behind when he'd returned to England. Now, when she needed them most, she realised her impetuous nature and quick tongue seemed to have deserted her.

'Perhaps you might like to apologise and admit you were wrong to accuse me of having designs on that chit's virtue.'

Bea bristled beneath his arrogant drawl. It spurred her on, firing her indignation. 'I accused you of nothing. I merely asked questions. Even had I assumed you guilty it would have been an easy mistake to make.' She stepped back from him, her blue gaze adopting a glacial hardness. 'When trying to warn me about your womanising, Colin said you had a mistress at either end of town and wondered where you might position another.' Bea tilted her head to a challenging angle, forcing her eyes to meet his squarely. 'If only I had known then what I know now I might have been able to tell him. India is the answer, is it not?'

Chapter Twenty-One

She watched carefully, and, yes, there was an unmistakable flicker of cynical acceptance that something hidden had been unearthed.

'Mrs Monk told you about that too?'

'She did…' Beatrice croaked, gripping at a chair-rail to steady herself. 'And I'm sorry that she was mean enough to do so. I'm certain you'd not reveal anything so personal to her, and don't know how she found out about your Indian mistress and the little boy.'

'Toby probably told her; from what you've said it sounds as though they've been in touch,' Hugh said tonelessly.

'I'm sorry if your brother has betrayed you…it is a very personal matter,' Bea repeated in a voice roughened by emotion. 'It was none of that woman's business…just as it is none of mine…' She gulped in a shaky breath. 'I must go now, but first will again apologise for intruding like this.'

She'd reached the door and half opened it before he spoke.

'Don't you want to know more about the affair?'

Bea twisted about, eyes blazing. 'What possible interest would I have in your family abroad?'

'I have no family abroad...'

'You are a very callous man to say so,' Bea whispered. 'What else are the mother of your child and a son...even a bastard son...but members of your family?'

Bea's fists clenched at her sides in rage and frustration. She had been wrong about him all along; despite his arrogance and philandering she had harboured a hope—a hope that had soared this afternoon—that he was an inherently decent man. He'd not denied the little boy's birth, yet had easily dismissed him.

'Have you finished?'

'Utterly finished... I've no wish to say or hear more on the subject. Good evening...' Bea had her fingers on the door, pulling it fully open, when his dark fist hit the panel overhead, slamming it again shut.

'I don't think you mean that, do you, Beatrice?' he said quietly. 'I think you're keen for every detail about Rani and Shay.'

Bea spun about, her back pressed into the door. She gazed up at him with glittering eyes, hating him for understanding her turmoil and for making real people of the ghosts in her mind.

'You're wrong!' she spat. 'I've had enough proof that your lechery causes hurt to innocent people. You will never hurt me in that way.' Tears trickled down her cheeks. 'How can you abandon your own flesh and blood in a distant land?'

'Shay isn't my flesh and blood...'

'What?' Bea whispered. 'Are you now going to lie—?'

'It's not a lie,' Hugh interrupted harshly. 'He's not my flesh and blood and, much as I want the best for him, I'm content to let Rani care for his welfare.'

Hugh pressed thumb and forefinger to the bridge of his nose, as though to ease strain.

'I want to tell you, Beatrice…let me tell you… And then, if you want nothing more to do with me, I'll try and accept your wishes and stay away.'

His hoarse words held a note of authority, and Bea realised he'd force her to listen whether she chose to or not.

'Sit down…please…' Hugh abruptly strode away from her, thrusting hands that ached to touch her in his pockets. One was withdrawn to gesture at the chair she'd previously used.

Slowly Bea approached the seat, perching again on its very edge, as though she might flee if the details of his foreign affair were too unbearable.

'Rani became my mistress shortly after I arrived in Hyderabad,' Hugh started without preamble. 'She'd had an arranged marriage when little more than a girl. Her husband was much older and they had no offspring. She craved a child to love…'

Bea's slender fingers gripped the chair-arm as though she would use its support to rise.

'Let me finish, Bea!' Hugh ordered with a note of pleading. He quickly resumed. 'There were many English families in the area connected to the East Indies trade. I became friendly with one fellow, Keith Wheeler, who had his wife and only daughter with him. They'd planned to return to England so the girl could make her come-out. Then they found out Louise was pregnant by a married Indian potentate.'

Hugh's mouth hardened at the memory.

'Once the seduction was done the fellow distanced himself, and there would have been a diplomatic incident and a scandal if he'd been pursued over the matter.'

Bea relaxed her tight grip on the chair, returned her fingers to her lap. She gazed at Hugh's profile, her mind racing ahead. But she remained quiet, breathlessly waiting for him to continue.

'Louise's parents were understandably distraught and keen to keep the matter concealed. When Rani discovered that a baby was to be born in secret and then given away she wanted it. She pleaded with me to make the necessary arrangements. I refused, so behind my back she spoke to the expectant mother and the parents…offered to pay them for the child. The Wheelers wanted nothing other than that the whole affair be dealt with as discreetly as possible.'

Hugh paused, threw his head back to sightlessly stare at the ceiling.

'The Wheelers begged me to put it right for them if I could. I resisted, and tried to dissuade Rani too, but her obsession with being a mother overrode all else and eventually I agreed to help them all obtain the longed-for outcome.' He gestured briefly. 'My liaison with Rani was in the open, and accepted by the locals as a practical arrangement. Rani's elderly husband didn't object to his wife sleeping with me. They were not peasants, but neither were they wealthy people, and the family welcomed my friendship and financial assistance.'

Hugh shifted position, lowering his moody features to the empty fire grate.

'Louise concealed her weight gain; Rani padded out her clothes and begged me to claim the child as mine. She didn't want to be vilified as a trollop, unable to name her baby's father, and a fair-skinned sire would be required as the baby was sure to look of mixed race. As indeed he does…'

A softening about Hugh's mouth caused Beatrice a pang of joy rather than jealousy. Despite everything, the little boy held a place in his heart. 'You love him, don't you?'

'I grew to adore the little chap…'

'And you named him Shay?' she asked, in a voice so quiet it was almost inaudible.

'Rani chose the name. Shay means gift…and that's how she saw the boy… Whereas I…'

'Whereas you…?' Bea prompted in a whisper.

'Whereas I knew word of Shay's existence would leak out, and I could see the problems and inconvenience that lay ahead in my becoming embroiled in such deceit.'

'But you did it anyway,' Bea said, her voice soft with wonder. She knew she believed what he'd said… Every single word was true—outlandishly dramatic tale though it was. A spontaneous sob of admiration and love for him welled in her chest. 'You must have loved her very much to sacrifice what you believed to be right so she might have her dream of becoming a mother.'

'No...' He grimaced wryly. 'I was fond of Rani, but we both knew I didn't love her—and neither did she love me. It was an exchange of basic needs that suited us both at the time.'

'It was good and selfless of you, nevertheless...'

'In the end I did it for Louise. My sister was compromised when young and it nearly ruined her future. I could understand why Louise's parents were fretting over what lay ahead for their daughter.'

'How did Toby find out?' Bea asked, puzzled.

'He came to India, uninvited, to try and wangle himself an interest in my mining company. He got nothing from me but of course he's used the knowledge of Shay's birth to his advantage. My brother has hinted at spreading what he knows...but up to now he's shrewdly kept quiet, fearing my revenge. I expect he's already worried that he'll not be able to extract another penny from me.'

'He's been blackmailing you?' Bea sounded outraged.

'In a subtle way... But it seems he's now burned his bridges, and in a way I'm glad. The gossip will spread like wildfire; Mrs Monk will make sure of that now she knows I've no interest in her daughter.'

'It will die down...' Bea reassured him.

Hugh shrugged carelessness. 'A few other people already know of Shay's existence. Of course Alex has had the full story; he's the only person, apart from you, to hear it from my lips. He said he's never had reason to mention it to Elise.' Hugh prowled to and fro in front of the chimneypiece. 'Lord Mornington was in India at the same time as me, attending to his investments. I expect he's told his close circle that I fathered a child abroad. I've noticed his sister looking at me oddly at times. But Lady Groves is obviously not a gossip or word would have already got round.'

Hugh gave another lazy shrug.

'It no longer matters who knows, and thankfully Toby never discovered the truth behind the boy's birth. Had he done so he'd have held the means to destroy many people's happiness.'

'What of Louise and her parents?'

'They returned to England and Louise was quietly married in Kent to a nice young fellow… I was invited to the ceremony…'

'A happy ending all round…' Bea gave him a tiny smile.

'Is it?' Hugh plunged his hands in his pockets, his eyes darkening. 'Why did you assume I was a deceitful villain before allowing me to explain?'

'I told Mrs Monk she was lying about you from the start. I was sceptical about your interest in her daughter even when she said you'd take Stella just to ensure Toby couldn't have her…' Beatrice rattled off, wishing she had a more robust defence to present to Hugh.

She had recklessly flown here in a fury, believing the worst of him. She'd called him names and quizzed him over being a liar…but now that her jealousy and indignation were no longer colouring her reason her earlier opinion of him had changed drastically. In fact he had moments ago provided her with yet more cause to adore him, she realised. He might be self-indulgent where women and pleasure were concerned, but he was not weak or mean. His kindness towards Rani didn't irk Beatrice; such consideration reassured her that, however nasty and corrupt his older brother might be, Hugh had escaped being infected with a similar nature. Hugh Kendrick was an honourable man, and she loved him.

Blinking back the heat in her eyes, she gazed at him, wanting him to say something, but he remained stubbornly quiet.

'I'm conscious that you have great trust in me to have disclosed your secret… I swear I will never betray it.' Still he said nothing, and Bea slowly turned away. 'I must go now, and hope that nobody knows I've been here other than your servants.'

'You took a great risk for a man you don't trust.'

'I *do* trust you…' Beatrice keened, swinging back to gaze at him beseechingly.

Hugh suddenly cradled her face in his hand. '*Do* you, Beatrice?' he demanded throatily. 'Prove it to me, then…'

Chapter Twenty-Two

'How can I? What do you want me to do?' Beatrice whispered. She glimpsed the smoky desire burning at the backs of his eyes and a piquant thrill rippled through her. 'I shouldn't have doubted you, but Mrs Monk is adept at stirring the pot…' She began a diffident mitigation.

'If you're curious about my past ask me about it and I'll tell you everything you want to know.' Hugh dipped his head to tantalise a corner of her lips with his own. 'Or perhaps you'll think me lying to cover up my sins… will you?'

'No! I won't! I trust you…' Bea's eyelids fell as the kiss continued.

'Good. But I'm after more than just your trust, sweet, you know that. I always have been.' His fingers smoothed over a warm satiny cheek, a thumb brushing lightly on her lower lip. 'I want us to finish what we started in Hyde Park this afternoon, before we were interrupted by those infernal people.'

He held her back from him a little, tilting his head to watch her bashful expression.

'Come…don't be shy; we both know it didn't begin today but years ago, and we've waited far too long to satisfy this need for one another. It's time now to surrender, Beatrice.'

'You want me to kiss you to say sorry?' Beatrice murmured, glancing at him from under her curly dark lashes.

'That would be a nice start…' Hugh sounded huskily amused as he moved his mouth to a position fractionally above hers, daring her to take the initiative and close the space between their lips.

Raising herself onto tiptoe, Bea kissed him with innocent sensuality. A scent of tangy sandalwood soap enveloped her as their bodies merged and she slipped her arms onto his shoulders, entwining her fingers in his tousled hair.

'You feel damp…' she teased, trying to temper the sizzling atmosphere between them. 'I'm sorry I interrupted your bathing…'

'There's time yet to finish that too before the night's out,' Hugh growled against her mouth. 'Will you wash my back?'

Bea stumbled back a pace from him, her smile uncertain. 'I hope you're joking…'

Hugh tracked her evasive paces until her spine was touching the library table. Indolently he placed a hand either side of her, trapping her between his muscular arms. 'No joke… I want you with me everywhere, Beatrice…even in my bath.'

Confused by an overwhelming mix of excitement and embarrassment, she clasped the solid forearm closest to her with two small hands. Sinew flexed beneath her palms as he resisted her attempt to move him. Bea's eyes roved features that displayed an uncompromising raw carnality. Slowly she exhaled a pent-up breath. Why fight him? She yearned for his loving as ardently as he would bestow it. She couldn't deny it. Neither could she deny that the idea of his sleek skin slipping beneath her wet palms as she soaped him was making her feel restless.

This afternoon she had been ready to take his terms and become his mistress. What matter if she yielded and agreed to go to his bed or his bath now? Hours ago it would have seemed a shocking notion: she'd always assumed Hugh would arrange for them to make love at a secret location so as not to cause outrage.

But the damage was already done: she'd shocked his servants, who no doubt imagined she was a harlot. Besides, Mrs Monk would be bent on revenge and would besmirch Bea for the sin of a single kiss. In Bea's rueful estimation she might as well get hung for a sheep as a lamb and stay awhile with the man she loved.

It *was* time for her to surrender and prove her love and trust to Hugh. When word got out about her visit to Mr Kendrick's Mayfair mansion she would be home in Hertfordshire. In time a new scandal would erupt to entertain the *ton* and gossip about her would fade.

Bea's reflections were interrupted by the touch of gentle fingers at her throat, untying her bonnet strings. Hugh tossed the hat to the table, his eyes capturing her vivid blue gaze as his fingers threaded into her silken hair.

'This afternoon when I came to meet you in Oxford Street I brought something with me to give to you.'

'I know…and my papa was as grateful as I to have those IOUs,' she said with trembling sincerity. 'I own I thought he might be livid that a gentleman had paid my debts, but he claims you did the right thing, protecting your family's honour and thwarting your odious brother's spite. You are still my papa's good friend.'

Hugh's mouth tilted wryly. 'And will he think me his friend after tonight?'

'I doubt he will if he finds out what we've done,' Bea admitted with a catch to her voice.

'And what will he think of you if he finds out what we've done?'

Bea averted her face as her eyes prickled, but she attempted a steady reply. 'He will be very upset, of course, but I think he will allow me to stay with him in Hertfordshire—although many would deem me unfit to again darken his doorstep.'

'Are you prepared to risk so much for me, Beatrice?' Hugh asked gently.

'Yes…' she murmured.

'Why?'

She knew she should tell him now that she loved and wanted him, and no other man would do. She should say she'd far sooner have an uncertain future with him than settle for respectability and the prospect of an arid marriage of convenience when her aged papa died and was no longer her companion. But an obstinate pride remained, blocking the confession in her throat. He might not love her, or want to marry her, but the least she required of him was that he allowed her some dignity, offering up some affectionate words first.

'Shall I tell you why I think you'd do all that for me, sweetheart?'

Beatrice nodded, the painful throb in her throat preventing her from voicing a need to have his fullest explanation.

'I think you would risk everything you hold dear because you love me as greatly as I love you. I also think you're hoping I'm not the immoral lecher others say I am, and will protect you with my name as well as my heart.' Hugh soothed her quiet sob by stroking his cool lips against her brow. 'I've loved and desired you for years, Beatrice. I've tried to force you from my memory by carousing, but you stubbornly resisted being put aside and curbed the worst of my excesses.'

His mouth slanted on hers, sliding with silky sweetness, his tongue teasing her with tiny persuasive touches.

'The worst of your excesses?' Bea echoed against his shoulder, although a quiet joy was burgeoning within. 'You keep *two* mistresses close by, sir. Did you restrict yourself then?'

Hugh bent his head, laughing soundlessly against her crown of golden hair. 'Perhaps in my immaturity I might have liked more, but now I have seen the error of my ways I have no desire for even one mistress, or any woman other than my future wife.'

Bea raised glowing eyes to his face, uncertain still,

yet daring to hope. 'You are to take a vow of celibacy then, Mr Kendrick...?'

'I suppose I must for the short duration of my betrothal...unless my adorable fiancée will take pity on me and let me love her.' Hugh gathered Beatrice in his arms, rocking her against his chest. 'Do you know how many times I've railed at myself for letting you slip through my fingers? From the moment I walked away from you three years ago I've bitterly regretted my decision to act the martyr, leaving you to enjoy your life with a worthier man who could give you what I could not.' He paused. 'When I found out you'd attracted another suitor so quickly I was sure you'd easily forgotten me.'

'Elise warned me I had fallen for Dr Burnett on the rebound. I remember feeling hurt and humiliated by your rejection and wanting somebody to boost my pride,' Bea admitted.

'I'm sorry, sweetheart, that I hurt you. At the time I thought I was the only one suffering. Your friend Fiona knew, of course, what a mess I was in, and kindly tolerated my pathetic courtship without taking offence. She told me bluntly to come back to you...but I'd heard Burnett was already courting you. I was a damnable fool! We might have started off as man and wife living in a garret, but we would have been together now for three years...'

'No...it would not have worked, Hugh,' Beatrice interjected on a sigh. 'We might have quickly grown bitter towards one another, constantly fretting over bills and hating feeling beholden to Alex, who would have offered loans of money,' Beatrice pointed out.

Hugh gave her a grateful smile for understanding so completely how humiliating such a situation would have been for him. His greatest fear had been losing Bea's respect.

Suddenly Hugh urged her towards a chair and made her perch on its edge. Then, dropping to a knee, he pulled out a grand-looking box from his inside pocket. 'Will you marry me, Beatrice, and keep me from slipping back into wicked ways?'

His teasing tone earned him a prim look from Beatrice. But soon her mock reproof was overcome by an expression of wonderment. Hugh had opened the casket to reveal a scintillating diamond ring nestling on a luxurious bed of satin.

'Is this the gift you brought with you this afternoon?' she asked, struck by its opulence.

'No…I wanted to give you your betrothal ring somewhere more appropriate than Oxford Street.' Again his hand disappeared into a pocket, to withdraw a smaller, plainer jewellery box. 'I brought this with me to show to you. I wanted to convince you that I was not toying with your affections when we first met. It was always my intention to propose to you, even if the best I could afford was a betrothal ring of very little value.'

'You have kept it all this time…?' Bea breathed softly. 'Show it to me…please…' she coaxed hoarsely when he hesitated in opening the lid of the little box. Reaching out a single digit, Bea stroked the tiny cluster of sapphires embedded in a thin golden shank.

'I bought it because the blue stones match your eyes.

I hoped you might be swayed to accept it with such a sweet thought attached to it. Then my pride took over...'

Bea raised her eyes to his face, seeing for the first time a bashfulness shaping his features, making him look appealingly boyish. 'Indeed, there was no need for you to have felt ashamed of your gift,' she reassured him. 'In fact, if you were to allow me to choose between the two...'

She reached out a hand and removed the small golden band from its resting place. Handing it to him, she extended her left hand towards him.

'I will marry you, Mr Kendrick, even though you have made me wait far too long to hear you ask me to be your wife.'

After he'd slipped the sapphires onto her finger she curled the digit, securing it in place.

Springing to his feet, Hugh whipped her up into his arms, making her gasp as he spun them both about. 'You've made me the happiest man, even though you don't like your flawless Golkonda diamond.'

'Oh, I do, Hugh!' Beatrice cupped his abrasive chin between her palms. 'Of course I do. But this is my betrothal ring...the one I always wanted...the one I would so proudly have worn three years ago.' She extended her finger, admiring the small blue gems. 'That other, finer gift you may give to me another time...perhaps on the birth of our first child...' she murmured, blushing.

Hugh let her feet drop to the floor in a way that sensually slid together their bodies. 'Well, I want to see you wearing that diamond, sweet, so we'd better start on making our family very soon.'

With a confidence that stopped her heart he covered her mouth with his in a kiss that was simultaneously demanding yet reverential. Keeping their faces fused together with a hand cupping her scalp, Hugh manoeuvred them slowly towards the armchair. He sat with Bea on his lap, deepening the kiss as he repositioned her to sit facing him, straddling his thighs.

Swift fingers worked open the buttons on her bodice and the ribbons of her chemise. With teasing leisure he lowered his mouth to the breasts he'd exposed, feasting on the plump milky flesh like a ravenous man. One of his hands swept up her skirt, his fingers caressing the soft inner skin of her thighs with long strokes that stopped a hair's breadth from their apex.

'Hugh...' Bea groaned, throwing back her head and squirming against the tormenting pulse rocking her body. 'Should we not go upstairs? I don't care—honestly I do not—if you make love to me properly before I go home. But I must return because they will all worry where I am...'

She gasped in a shuddering breath as his hot mouth and tongue tantalised a rigid nipple. Bea gave herself up to the tension building within, parting her thighs to his artfully sliding fingers. Her panting grew shallow as her back arched, then an explosion of pleasure made her buck wildly against him.

Hugh drew her face forward, soothing her bruised lips with a courteous kiss. 'Did you like that?' he asked gently as she collapsed like a rag doll against his shoulder.

Bea nodded slowly, feeling too enervated to speak. A moment later, when her heartbeat had steadied, she glanced up at his shady jaw. 'Do you want me to take off my clothes so you might also like it?' she asked shyly.

Hugh buried his lips in her hair. 'I'd like that more than anything, sweet, but not now…it's not right…'

'I want to please you. I don't care what you do…' Bea started, but a gentle finger laid on her pulsating lips silenced her.

'But *I* care, sweetheart,' Hugh said. 'I'll not take your virginity like this. I want to savour every second of our first proper time together. I want us to share a feather bed covered in silk sheets. I want to enjoy your beautiful body for hours and hours—not snatch a few minutes' release on an armchair with the servants listening at the keyhole.'

Bea started in his arms, darting a horrified glance at the door. 'Do you honestly think they are?' she wailed in a whisper.

Hugh chuckled. 'No… They wouldn't dare, if they value their employment with me.'

'Mrs Monk will do her best to smear my name.'

'Your name will soon be my name, and after that nobody will give a damn for a word she says. And neither should you…' Hugh terminated his concise reassurance with a light kiss on her brow. 'Besides, I'm conscious of the fact that I've been a rank hypocrite where you're concerned. I've protected my sister and Louise from ruined futures, yet would have made you my mistress and put your reputation in jeopardy.' He dropped forward his head, quite bashfully. 'I'm sorry… I can't help wanting you, so I'd do anything to have you and keep you always with me…'

'You don't have to do anything but love me…that's enough, Hugh,' Bea said softly.

As she snuggled, satisfied, into his shoulder Hugh neatened her clothes, doing up buttons and laces with an expertise that might have worried Bea had she not been still pleasantly dazed with sensuality.

'I'll get a special licence and we can be married before the end of the week. Just a quiet affair—if you're happy with that?'

Bea nodded dreamily, feeling utterly content. 'There is just one thing I would ask for…'

'You can ask me for anything, sweet, and I'll grant you your wish,' Hugh said.

'I should like us to honeymoon in India… I should like to meet Shay.'

Hugh's eyes whipped to hers. 'I was going to offer to cut my ties with them if you wanted me to. I never thought I would ever do so for anyone. I'm very fond of my…of Shay,' he corrected himself. 'But I realise you might find the situation hard to accept.'

'I understand why you keep in touch with Shay and his mother,' Bea said softly. 'I expect you support them financially, don't you?' She tilted her head, watching his expression. 'I really don't mind…in fact I think it is very worthy of you to do so.' She kissed his stubbly cheek. 'I'm not jealous of Shay or of Rani. I believe you, you see, when you say your future wife is the only woman you want.' She urged huskily, 'Take me to India, please; I should love to meet your adopted son, and you said you would grant me anything I wished for…'

Hugh turned to her, a new depth of adoration for

her burnishing his golden eyes. 'Of course I shall take you to see my boy,' he said huskily. 'And when we have our first child, and he or she is old enough, we shall go again, if you would like to, so the children can get to know one another.'

'That sounds perfect…' Bea cuddled into him.

Hugh suddenly buried his face into the warm curve of her shoulder. 'It is time to go and see your father and tell him our wonderful news.'

'You will certainly be his good friend now.' Beatrice choked a little laugh, tangling her fingers in his glossy hair. 'I know I have driven him to despair on occasion with my recklessness; he will be pleased to be rid of me, I'm sure.'

'He has my sympathy.'

Hugh lifted his face. His lashes, wet earlier from his bath, were again clumped with moisture.

'You are a wild and wanton young woman,' Hugh scolded on a sniff. He took her mouth in a kiss that bordered on bittersweet pain before transforming into a tender salute. 'But I think I know a way of taming you, Beatrice, that we'll both like very much…'

* * * * *

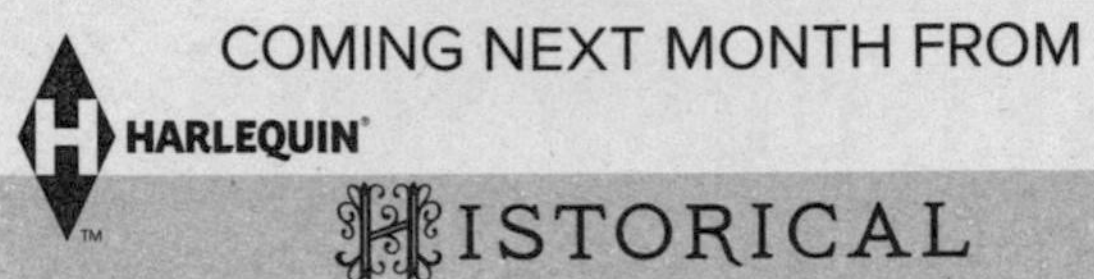

Available August 19, 2014

THE LONE SHERIFF

by Lynna Banning

(Western)

Sheriff Jericho Silver's backup has arrived, and *she* sure spells trouble. Determined to fill her days with daring deeds, widowed Madison O'Donnell just won't take no for an answer!

LORD HAVELOCK'S LIST

by Annie Burrows

(Regency)

When orphan Mary Carpenter discovers her new husband Lord Havelock's list of wifely requirements, she's hurt—and incensed. Perhaps it's time for Mary to make a list of her own....

THE GENTLEMAN ROGUE

by Margaret McPhee

(Regency)

In Mayfair, Emma Northcote stands transfixed by Ned Stratham's unforgettable gaze. Their past is mired in secrets, but what will happen when Emma discovers they share a deeper...darker connection?

SAVED BY THE VIKING WARRIOR

by Michelle Styles

(Viking)

With the beautiful Lady of Lingfold as his prisoner, Thrand the Destroyer dreams of starting anew. Can they both leave revenge to the gods and forge a new life together?

YOU CAN FIND MORE INFORMATION ON UPCOMING HARLEQUIN® TITLES, FREE EXCERPTS AND MORE AT WWW.HARLEQUIN.COM.

HHCNM0814

SPECIAL EXCERPT FROM

HARLEQUIN

HISTORICAL

What exactly are the qualities that Lord Havelock desires in a wife? And will orphaned Mary Carpenter fit the bill? Find out next month in this spirited new tale by Annie Burrows.

Read on for a sneak preview of LORD HAVELOCK'S LIST...

A *Mouse,* the heavier hand had scrawled next to the bit about the ceremony, and underlined it.

Not of the upper ten thousand, her shocked eyes discovered next.

Preferably an orphan.

Her stomach roiled as she recalled the look on Lord Havelock's face when she'd told him, that fateful night at the Crimmers, that she'd just lost her mother. She'd thought he couldn't possibly have looked pleased to hear she was all alone in the world, that surely she must have been mistaken.

But she hadn't been.

She tottered back to the tea table and sank onto the chair the waiter had so helpfully drawn up to it. And carried on reading.

Not completely hen-witted, the sloppier of the two writers had added. And she suddenly understood that cryptic comment he'd made about finding a wife with brains. Suggested by someone called...Ash, that was it. How she could remember a name tossed out just the once, in such an offhand way, she could not think.

Unless it was because she felt as though the beautiful little dainties set out on their fine china plates might as well have been so many piles of ash, for all the desire she had now to put one in her mouth.

Good with children, not selfish, the darker hand had scrawled. Then it was back to the neater hand again. It had written, *Modest, Honest* and *Not looking for affection within Matrimony.* And then the untidier, what she'd come to think of as the more sarcastic, compiler of wifely qualities had written the word *Mouse* again, and this time underlined it twice.

But what made a small whimper of distress finally escape her lips was the last item on the list.

Need not be pretty.

Need not be pretty. Well, that was her all right! Plain, dowdy mouse that she was. No wonder he'd looked at her like—what was it Aunt Pargetter had said—like his ship had come in?

Getting to her feet, she strode to his bedroom door and flung it open. Somehow she had to find a sample of his handwriting to see if he'd been the one to…to mock her this way, before he'd even met her. And then she would… She came to an abrupt halt by his desk, across the surface of which was scattered a veritable raft of papers. What would she do? She'd already married him.

Don't miss
LORD HAVELOCK'S LIST,
available from Harlequin® Historical
September 2014.

HHEXP0814